Salvation Jane

By S.V. Pinnegar

ISBN 13: 978-0-473-31111-7 (Softcover)
ISBN 13: 978-0-473-31112-4 (Mobi)
ISBN 13: 978-0-473-31113-1(Kindle)

S.V. Pinnegar is a freelance writer and newspaper copy editor of many years. He now lives in Auckland, New Zealand. He wrote this book, with its present title, in 1986. Mainly because of the share market crash of the late 80s, the manuscript languished in a drawer until April 2013, when the author further worked on it.

Table of Contents

Synopsis

Peter Mitchell is a troubled 15-year-old, suffering from an undiagnosed attention deficit disorder who finds himself, among other fantasies, fighting off Martian hordes trying to attack Earth rather than concentrating on his school work. Then, one fateful day, he is torn from his friends and delightful haunts in his beloved England when, despite his protestations and those of his older brother, his parents decide to find a new life in Australia. After a four-week trip by sea where he is assailed by loneliness and seasickness he is dumped with a busload of other immigrants at a former army camp, turned into a migrant hostel, in the middle of nowhere. However, he is delighted to find there are many girls at the hostel — only trouble is, he falls in love with them all. Struggling into adulthood, he is soon to make new friends and meet new challenges as well as to find love and hope among his despair.

Salvation Jane is a sad-happy and humorous story. It contains a tender sexual theme and strong language.

Also, under Stan Pinnegar, Lucy Leader 44 Butterfly Drive, a fabulous romp through time and space, e-book, on Amazon and as a paperback from CreateSpace..

stan@almostnearlyfamous.com

Salvation Jane (Echium plantagineum), also known as Paterson's Curse, was introduced to Australia from Britain in the 1880s, apparently by a Jane Paterson. It spread like wildfire in its new home and was branded a curse and a noxious weed. However, during a terrible drought which left cattle with nothing else to eat, the plant flourished and was credited with saving the animals, thus its new name, Salvation Jane. The plant's beautiful purple flowers once adorned the northern hills of Adelaide.

Acknowledgments

For my dear friends the original "Smithfield-ites and the original "Elizabethans", thank you for your teenage camaraderie and all the fun we had together.

For Marlene, my darling wife of more than 50 years, without whose patience and support this book would not have been possible.

In loving memory of my brothers Frederick Godfrey (Goff) and Peter Michael and my parents Frederick George and Helen Margaret.

Grateful thanks to Amy, who tirelessly scanned this book, page by page, onto Microsoft Word.

For that young stationmaster who bought sandwiches for a lost and hungry boy all those years ago.

A salute to the 1950s, the final decade of innocence.

HAD I the heavens' embroidered cloths,
Enwrought with golden and silver light,
The blue and the dim and the dark cloths
Of night and light and the half light,
I would spread the cloths under your feet:
But I, being poor, have only my dreams;
I have spread my dreams under your feet;
Tread softly because you tread on my dreams.

W.B. Yeats

Chapter 1

New Beginnings

The mirror cleared quickly in the cool, alien August air. So much had happened since December when he had rubbed on the onion juice, yet still there was not a single hair on his chest. He flexed his arm muscles and gazed approvingly at their reflection before letting his eyes wander down, past his bellybutton to the soft mound of dark hair from which his penis rose with agonising stiffness. Standing sideways to the mirror, he cupped his hand around the fascinating thing and pushed it forward, the bottom of his hand pressing against his testicles. He was delighting in how big it looked, when the outside door crashed open, rushing cold air to his skin. Terror-stricken, he cupped both hands over his private parts, his penis thrusting out defiantly, and dived into the shower cubicle, slamming the door and latching it behind him, his breath coming in short, frightened gasps as he fumbled for a towel.

Numbed by the shock of exposure to other eyes, he was at first barely aware of the soft, lilting voice seeking and then demanding his attention.

"Sorry — what did you say?" he finally choked out.

The few seconds silence roared like Armageddon before the reply came: "I said I have seen many a worse sight than that and will no doubt again before I die." Then, musingly, "Mind, I have seen many a better sight too, so I have."

The friendly cheekiness of the man horrified the boy. He dressed quickly, leaning against the cubicle door for added safety, tore open the latch and fled.

Peter Mitchell wore English-made, rubber-soled shoes and grey worsted flannels, a white shirt and blue pullover. He preferred rubber soles because they gripped better, especially in an English winter when the footpaths were covered in ice or snow. But on this day, speeding from the toilet block, the rubber soles could not save him as he skidded into the loose metal beside the tarsealed strip that ran between the grey, oblong huts of the migrant hostel. His years of play and survival in the back streets of Birmingham failed him, and he sprawled almost sideways on to the sharp stones, towel and soap flying in different directions. He lay there in anger and pain, a gashed right leg pouring blood through his trousers and bits of gravel embedded in his right hand. Embarrassment flooded him for the second time that day — and he hadn't been out of bed an hour.

"Are you all right?"

He looked up with practised nonchalance. She was blond and narrow-featured, but pretty. She would be prettier without her hair tied back so tightly.

"I've cum unstuck." He managed a grin and refined his accent, "I just slipped, thanks."

"Are you going to stay down there for the rest of the day, or what?"

"I wouldn't mind," he replied. "Things haven't started off too well this morning."

He wished a silent wish that she would go away. Each time he tried to get up, he slid helplessly back into the gravel and his face deepened crimson with each attempt. Finally, she grabbed his arm and helped him up.

"Watch where you're going next time," she scolded, "it's a long way to Tipperary."

"I will."

He rescued the towel and wiped his hands with it before pulling up his trouser leg and tying a handkerchief from his pocket around the sore part on the side of his knee. "I'm bleeding quite a bit."

"You'll survive," she assured him cheerfully.

They walked side by side, keeping to the middle of the tarseal.

"I slept in," he offered. "The others have probably finished breakfast."

"You must be a lazy beggar," she observed, tossing back hair which could not possibly be tossed back. "Why is your face so red — am I an embarrassment?"

"Of course not. I've just had a hot shower, that's why."

She stopped beside one of the huts. "I live here. Enjoy your breakfast. It's awful, but enjoy it. 'Trah."

He watched her skip away into the hut.

Breakfast really wasn't bad — not that he was a fussy eater, anyway. The cornflakes were fresh and crisp by anyone's standards, the bacon wasn't shrivelled or burned and the toast looked and tasted like toast, perhaps a little dry. There was even marmalade. He poured his own tea from a large but almost empty urn at the servery and said a shy "good morning" to the women washing the dishes. He sat at a long, wooden trestle which was covered by three square, white tablecloths. Somebody had spilled tea on one of the cloths so he chose a seat away from the stain in case the staff thought he had done it.

It was 8.50 am on his first full day on Australian soil and as he took a mouthful of cornflakes, he wondered crazily whether he would ever eat shredded wheat again.

After breakfast he put on his jacket and St John beret and went for a walk, discovering a dirt track winding south at the rear of the hostel. He kept a vigilance for snakes, remembering the warning they had all been given on the ship that South Australia was host to many poisonous snakes and spiders. To his left, the other side of the scarred, brown paddock, ran the railway line — the main northern line, the coach driver had told them on the trip from Port Adelaide. To his right were more paddocks, uninspiring, light brown with only occasional tufts of green in deference to the winter rains.

He walked under a darkening sky and pulled the collar of his jacket up so it reached the slanted rim of the beret. The air smelled of rain. A large stick on the pathway offered itself as a weapon. He turned it over gingerly, but felt safer once it was in his hand and swished devil-may-care at the stubby grass beside the path.

Had it really been little more than a month since he had slashed such a stick into the lush green grass of the bluebell woods behind Handsworth Park on that singing English summer day?

"You'll soon make new friends," his mother told him.

"We're heading for a better life," his father tried to placate him, not sounding too convinced, his father, who had worked 12 hours a day when work was available and when he wasn't forced out on strike, to keep his family fed and clothed in their Thornhill Road semi-detached home. Peter had never wanted to move to Australia. His friends meant too much to him and there were so many adventures not yet pursued in his beloved England. And there was Margie. Dear, sweet Margie. Most of his life he had loved Margie, though it wasn't until he was fourteen and she thirteen that he made any serious attempt at romance. He threw a note down to her from his upstairs bedroom window as she walked by one evening on her way back from the corner shop.

"I love you, do you love me?" the note said.

She rescued the note from the breeze and tucked it into her coat pocket without reading it, lifting her face to give him a delightful, frowning smile before walking on.

He had thrown himself prostrate on the bed afterwards in shame, wondering how he could ever face her again. He worried for hours that her parents might find the note and come knocking at the Mitchells door. After all, he was a teenager and he supposed he should have known better.

The next day his friend John Crooks came round and with a sly grin thrust a note into his hand. It was from Margie and it said, "Yes, I do". Excited, he called on her straight away, forgetting his fear that her parents might have seen the note.

They went to the markets on the Soho Road, the main road through Handsworth, walking mostly in silence — he feeling shy and awkward and she deep in secret thoughts of her own. A whole seven pence jingled in his pocket, and he would have given it all for the knowledge of what to say to Margie that first time they had "walked out" together. But he had to content himself with standing as close to her as he dared while they gazed longingly at the wares on display and with a rare, unblemished apple each he bought with most of his money. Then they walked to the park and joined the gang in a game of rounders and for a little while quite forgot they were supposed to be dating.

Peter walked her home after their playing was done, and the rest of the gang tagged along too.

He hadn't seen her for two weeks after that. She went to an aunt's in Gloucester for the school holidays. But when she returned, they walked out together again · holding hands and enjoying their new-found togetherness. His mother just about had a fit when she found out and barred him from seeing Margie.

"I've known her for years," he protested.

"I don't care," his mother shouted, "you are forbidden to go with girls. Don't let me hear of you going with a girl — is that clear?"

"It's only Margie from up the road," he protested further.

"I know who it is. You've got something else on your mind and I'll stuff your mouth with soap if I ever find you've been seeing her. I want you to stay home week nights in future."

The tirade almost tore his mind out and after he had shut himself in his room and found some normality of thought, he worried about the soap threat because he hadn't been swearing and he thought his mother must have believed he had been. He wanted to tell her that he hadn't been swearing but decided to wait. Hurt and bewildered, Peter let a few days go by before again raising the subject of Margie.

"What if all my friends are with us? She plays with my friends, her and Cynthia, I can't play with my friends if I can't even see her."

"That isn't what's been happening lately, though," his mother was calmer.

"I don't know," Peter shrugged. "I don't understand what you're talking about . . . And I never swear."

"Just as well you don't," she said. And she relented. He was allowed to play with Margie again, but only in the way he had before. There was to be no walking out together. And he was still to stay home at night.

Funny, he thought, how his parents had gone to so much trouble to ensure their children were brought up properly, yet he could not be trusted to walk down the road with a girl — a very respectable girl at that. Still hurting, even if relieved at being able to see Margie at all, he tried to bury himself, if unsuccessfully, in his schoolwork and even avoided being caned that term. But he saw Margie at weekends and during the Christmas holidays and by then was allowed out at night again because his mother was sick of looking at him mooning about.

He kissed Margie in his fourteenth summer. It was midseason and daylight had lingered late into that magical evening. It was his first kiss except for the cheeks of visiting aunts when he was small. That first kiss, soft and tender and innocent, electrified him with feelings he had never known before and he had held the lower part of his body away from her so she wouldn't feel the swelling in his groin. She was thirteen but her lithe young body was already beginning to ripen into womanhood. He hadn't consciously thought of her in that way, though. She was just wonderful Margie to him and he loved her.

Peter came to an abrupt halt on the path. Ahead stood three men poring over a large document spread out on the bonnet of a red ute. They looked incongruous in suits and ties and large Wellington boots which reached almost up to their knees. One of them began writing on a clipboard. Nearby on a tripod was a surveyor instrument. Peter knew it was called a theodolite. They looked up and smiled as the boy approached.

"Hello," Peter called nervously. He felt silly with the stick and swished it at the grass so they would think he was being casual. "Seen any snakes?" But the men were now in deep conversation and didn't hear him.

He turned and retraced his steps, not wanting to have to greet the men again on his way back. He was almost at the hostel when he saw the girl he had met earlier that morning standing with the air of a person waiting for somebody. He dropped his stick and waved. She sprinted to stand beside him. "How did you know where to find me?" he asked.

"What makes you think I was waiting for you?" Her voice was sharp.

"Sorry," he muttered, his face reddening, "I shouldn't have assumed that you were."

She gave a small, satisfied, smile. "But now you are here, you can escort me to the rec."

"What wreck?"

"The recreation hall — the rec," she said impatiently.

"Oh, the rec." He grinned, "That's what I thought you said. By the way, my name's Peter — Peter Mitchell. What's yours?"

"Petula," she said seriously, "Petula Pumpkin."

He sneaked a sideways glance at her.

"Do you think my name is funny?" she demanded.

"Of course I don't."

"Well, I do — I don't think the name suits me at all. Do you think it does?"

He didn't answer. There was suddenly thin ice under his feet. He wasn't sure whether she was joking, and she was a bit scary; a bit strangely sophisticated. Perhaps she was older than he first thought. You couldn't always tell with girls.

"What if your name was Peter Pumpkin, then? Would you change it?"

"Probably," he replied, but thinking that if his name were Peter Pumpkin, he almost certainly would change it. "I would get the pip over it," he grinned so she would see the joke.

"You're making fun of my name."

"Sorry."

"Just as well my name isn't really Petula Pumpkin — for your sake." She gave him a freckly smile and screwed up her eyes.

"Do you always do that?" he asked.

"Always do what?"

"Make fun of people?"

"I didn't realise you were so sensitive."

"I don't think I am sensitive, but you nearly had me fooled. Do you have a real name?"

"Yes, better than Petula Pumpkin, too." She took his arm as though she had always known him as they approached the white and pale-yellow washed hall which stood palace-like among the grey, featureless huts.

"This is where you get to meet the hostel manager and the other people," she told him. "If you're extra lucky, you might get to meet me."

"I can't wait," he replied.

There were about forty people inside, including his parents and George, and Peter realised with a start that he was standing before them arm-in-arm with a girl. He unhooked himself from her and whispered an urgent "cheerio".

"Trah," she said loudly, and, "Don't you want to know what my name is?"

"Of course." He glanced nervously over at his parents.

"What's wrong?" She frowned, "have you got ants in your pants?"

"I've got to go — my parents are waiting."

"I'm Pauline — Pauline Nicholls."

"Pleased to meet you — I'm Peter Pumpkin." He felt his face redden as always. He would be sixteen in November but he wasn't sure whether he was still barred from "seeing girls".

"Sixteen, he knew, was the age of consent for girls. He didn't know if it applied to boys. He felt fairly certain that the term "age of consent" meant girls could have sex if they wanted to. Though it could mean that girls were allowed to get married at that age — or it could mean both things. He knew parental consent was still needed to get married, even if you were sixteen or older, because both his brothers-in-law had sought permission from his father even though his sisters were eighteen.

Pauline joined a small group of other girls at the far end of the hall. There were several boys, some looked to be younger than Peter and some older. He sighed inwardly. He would bet there wasn't going to be any boys his age. This was going to be one lonely existence. He would bet on that much. He moved towards his parents.

"What are we here for, Mom?" he whispered.

She turned on him, a mixture of anger and relief on her face, "Where have you been?"

"Out walking."

"Your brother has been looking everywhere for you — we were worried."

"I was only walking."

"This is a big country — you can't just go walking here, you'll get lost."

"I used to get lost in Handsworth," he pointed out.

"Exactly."

"What's going on Mom? Why are we here?"

"We are getting told about the tariff and facilities, I think." She fixed him with a gimlet eye. "If your father wasn't so busy talking he would have a word with you."

"That girl was only showing me where to come."

"It's nothing to do with that."

"What have I done then?"

"It's what you haven't done — you'll see," she said mysteriously and in a softer tone, letting him know that he wasn't in very big trouble.

He looked round at his father's touch on his shoulder.

"When you went out this morning was there anything you forgot to do?" His voice was almost jocular. George Mitchell senior was a kind and humorous man, but his 6ft 3in frame was not to be trifled with, especially by fifteen-year-old boys, and more especially if their name was Peter Mitchell.

Peter thought rapidly, "Sorry, I forgot to make my bed."

"Try to remember in future, because it upsets your mother and then I get upset."

Peter searched for an excuse, "I thought I had done it and I remembered I hadn't when I was out."

"You thought you had but you hadn't?" His father stood back with hands on hips and stared at him, "Now where have I heard that before?"

He moved off with a vague smile, saving Peter the obvious answer. He had escaped, too, a quote or phrase from his mother. She might have said, "You know what thought did don't you?" And when he said "no", she would say, "Thought he did but he didn't." Or she might clip him across the ear for not remembering.

Such admonishments, though, were usually made with good humour, Peter playing his part with mock chagrin. The trouble was, one could never be really sure just how serious parents were going to be. The secret to handling grown-ups was to know when they were in the mood for fun. And Peter quite often got it wrong. But there was no one in the world he loved more than his parents. He accepted his strict upbringing as necessary, as did all of his friends accept their tough upbringing. Children needed discipline — both at home and at school.

The number of people in the hall had swollen by the time the camp manager took the microphone and welcomed the newest arrivals. Peter barely listened. This was something for the adults. But when the man finished by asking everyone to mingle and introduce themselves around, he made himself invisible. He hated his shyness but had to live with it and when he made himself invisible, people rarely noticed him. Not that they noticed him much when he was visible.

He learned later that the camp manager had told them nobody needed to pay the tariff until they had found work and received their first wage. Most of the men in the camp, though, had been guaranteed work by the Commonwealth of Australia. Peter's father had obtained a job before signing the immigration papers. The letter confirming the job arrived one fateful day in December, while Peter was looking excitedly towards Christmas, having finished school for good and not realising it was to be his last English Christmas.

His father was to work at the Weapons Research Establishment, in Salisbury, South Australia. The letter said it was situated near the migrant hostel where they would be temporarily housed.

The Mitchells arrived at Port Adelaide with only seven shillings and sixpence between them, but were to receive a gift of £2 10 shillings from the Australian Government as soon as they reached the hostel. The two Mitchell girls, not Mitchells any more, stayed tearfully behind with their husbands.

Peter managed to avoid meeting anyone as the older folk began leaving the hall. The young people lingered in groups. They were off earlier ships than Peter and so had already made friends. He guessed they had come into the hall to see who the new arrivals were. And he guessed that he had come under more than a little scrutiny from the other teenagers. Pauline was in conversation with a younger girl and he decided not to interrupt them.

"Don't worry, everything will be all right," he heard his father say to his mother. Peter moved closer to them as they made their way to the exit. "You can look for work on Monday," his mother told the boy. "We are not taking charity in this place and the tariff is quite high."

Peter had worked for nearly six months in England, first in an electroplating factory, then in a grocer's shop and finally as an office boy at a large factory called Canning's. Something of a miracle, the Canning's job, considering the lies the teachers had written in his final school reports and the fact that he had sat and failed grammar school three times, technical school three times and art school twice. They hadn't let him go back for any more attempts. His report from Rookery Road Secondary Modern School had made dismal reading:

"Peter is lazy and disinterested. He will need to make a major effort to get anywhere in the world. We fear for his future." None of it was true, of course. He was almost top of the school in English and science, and although he was almost bottom of A-grade in everything else, his poor marks had nothing to do with laziness.

It was easy to teach kids who were particularly bright and scholastic or had photographic memories or who hung on every word uttered by a teacher. But what about kids like him? How could kids like Peter Mitchell be expected to learn things when teachers wrote something on the blackboard, burbled on about it and then wiped it off without giving their young minds a chance to home-in? Peter couldn't help what happened to him in class. He had no control whatever over just when a fierce battle was likely to erupt on the planet Mars or when a maiden in distress might need rescuing on Earth. Yes, it was all very well for the kids with photographic memories or those who didn't have a whole lot of dreams to dream.

"Think, Mitchell, think!"

"I am thinking, sir."

"If you were thinking, Mitchell, you would know the answer."

Sometimes Peter thought so much that the words and pictures got too big for his head so he had to look round to see if they had spilled out or to see if anybody had noticed anything strange about him.

He mostly hated school and many of the teachers. Only the English and science teachers bore any resemblance to human beings. He hated the others as much as he thought they hated him. And even the English and science teachers were capable of caning a trembling outstretched hand on a freezing winter's day. Winter was the worst time to be caned — across the inside of knuckles blue with cold.

Yet he had felt sad on his last day at school. Comradeship had been good in the face of adversity from both bullying teachers and some of the rougher kids who stayed in B-grade or C-grade and tried to make life miserable for a few of those in the A-grade. Each year, Peter's various teachers would announce to the entire class of 48 pupils that, "Mitchell has stayed in A-grade for next year by the skin of his teeth". Not that the B- or C-graders worried Peter much. He had learned to be tough, too, and had his own band of close friends who could look after themselves. Few thought that because Peter was generally polite and well-mannered he was therefore a weakling. Peter could survive in the Handsworth jungle. But more importantly, he had his big brother, and even though George left senior school as Peter was starting there, his brother's reputation stayed on. George, who tried to teach Peter to box, won fifteen junior fights in succession before his mother made him hang up his gloves. Unfortunately, George had left his reputation behind with the teachers, too. And particularly with a couple of them who believed as much in sparing the rod as they believed in Father Christmas.

Chapter 2

Oh, Donna!

So, with no school reports, he would catch the train to Adelaide and look for work. But today was only Wednesday — he had a few days of freedom left, which just showed how readily he took things on trust. The next morning he awoke to find his mother thrusting the morning paper at him.

"Have a look for a job — there are plenty of early trains. George will take you to the station when you're ready."

"You said Monday," he protested.

"Never put off until tomorrow what you can do today."

"I don't need George to take me — it's only a half-mile up the road."

"Suit yourself, but don't get lost."

Peter sighed. He was sure he had been born with some directional dysfunction. How many times had he walked out of a shop or cinema, turned the wrong way while deep in thought and become lost? He had spent almost his entire childhood playing in the streets of Handsworth, yet only about a year ago had become utterly lost in thick fog and found himself outside the forbidding gates of Winson Green Prison. They hanged murderers there and Peter felt real terror for the first time. He pressed the bell outside, ready to run if accused of anything, but the man who answered laughed and told him Thornhill Road was in the opposite direction.

He showered slowly, sauntered off to breakfast and picked at his food in the forlorn hope that he would miss all the trains or his mother would decide he was sickening for something. He slouched gloomily off to the station but brightened at the sight of Pauline and another girl on the platform. There was also a short, thickset man who smiled at Peter and said "hello" and sounded Welsh. Peter wondered if he was the same man who had seen him in the shower room.

He bought a ticket and stood next to Pauline nervously studying it.

"You going for a job?" she asked at last.

He nodded, "Are you?"

"This is Donna . . . she lives in the hut opposite yours."

"Pleased to meet you, Donna — are you looking for a job as well?"

"Where are you from?" Donna asked.

"Burrming—umm."

"Burrming—umm," they both mimicked.

"He's from Burrming—umm," Donna said to Pauline. "Have you ever heard of Burrming—umm?"

Peter felt the familiar warming of his face and wished they would stop. The Welshman and other people who had arrived for the train were now taking an interest.

"We're both from Liverpool," Donna said churlishly, "and we don't have an accent, or hardly. Liverpool people don't."

They could have fooled Peter. He was surprised that he still had a broad accent. His mother had always corrected their speech and when other Birmingham people sounded broad to him, he had supposed it was because his mother's insistence that they talk "properly" had wiped away the rough edges. His mother never let him get away with slang or poor pronunciation. Nevertheless, they had all cringed when one of his brothers-in-law had brought home a Grundig tape-recorder and sneaked it on while everyone was chatting. They had all sounded so strange when it was played back that Peter vowed to rid himself of his accent. That had been two years ago.

"How old are you?" Donna suddenly interrupted his thoughts. Was she taking a special interest in him?

"Nearly sixteen — how old are you?" Peter replied.

"When are you sixteen, then?"

"In November — November the sixth."

"Oooh, you missed Guy Fawkes. Was your mother frightened by fireworks?"

He grinned. That was exactly what his mother had told him, forgetting, he had presumed, that she always maintained he had been found in a cabbage patch or that George was discovered in a gooseberry bush. He didn't think he ever really believed that, but when he was younger there had been a marked absence in Peter's mind of any other explanation.

He had found out about the birds and the bees from an older friend when he was eleven. He hadn't believed it at first, but as the months went by more and more information filtered through to him from other boys, confirming the likelihood. He remembered his first and only sex lesson at school. He was thirteen going on fourteen and by then, like the rest of the class, already knew just about everything they were being told. The summing-up of the lesson had been quite brutally simple and, although they hadn't known it at the time, deliberately understated.

"The male inserts his penis and wiggles it around for a while. . . One boy fell off his chair and others in the class turned red and purple trying not to laugh. It had been difficult enough not to grin at the teacher's obvious discomfort.

Lucky, Peter had observed to Yeoman afterwards, that the teacher hadn't had to tell a mixed class. Lucky it was a boys' school. But Yeoman had destroyed Peter's delightful images, pointing out that the girls would have been taught by a woman teacher. Bloody spoilsport Yeoman was sometimes.

"You're hardly the eternal chatterbox, are you?" Pauline interrupted his reverie.

"A penny for your thoughts," said Donna,

Peter blushed, "I was miles away."

"I wish I was — ten thousand of them," Donna said mournfully, "better than being in that terrible camp."

Pauline sat facing him and Donna close beside him. He would have preferred it to be the other way round. He didn't think he was too keen on Donna.

"They're having a great summer over there," Pauline said, "just our luck to be missing it."

"There were so many things to do," Peter sighed. "So many things . . ."

"We'll find plenty to do here," Pauline's voice softened. "We're here now and there's nothing we can do about it."

"Nothing," said Donna.

Peter glumly nodded his agreement.

They fell into silence and he allowed his thoughts to again wander back across the oceans to the summer he was missing: warm days and balmy nights to beckon a boy on thrilling child adventures. And now, at fifteen and three-quarters, wasn't there a chance too of peeping into adult adventures? And then there was the gang. How would they get on without him? Why hadn't he said more than "cheerio" that last morning at Handsworth Park, shaded under the conker tree from the beating sun?

They had all turned up, even his friends from Handsworth New Road School, where he attended briefly before moving to Rookery Road. And, stupidly, he hadn't realised why they came. They hadn't said. He supposed he must have assumed they were all there because it was such a beautiful day for lolling in the park. Why hadn't they said? Then, maybe, just maybe, he might have said more than, "I have to go now — we're getting the train to London this afternoon. Cheerio." Some had just looked at him, some had waved. Some had looked away. They would be having adventures without him, now. But the one-time Black Hand Gang, otherwise once known variously as Robin Hood and his Merry Men or the Knights of the Round Table, was without its leader. Its leader was stranded on the other side of the world. Of course the gang didn't really have a name any more. They were sort of growing out of that. Peter sighed. His lost summer had promised so much. Nobody should have taken that away from him.

Donna was pressing very close to him by the time they began entering Adelaide. Peter kept his leg away from her the best he could, but now it began to jiggle and the more he tried to control it, the worse it became. In desperation he closed his knees together and held them there with his hands. This jiggling had happened to him before and the best way to cure it was to merely allow his leg to relax sideways. But when you were sitting close beside a girl you couldn't do that. She might think you were getting fresh with her. He pretended to be interested in their conversation, watching their faces in turn. Donna kept glancing at him while she talked to Pauline. She was plump and her dark hair was pushed up on the top of her head. She had a well-shaped nose and mouth spoiled slightly by a crooked front tooth. Her already large breasts tended to merely sit rather than point upwards. She had overdone the make-up on her eyes — big and blue, with green-blue colouring stuff on the lids, and dark, curling eyelashes. Nevertheless, he didn't find her unattractive.

Pauline's features were much thinner, with pale blue, twinkling eyes and a strong, slightly Roman nose. Her blond hair looked untidy, even when it was tied back. She had a pale, lightly freckled face and white, even teeth. She was smiling now, while talking to Donna, and looked startlingly pretty. Her eyes screwed up and joy danced all over her face and Peter became even more attracted to her.

So busy was he surreptitiously studying the girls and trying to look debonair and intelligent in their company at the same time, he lost track of what they were talking about, but it was mostly female talk.

The train ride gave him an erection so he let the girls get out first when it finally stopped at Adelaide, and he doubled over while getting out so nobody would see his embarrassment.

He had caught only glimpses of Adelaide during the trip from the port to the hostel. The city was so clean and sparklingly tidy. He would learn that Adelaide was a deliberately planned city which had not been allowed to just "mushroom" without attention to design. It was a model for the world to copy. The main thoroughfare, Rundle Street, was teeming with people on their way to work or wandering around waiting for the myriad fascinating, boy-beckoning shops and stores to open for the day. The side streets lured those looking for rare prizes, if only to gaze at through plate-glass windows, or waited to tempt the hungry with coffee shops and restaurants offering cuisines, it seemed, from just about every country in the world, with Greece, Italy, France, Spain, Yugoslavia, Russia, Germany and China particularly represented.

Peter, still walking behind the girls, jingled the few pennies left in his trouser pocket and checked again that the return train ticket was safe in the top pocket of his jacket. It was not yet 9 o'clock and it had said in the paper to report to the department store at 9.15. Both girls had jobs to go to, it turned out, but they showed him where the department store was before hurrying on their way with a "Trah," and "Good luck".

He entered the huge store, which was just opening, with a fatalistic air, knowing that he might have to exaggerate somewhat if he were questioned about his scholastic achievements. And his few weeks in a grocer's shop might have to be stretched to a few months. Even then, he was hardly brimming with assets for any employer. Still, the advertisement had said: "Boy wanted for china department, full training given."

"You are so clumsy, Peter," his mother's words came back to him as he remembered breaking yet another cup or saucer. When he thought about it, he had broken lots of china at home. But it hadn't always been his fault. Many a cup, for example, had deliberately waited for him to pick it up before parting with its handle. Still, he would have to be careful if he found work around china crockery.

He started work that morning and was entrusted with setting up the finest Noritake as well as the cheaper lines and didn't break a thing. He was kept very busy but enjoyed the work and made an immediate hit with the other staff. Two elderly Australian men out the back, who packed up the orders in big cardboard boxes, were delighted to meet a young "new chum" fresh from the mother country. His immediate superior was an impeccably dressed cockney, small and dapper, charcoal-black suit, white shirt and bowtie, who sneaked off into the back a couple of times for an illicit cigarette. He reminded Peter of Dickie Valentine, the heart-throb singer of British housewives.

His pay was to be just over £5 a week, twice the sum he had received in England. He would hand £4 to his mother towards board, clothes and train ticket and the rest was his, nearly 17 shillings after the taxman's small cut. The hostel canteen staff made up sandwiches for the workers, so he didn't have to buy food, except for that first day, when he scraped up nine pence for a filled roll at midday.

He was so delighted at the prospect of having money in his pocket again that he wrote to Margie and told her he was saving to come back home. When his first pay came he put his pocket money in a tin beside his bed and vowed to be back in England in a year or so. He travelled to work with Pauline and Donna each morning and back home with them each night.

As the hostel filled with new arrivals, a few more teenagers caught the same train so they all sat in the longer seats at the back of a carriage. And as more people came into the hostel, so the recreation hall began to jump on a Saturday night and on a Sunday night they showed old movies, which also attracted young and not so young alike. The teenagers always sat in the back rows of the movies, too, and the older folk by silent consent sat as far away from them as they could.

Peter quickly assumed the role of friend and guardian to Pauline. They went everywhere together, arms linked more often than not, so to the casual observer they were going steady. But it wasn't quite like that. Peter had fallen for her all right, and hadn't failed to notice how well they got on together, not to mention her fine figure, but he was somehow too nervous of her to make any strong romantic moves. And so far as he could tell she showed no positive romantic inclination towards him, despite their linking arms and, on cold nights, her hand joining his to snuggle in his jacket pocket, after she had refused his offer of putting the coat around her shoulders. So he contented himself with being Pauline's close friend for a while, believing that romance would one day perhaps blossom between them. But, she became more and more like a sister to him.

October brought wildly fickle weather. Peter went to work one morning dressed in jumper and jacket and still feeling a bit chilly. But at lunchtime he walked out of the air-conditioned store into a sweltering 32 degrees Celsius. The next day he went to work in white shirt and tie, leaving both his jacket and jumper behind and shivered on the way home because the temperature had plummeted to 12 degrees.

On the colder nights, when there was no adult to open the recreation hall, the teenagers crowded into one of the small boilerhouses from where the camp's hot water supply was fuelled. Here they swapped yarns or in some cases paired off for kissing and snogging in a dark corner. Peter did not pair off with anyone in that way, though Pauline usually stood a bit closer to him in the privacy of the darkness, and he would often catch the eye of one of the other girls in the flickering light from the boiler fire and wish he could become more romantically involved.

Then Pauline's younger sister Veronica, the girl Pauline had been talking to in the rec on his second day there, turned 14 and began accompanying them. He took her under his wing as well.

Sometimes, Donna would brush against him in the darkness of the boilerhouse or stand very close to him. One night, after Pauline and Veronica had gone home, Donna moved so close to him her head was nestled under his chin. She had her back to him and he put his hands breathlessly on her waist. She leaned back against him and they moved slowly back to the corrugated iron wall beside the boiler. There were only a couple of others left in the boiler room by then, so they waited, making small talk until they were alone.

Peter kissed her on the cheek first, gently, but she urgently sought his lips and soon they were kissing passionately. His hands moved for the zip at the back of her dress and he pulled it down, slowly, carefully. The zip worked down cleanly, without snagging, and he reached to undo her bra, but the intricacies of the garment confounded him. Impatiently she reached behind and undid the hooks herself. He had never dreamed anything could be as soft and wonderful as those breasts. He stroked them gently and worked his fingers to her nipples, brushing them lightly with this thumb, taking care not to hurt her. She moaned softly and he stopped, trembling with desire.

"Are you all right"? he asked, fearfully.

"Oooohhh," she gasped.

He became more uncertain. What had he done to her? Was she going to faint? "Oooh, oooh," she cried, "don't stop."

Wondering when his knees were going to give out completely he moved his hands back to her breasts. Her groin was thrusting into his now and he began to feel dizzy. She moved one of his hands and placed it up the top of her skirt. His hand sought and found the soft mound.

It was just as he had imagined — warm and wet and readily accepting his finger. Her moans were becoming more desperate and through the thick haze of passion he worried that someone might hear her. He was getting in too deep, he knew that, but there was no turning back. He wondered if she was a virgin and tried to ask her, but she pushed her mouth against his so hard that he couldn't move his lips. When she suddenly let herself fall backwards he grabbed her and managed to lower her gently to the floor. She reached up for the front of his trousers and worked out each button. He knelt over her and she lowered his trousers. Relief came as she took hold of his stiff penis and tried to force it under her skirt. It came in fiery spurts of warm liquid that threatened to take away whatever breath he had left. He lay in ecstasy beside her, still spurting the fiery stuff over himself, the floor and her dress.

"What's wrong now?" she demanded.

"I can't do it," he said. "I mean . . . I've already done it."

She had been so close to getting what she wanted, she was not easily going to be denied.

He half stood and awkwardly pulled up his trousers. But she pounced before he could fasten his buttons.

She felt it — temporarily small and soft.

"You've come," she said, "you useless bastard."

He couldn't get out of there quickly enough. He did his belt up at the doorway and waited impatiently for her. "I'm sorry about that," he choked out, "I'll see you home."

She was clearly upset but didn't speak again. He watched her go up the steps of her hut. He felt weakened yet strangely elated.

In a way, he was glad he had spoiled it. After all, what sort of reception would await him if he got a girl pregnant? His mother would have a blue fit.

He bounced into the small lounge of their hut cheerfully and then sped out again as he realised his flies were undone.

Sleep was a long time arriving that night. He was "overtired" he told himself. But it was more than that — he felt vaguely dirty and scared. He must get out. He must escape to his crew on board the spaceship he had left in orbit before leaving England. Before he could even tune-in to outer space, the song popped into his head. It was the one he had sung at Sunday school with Margie . . . how long ago?

At the end of the day
Just kneel and say
Thank you Lord
For my work and play
I tried to be good
For I know that I should
That's my prayer at the end of the day.

He turned his face into the pillow, trying to blot the words from his mind. Why did he have to grow up . . . why couldn't he stay like Peter Pan forever in that magical garden of childhood?

He thought about Peter Pan and Wendy. If she grew up and he didn't, she would have had to find herself a new boyfriend one day.

Dawn wakened him with the raucous squawking of magpies. That was another sad thing for him to reflect on. He had counted about a dozen birds since his arrival, mostly what they called Murray magpies, and he was sure there weren't many others in the state. Where would they live? Birds needed trees, and in an expanse of about 20 miles he would bet there were no more than a dozen trees.

Donna was at the station as usual. Their greeting was restrained. Pauline stood sniffing in a thick overcoat with the collar turned up. It was cool but not really cold. She looked paler than usual and he guessed that she had the flu but was going to work. Jobs were too precious to risk getting sacked. His job was still meandering along. He was kept busy but there was little strain on his intellect. He enjoyed the companionship as much as the work. The elderly packers talked to him about

Australia, about the Aborigines and told him what they knew of Dreamtime.

"We like to call them Aborigines," one of them had politely told him when he inquired about the "dark people".

"We don't say blacks, or niggers," the other one had added.

Heaven forbid. His parents would never let him use those words.

They told him much about the Aborigines. How they could walk a thousand miles through the Outback, finding sustenance and water where no European would ever find it and how they had been doing that since time began. They told him, also, of the didgeridoo and the boomerang, though he had learned about those at school.

The department store was a good, friendly firm to work for, but he had saved little money. England was as far away as ever.

Not long after, Pauline told him she had been moved to a branch office in nearby Salisbury. She would not be catching his train any more. Donna had become reasonably friendly with him again, but he found it difficult to look her in the face and he felt stupid sitting next to her on the train. There were still a few other kids he knew on the train. But they came and went — sometimes getting earlier trains, sometimes later ones. The train journeys were no longer the fun they once were.

One night he stepped from work into bitterly cold air. The inside of the train was warm, though, and the clackety-clack of the wheels made him drowsy. At first he dozed and awoke with a start, looking around to see if anyone had noticed. By the time the train reached Dry Creek a few miles on, he was sound asleep and didn't wake up until miles from Smithfield. His carriage was empty and it was dark outside. The train had come to the end of its run. He walked out into a black, threatening night.

The young, kindly stationmaster told him at the otherwise deserted platform that there was not another train until 10.30 pm. It was now 7.38. The train had arrived at Gawler North at 7.01 but he had slept on in the stationary carriage.

He waited in the tiny tin shed with a sense of hopelessness. Everyone would wonder where he was. They would laugh when they knew.

The stationmaster bought him some sandwiches from the township, which he accepted gratefully and ate hungrily. He had no money — just his weekly train ticket, a few cigarettes and some matches. He lit a precious cigarette and blew a cloud of smoke into the black sky, beyond the range of light above the shed. There was something in the air. He could taste it, feel it against his skin and was electrified by it. It was almost like just before the first snow fell over Birmingham, only much more threatening.

It came suddenly, the most fearful hailstorm he had ever known crashing against the tin shed in maniacal fury and slashing on to the pathway in front of him. Huge hailstones, big enough, he felt sure, to kill if you were out there. Numb with fear at the deafening noise on the roof, he pressed his hands to his ears to help shut out the din. It went on and on until he thought it would never stop, but finally it did, as suddenly as it had started, leaving a deep, white carpet of ice before him. He reached from the shed and grabbed a handful, meaning to make a snowball but it was so cold it burned his skin and he dropped it quickly, rubbing his hands on his coat for warmth before putting them in his pockets.

"I'm off now — you'll be all right?" It was the stationmaster.

"Yes, thanks," he grinned bravely at the man.

"The storm will have blown itself out," the man added, "look after yourself." Then Peter was alone in the eerie darkness.

He had no watch and had forgotten to ask the man the time. He guessed he had been there about an hour. Time still stretched interminably ahead of him and the longer he was there, the colder he became.

Back at the hostel they organised a small search party for him. His mother was anxious that he might have fallen in a ditch or somehow come to grief in the half mile from the Smithfield station to the camp.

It was nearly 11.15 pm when he arrived home, scared and cold. She made him a cup of tea and scolded him for causing all that worry. He threw a sickie the next day, taking advantage of some lingering sympathy in the household.

He told himself that he didn't feel all that good. Perhaps he was getting a cold. Sometimes, as on the next morning, George caught a train so early that it was still dark when he reached work. His father left soon after. So when he awoke only his mother was still there, still comfortably there.

<h1 style="text-align:center">Chapter 3</h1>

<h1 style="text-align:center">Hello Jim</h1>

There was a scattering of people at the camp during midweek days, mostly young mothers and older women. His mother went to town with a couple of the women around 10.30 that morning, leaving him to his own devices.

He put on his brown corduroys and light grey jumper and set off to walk the same path as on his first morning. His stick was still lying where he had left it a couple of months before and he gathered it, again carefully, before proceeding. It had rained over Smithfield through the night, but the path was now barely damp.

Alert for snakes or anything else that crept or crawled or slithered in the grass, he was almost upon the other youth before he saw him. He had brilliantly red hair, a classical ginger, and a complexion to match. He wore blue jeans and a light-brown check jacket, his white shirt was unbuttoned to halfway down his chest. Well-built, almost plump, the youth would have weighed about the same as Peter, though he was a couple of inches shorter — about 5ft 9in.

Peter's greeting froze in his throat when he saw the pistol. It was pointing straight at him. The silence between them stretched interminably. Peter was trying to say something, anything, but words wouldn't come. He was as transfixed as that time in Handsworth when he came across a Teddy boy shooting an airgun at the feet of two young girls. The girls were screaming each time the pellets ricocheted on the paving, sometimes striking their dresses, threatening their legs.

Peter had known he must do something, yet he couldn't move. It wasn't the airgun so much, it was just fear of a situation. The youth was older but only a bit taller — and was reloading the gun with incredible speed, obviously having practised long hours at it.

"Leave them", Peter finally yelled: "Leave them or I'll call the police." The Teddy boy only glanced at Peter, a strange excitement blazing in his eyes. Then, just like in the Westerns, when the cowboys were pinned down by hundreds of warring Indians and had run out of ammunition, the cavalry arrived — George and a friend came speeding round the corner on their bicycles having decided some months before, rather wildly, to train for the Tour de France.

George stopped beside Peter giving him a quizzical look when he saw what was going on.

"Is he with you?" he asked,

"No," Peter was most definite. "I've told him to leave them alone but he won't."

The Teddy boy, suddenly aware of the two cyclists, swaggered over to them. He placed his hand on the handlebars of George's bike, and George knocked him out. Just like that, George hadn't even looked at the Teddy boy, hadn't even looked away from Peter.

The youth lay in the gutter, well, half in the gutter, as the airgun skidded away across the pavement. The girls kept saying "thank you" to George and they even said it to Peter, who felt really proud of George and himself, and the United States cavalry.

Peter spent much of the next day in class knocking out imaginary villains without looking at them. He told all his friends about what had happened, and those who believed him were almost as impressed as he was.

But today, in this vast paddock in the middle of nowhere, Peter was on his own and staring at the barrel of a gun. Gene Autry or Roy Rogers would have whipped out their own guns and put a bullet through the hand of the villain.

"You . . . you shot the gun out of my hand," the baddie would have spluttered unnecessarily.

The youth moved closer to him, still silent, apparently awaiting some reaction from Peter. It didn't look all that powerful an airgun, and some of the fear left Peter. He decided to wait until his adversary came even nearer and then rush him.

At long last he heard himself talk: "What's the problem?"

The youth continued to gaze silently at him and the seconds ticked away in Peter's brain.

"What's the problem? What's the problem?" The youth finally repeated back at him. "What's the problem? What's the problem?" He repeated again. Now he had his head cocked to one side at Peter, who wanted to make himself invisible, having decided that the youth was quite mad.

"I'll tell you what the problem is," the youth said.

"The problem is that you are trespassing aren't you?"

"I thought this was public land," Peter said, genuinely puzzled.

"Is it fuck it's my land."

"Sorry," Peter shrugged, though not knowing whether to believe the youth. "I'll remember in future."

The youth lowered the gun and moved right up to Peter. Close enough for a punch on the jaw if necessary.

"When did you buy it?" Peter asked nervously.

"Buy what?"

"The land."

"I didn't buy it, I had it given to me," he offered Peter a thin smile. "The Aborigines gave it to me."

"Did you give them some beads or something?"

"Don't be fuckin' smart. Do I look as though I would walk around with beads?"

The youth's face had reddened even more, making Peter think of carrots. "Shall we call a truce and have a look round together?" Peter suggested, all fear having left him with his instinct recognising that there was little real menace in the youth.

"*Y'rre* awwri", the youth said, lapsing deeply into his native accent. "Where yuh from?"

"Burrmingumm," Peter said, wishing he had said it correctly.

"Manchester," the youth offered. "Have you heard of it?"

"Of course," Peter said, "the ship canal."

"There's more to Manchester than a ship canal."

"And lots of rain," Peter offered. "More rain than in Brum."

"That's right," said the youth with a touch of pride.

"If there's more rain in Manchester than in Birmingham, there must be a heck of a lot of rain in Manchester," Peter observed. "A heck of a lot."

"There wasn't any fuckin' rain when I left, was there?" the youth replied. "I had to come to fuckin' Australia to get wet."

Peter laughed. "What's your name?"

"What's yours?"

"Peter Mitchell,"

The youth extended his hand, "Jim Brown, howd'y do."

Jim, it turned out, lived at the hostel as well, but Peter had never seen him before because glandular fever had kept the youth indoors for weeks and further incarceration had been forced on him for studies.

"That's why I'm here," Jim told him. "This is my home now — this fuckin' paddock and the stars."

"Wow," Peter marvelled, "have you left home?"

"Yeah, I've been here for three days."

"What were you studying?"

"Building trade," Jim spat into the grass. "What for?" he demanded of Peter.

"I suppose it's a good trade," Peter said. "Good money."

Jim rounded on him, almost angrily. "Do you know where I've just been?"

"No."

"I've been down the fuckin' building site, that's where." He was walking backwards now, directly in front of Peter. "And," he swept his arms out, "do you know what happened? I got a fuckin' job."

Peter had to anticipate: "So why study if you can get a job anyway?"

"Dead fuckin' raaght."

"Can I have a go with your air pistol?"

"No — you couldn't hit a barn door at two paces. And I haven't got any slugs."

Peter sighed inwardly, at least in Handsworth people were either nice or nasty. Since arriving in Australia he had met some very strange people. Jim Brown was going to be no exception.

"Did you take your gun with you to look for a job?"

Jim shook his head, "I hid it before going on to the site. I'm not stupid."

"What sort of money do they pay?" Peter asked.

"About £5 a week to start. You get a rise after three months and then after each birthday."

"Where is it?"

"Just down there," Jim pointed in the direction Peter had seen the men studying a map.

"Any more vacancies?"

"Yurr," Jim said, "just go and ask for Joe."

"Not today," Peter said, "I'm off work with the flu."

"Where are you working?"

"In Adelaide."

"Save your train fare. You can walk to work . . . Mind you, you'll have to buy tools, but you can get those on tick. You don't sound like you've got the flu."

Peter walked to the building site the next day and was told he could start as an improver carpenter the following Monday. Peter wasn't sure whether an improver carpenter was the same as an apprentice, and he didn't like to ask.

He told Joe, the site foreman, that he should give a week's notice where he worked.

Joe agreed, "Start as soon as you've worked your notice out then. If I'm not here, ask for Clive."

Clive was typically Australian, Peter decided, big and lean with a voice to match. Nobody messed with Clive, but he was kindly and generous to his gang of men. Peter became part of the Clive carpentry gang with some trepidation. There were ten of them, counting Peter and old Charlie.

Ronnie was the tall, angular apprentice who had only a year to go before he became a tradesman. Bluey was so called, Peter found, because of his alleged red hair (which actually was a light golden colour). He was tall, broad and wore a sleeveless

T-shirt which showed off rippling arm muscles. Peter wondered how George would fare in combat with Bluey.

Dave was a couple of inches shorter than the others and a bit plump. His dark hair was receding but he still looked only 30ish. Dave was the friendliest of the men and the least ruffled when tempers flared. Chris wore shorts so badly ripped they hardly existed. He was the quietest and wore thick-lensed glasses. He had come to Australia from Switzerland as a child. Peter was never sure about Chris, who answered his questions rarely — and then virtually in monosyllables. Helmut was a short, stocky German in his mid-40s. He spoke precise English, when he spoke at all. He had the most brilliant blue eyes Peter had ever seen. But there was something about Helmut that he did not like. Nothing you could put your finger on — he just gave Peter the creeps. Mush, a very large, fat Greek with a sumptuous black moustache, spoke little English but always had a smile for Peter, who liked the man, except during meals. Dopples was a Cypriot Greek in his early to mid-30s. He spoke good English and talked often of the new life he had come to with his wife and family. He was pleased to be away from the troubles in Cyprus and had high expectations for the future in his new land. Peter and Dopples hit it off straight away and became good mates at work. But the Australians hated Dopples for some reason or possibly for no reason. The other member of the gang was inherited from the brickies for lunchtimes and smokos. They claimed they couldn't stand his bullshit any more. Charlie, a labourer with the nearest brickie gang, claimed to be 63, but some said he was 80 if he was a day. Peter could believe he was 80. Charlie wore blue bib-fronted overalls with nothing on underneath. His skin had once been as tough and as hard as parched leather, but was softened and wrinkled now, having seen too many blazing summers as much as too many birthdays. He walked hunched rather than stooped, which he claimed was through carrying too many bricks on his shoulders. And he was so bandy they reckoned you could push a wheelbarrow between his legs when he stood with his feet together. His white hair and white stubble on his chin were always the same length, his hair almost to his ears and the stubble about an eighth of an inch. It was said that Charlie shaved with the end of a broken bottle. He reminded Peter of an old goldminer or the American character actor Gabby Hayes.

A natural affinity grew between the old man and the boy, who lent a ready and patient ear to some of the biggest bullshit it was possible to concoct. Peter, who had never heard his father use a bad word, soon learned to swear among the Australians, though he was careful to use those words in quiet mutterings to himself and he never even muttered them in front of Clive. He didn't see Jim at work — about two miles separated their gangs. This would be a big city one day, he was told.

Peter liked the open, expansive nature of the Australians, in the carpentry gang and most of the other building gangs he had contact with. But he was bewildered by the way they treated the so-called New Australians — the Greeks, Italians and such. It didn't take him long to discover that many of his countrymen, too, could be given virtually second-class citizen treatment, especially if they moaned too much, when they became known as "Pommie whingers"; though still they received nothing like the treatment meted out to those whose mother tongue was other than English.

Many of the New Australians throughout the building gangs sat apart from the Australians and British-born workers, so they could speak to one another, where possible, in their native tongues. It was an indulgence the born and bred Australians could not abide.

Peter was loaned the use of tools for the first few weeks, during which he was given simple tasks. Among his duties was fetching the morning tea and lunch orders from a caravan about half a mile away, and boiling up the large copper for making the men's teas. They showed him how to make "tea that would make England weep" and how to whirl a filled, scalding hot billycan round and round in the air without spilling a drop. The men liked to put the tealeaves in their own billies. A slither of wood across the top of each can was mandatory as was the whirling of each completed billy.

Peter struggled twice each day to light the fire for the teas; it was especially more difficult in the rain. No matter what the weather, he could not be late. The men sat down for a 10-minute break at 9.50 sharp and at midday for a half hour, and if they took longer than was strictly allowed — it had better not be because their teas or orders were not ready. Old Charlie gave the boy an ancient billycan for his own use and with it Peter pretended he had developed his special way of making tea. At first, he took milk and sugar, which the Australians said was a waste of a good brew. Eventually, he took his tea black and unsweetened. Charlie tasted it and pronounced it "quite nice but a bit weak". Charlie, though, drank tea so strong you could dye your hair with it or, as the old man had once put it, would make a mule shit stones.

Chapter 4

Girls, Girls, Girls

On Thursday, October 20, Pauline celebrated her 16th birthday with a small gathering in the Nicholls' hut. Her parents disappeared to a neighbour's so their daughter could enjoy the company of friends.

Peter, usually so conservatively dressed, looked rather sartorial in a green and yellow check shirt, red tie and grey worsteds, freshly pressed, on which he had made a good patch job after his fall into the gravel. He kept his corduroys now for the building site and for just knocking around in. They were no longer suitable for formal occasions.

He sat on a wooden chair next to Donna, whose grey, pleated skirt rode a good few inches above her knees. She had left an extra button undone on her yellow blouse and had crinkled her hair so it fell in waves to her shoulders. She gave Peter a big, cheeky smile when he arrived, making him hope she hadn't said anything about their attempt at lovemaking. There were seven of them. As well as himself and Donna, there was Pauline, Veronica, Shirley, who was the newest teenage arrival at the camp, Jim, and Lisa, a small, slightly built girl who was a friend of Veronica's. Lisa giggled and whispered in Veronica's ear a lot. Veronica pulled a face at Peter and made him blush. Peter hoped like hell that Lisa didn't decide to come over and talk to him. It was bad enough putting up with Veronica, sometimes.

Jim was in earnest conversation with Pauline, which irked Peter a bit and he decided he should move away from Donna in case Pauline thought they were together. However, he didn't want to appear rude to Donna, who just then nudged him in the side to get his attention.

"You're blushing," she said.

"No. I've been running," he lied.

"Were you running because you heard I would be here?"

"I ran because I felt like it," he replied, aware that his face was turning even redder.

"It's not far to run — you only live across the road."

"I went for a run, I mean, along the back of the hostel."

"You seem very nervous," she continued, determined to tease.

"I'm not even a bit nervous," Peter said nervously. "Why should I be?" She shrugged, "No reason that I know of."

It was obvious to Peter that as well as teasing, Donna was trying to get off with him again. And she wouldn't have to try too hard to lure him back into another attempt at lovemaking. After all, he had his pride to repair. Then again, hopefully, he might resist her. He was too interested in Pauline and he didn't trust Donna to keep her mouth shut. Already he had gone too far with her and he worried that she might tell any one of them, let alone Pauline. He was relieved when Donna got involved in a conversation with Veronica and Lisa.

Shirley attracted some of Peter's attention. He was sure she had glanced at him more than once since his arrival and when he caught her eye he was rewarded with a lovely, happy smile. She had a bubbling personality   always smiling or laughing, yet exuding a special charm and intelligence lacking in many of the teenagers. He wanted to move across the room and speak to her, sit close to her, but once again he felt constrained lest he be seen to be snubbing Donna. He had to talk to Pauline first, anyway. And therein lay another problem.

Should he wish Pauline 'happy birthday' and kiss her on the cheek or on the lips? Could he kiss her in front of everyone? Not really. That would be too embarrassing. It was all right for others to kiss someone in front of people, but they didn't get as embarrassed as Peter Mitchell. Just about everything made him blush.

The Nicholls' lounge was furnished simply, as lounges were in all the huts. Six straight-backed wooden chairs around an oblong Formica-topped table. Hard-wearing but cheap linoleum over which was thrown a couple of large mats . . . hardly the comforts of home for any of them, he suspected. Peter's mind wanted to wander back to Thornhill Road then, but Pauline suddenly interrupted his thoughts.

"Hey, dreamer — I'm talking to you."

He smiled, pleased that she had at last taken notice of him.

"By the way," he said before she could elaborate, "Many happy returns of the day." Wow, he didn't blush.

"Thank you, Peter." She gave him what he would have sworn was a rare, special smile; almost conspiratorial.

Was there a conspiracy of love between them? Peter didn't know. If there was, then he had missed his part in it somewhere. Perhaps it was only their friendship her smile alluded to, not a budding love of which he had yet to glimpse the first petal. But then, it was early days.

"We were saying that the dance should be fun on Saturday — they have some new records," Pauline said.

Peter was startled. Had Jim asked her to the dance? But surely she would have told him that she went everywhere with Peter. Surely . . .

Peter was not always aware that he assumed too much. But he knew he had no right to expect Pauline to reserve herself for him. After all, they weren't going steady or anything. They knocked around together because they kept getting in each other's way, really.

But what the Dickens could he do about it? He daren't ask her formally to go steady. God, what if she laughed? What if she laughed and said: "Don't be silly, you're too young," or something equally as embarrassing? What if it spoiled their friendship?

Peter made no outward sign of being possessive with his friends, learning through childhood that no one liked being crowded. Indeed, he respected freedom himself and valued immensely the times when he could be alone with his own thoughts and dreams. But deep inside, he was possessive.

He wanted to say to Pauline: "I'm taking you aren't I?" Or, "What time shall I call for you on Saturday?"

But he said: "Are you going?"

"I think so," she said, "ask Veronica, she'll go if you ask her." He didn't mind asking Veronica but he hesitated. He wasn't sure what Pauline meant. Veronica was too young for him to take out. Margie was young, too, but she was different. He hadn't grown up with Veronica. Pauline probably meant merely that she didn't want to go out on Saturday night and leave her kid sister at home.

Peter knew the power of words. He knew that if he wasn't careful about what he said he could hurt Veronica or exasperate Pauline. He took a deep breath and tackled the problem head-on.

"Pauline," he interrupted her conversation which had restarted with Jim, "Do you want me to take both you and Veronica to the dance?"

"Yes, of course, but Veronica needs a dancing partner."

"Veronica," he said, amazed at his own boldness. She turned to look at him. "Do you want to come to the dance on Saturday with me and Pauline?" She smiled and nodded. Then she gave Pauline a puzzled look and went back to her conversation.

Peter wanted to quit while he was ahead and asked if he could put another record on.

An hour later her parents came in bearing a cake ablaze with 16 candles. They all self-consciously sang *Happy Birthday* and Pauline took two puffs to blow out the candles. Jim gave Pauline a kiss in front of her parents which made Peter suddenly turn to Shirley and say something stupid, like "How's your little brother?" in case he was expected to kiss Pauline as well.

He lay in bed wishing he had brazened out his shyness and kissed Pauline. Had she been expecting him to? But he wouldn't have kissed even Margie in front of somebody else, especially in front of her parents. He decided that Pauline had not expected him to kiss her. In fact, the more he thought about it the more obvious it became that Pauline would have been delighted he had spared her that embarrassment. Trust Jim to upset her by kissing her like that. He must have a word with Jim . . . or at least keep an eye on him.

Peter had the most delicious wet dream that night. He was helping a beautiful maiden to cross a stream, like the one at Handsworth bluebell woods. The water ran freely and he kept saying to her, "Watch the stones, they're slippery." But she slipped and would have fallen had he not grabbed her in his strong arms and helped her to the bank. Then he was holding her tightly to him and they kissed long and passionately and sat down in the bluebells. She took off her coat and jumper and he saw that her top two blouse buttons were undone. He kept meaning to tell her she would catch cold, but suddenly he was picking the wild bluebells for her and as he turned with them bunched in his hand he realised he was naked and it was Donna waiting to receive the flowers. She gently took him to her. They caressed and he again felt her soft breast beneath his hand. They were about to couple and waves of joy washed over him as he triumphantly surged forward to enter her, then he ejaculated in fiery spurts into the grass beside them while she burst into hysterical laughter. He awoke in the darkness with a warm wetness between his legs, feeling strangely peaceful and happy. Even in his dreams his virginity was protected. He clasped his hands together:

At the end of the day
Just kneel and say
Thank you Lord for my work and play,
I tried to be good
For I know that I should . . .
Matthew, Mark, Luke and John,
Bless the bed that I lay on
May four angels round my bed
Trap my heels . . . Peter fell asleep.

Friday was a day for dreaming rather than working. He had girls on his mind more than usual.

In his daydreams Veronica had become his young sister who looked up to him for guidance and advice. When boys came calling for her he studied them first and almost invariably suggested that they were not very suitable. Such mental play-acting protected him from having sexual thoughts about Pauline; to think of her sexually trespassed in a way Peter didn't quite understand. He reserved any carnal thoughts for Donna, who spent most of the morning begging him to take her to the dance. And in the afternoon he had a great time laughing and joking with Shirley, until he split the side of his thumb with the side-axe.

The men told him he was "lucky" as he sat with his head between his knees waiting for the faintness to subside.

"Another flea's leg and it would have been curtains for that thumb," Ronnie said.

Clive told him he was a "great galah" and wrapped a large towel round the thumb to stop some of the bleeding before driving him to a doctor's surgery in Salisbury where the wound was stitched.

Before Peter went to the dance the next night he unwound the bandage from his thumb and replaced it with a small plaster. It was on his left hand and he didn't want to be dancing around with a huge bandaged thumb sticking in the air. He had gained enough mileage from his accident anyway.

"Just a fraction more and I would have chopped my thumb off," he had told a suitably impressed George at breakfast. Pauline and Veronica made so much fuss about it that Peter felt a bit of a twit; but Jim, making one of his rare appearances at the breakfast gathering, told him to "fuck off while I'm eating".

He decided he must not overdo the martyr bit. After all, it was a very minor injury and he certainly hadn't mentioned that he had nearly fainted because of it.

On the threshold of manhood stands the boy.

Dare he step forward?

Does he know he can never step back?

Chapter 5

Sad Songs

It was 8 o'clock when they arrived at the hall, Pauline holding on to his right arm and Veronica his left. He wondered whether other boys had the same problem trying to walk straight with a girl on each arm. It wasn't easy. But it was worth it.

Peter extricated himself before entering the hall. He had no wish to invite stares or leg-pulling catcalls. The girls had seemed quite willing to enter with their escort trapped in the middle. It was easy to disengage though because he had to open the swing doors for them anyway.

The Saturday night dances attracted a wide age group. Children were packed off to bed first. The music and singing reflected the homesickness of many and a general love for the nostalgic among the rest. Saturday nights were a long trip down memory lane. George was there, stony-faced beside their parents. Peter noted thankfully that they were sitting a good distance from the teenagers' table.

When the record player was turned off and it was singsong time, you could lay a certain bet on the Scottish immigrants opening up with songs like *I Belong to Glasgow, Bonnie Scotland, Just Aweadoch and Doris.* Then the English would come forth with *Maybe It's Because I'm a Londoner, Roll Out the Barrel,* then songs like *The Happy Wanderer, Mocking Bird Hill, Show Me The Way To Go Home,* and *Side By Side.* Peter knew most of the songs as did the other young people and they joined in lustily with the adults.

Then inevitably the master of ceremonies would call someone up to do a solo spot and most of the others would squirm in their seats fearing they might be next. The solo artists were reasonably good singers, those who weren't usually refused to go on stage, though it wasn't unknown for people to be carried bodily before the microphone. Peter liked listening to the singers. He had been given duty as a St John Ambulance cadet when Johnny Ray appeared at the Bingley Hall, in Birmingham, and the adoration of the fans and the number of times he had to produce the smelling salts had not been lost on him. As well, hadn't he and Margie and a couple of the others put on small concerts for their friends?

One of the teachers at Rookery Road School once told him he should further his singing.

But the longing to entertain in the way the pop stars did was something Peter kept well buried, particularly since his most awful experience ever at school. He had been chosen to sing before the entire assembly one Christmas break-up. Peter thought it cruel that he hadn't been warned. Had he been, he could have put on a suitable act of sickness to fool his mother and stayed at home. But children are no match for the cunning of adults, particularly teachers.

He knew his class, 2A, was to sing *I Drew My Ship (Into the Harbour)* and *All Through the Night* before the assembly that day. They had their songbooks with them to prove it. Like the other boys in the assembly, he began by only half-listening, with a bored indifference, knowing he would be anonymous in the crowd of 50 boys from 2A, thinking more of the holidays ahead as the headmaster told them about the real meaning of Christmas and how each should try to do a special act of kindness at this time of the year.

"Because that is why Christmas was given to us. Not just for stockings filled with gifts and sweets and nuts. Christmas is a time for goodwill to all men, and it is a time when we can quietly contemplate our good fortune when so many are sick or suffering in poverty. Perhaps too we could remember those who sacrificed their lives during two world wars so that this land of ours might stay free and its people be not dominated by a foreign power at any Yuletide."

Then he mentioned those Old Boys of the school who had lost their lives in war and whose names were on the big brass plaque in the assembly hall. He asked for two minutes' silence in remembrance of them. Peter had been about to hurl himself over the trench with bayonet fixed when the two minutes passed and the headmaster's voice crashed into his thoughts.

"They have not died in vain, their spirit lives on in this school and, indeed, throughout this free land of ours." Peter was moved almost to tears as sadness and pride welled up inside him. He would do that. He would fight for and die for England if it were necessary — his England, wonderful, beautiful England. Two boys sniggered behind him and he realised he was standing to attention — chin up and shoulders back. He relaxed, put his hands behind his back and stuck two fingers up at them, risking a caning before the eyrie of eagle-eyed teachers.

The assembly sang *Lead Us Heavenly Father Lead Us*, followed by *Abide With Me, O Come All Ye Faithful* and *The First Noel*. Then a boy was called forward to recite *Love Of Country*, and another boy, whom the headmaster said wanted to be a horse race caller one day, gave a fine rendition of calling the English Derby, which captured everybody's startled attention.

"Now, would Peter Mitchell, from 2A, please come up here."

Terror and panic filled Peter as he walked out of his line and up to the front, before the stares of hundreds of boys and a dozen or so teachers. He thought he had been seen giving the fingers sign and was to be punished in front of the entire school. The severity of punishment for such an act was well known ever since his friend Lenny had pleaded unsuccessfully to a teacher in the playground one day that he had been merely imitating Winston Churchill. Six of the best, Lenny got.

He walked up the three steps on to the stage and stood nervously before the headmaster — a small and dapper, elderly man with a neat, white moustache and a kind face. An ex-military man, fair but firm, he had personally caned Peter the year before for firing a pea-shooter at a teacher on a bus. But there was no admonishment, no reproach this time as he gently steered the boy to the microphone.

"Mr Binstead tells me that 2A are very keen on music, especially singing, and that Mitchell has a particularly fine voice. He will sing for us — *Tom Bowling*, I believe — and then 2A will join him with two more songs. The whole of his class was coming forward now, while Peter skimmed hurriedly through his book trying to find *Tom Bowling*, even though he knew it by heart. His classmates filed behind him, silent but for the whispering pages of their books and the occasional scuffing of shoes. And Peter couldn't find bloody *Tom Bowling*.

"What page?" he asked urgently of a boy, "what page is it on?" The boy shook his head mystified. Peter gave one final, desperate flick of the pages amid a few giggles in the hall, and found himself staring at the *Ash Grove*. He turned urgently to the headmaster, "Sir, can I sing the *Ash Grove*, instead?" He dared not say that he couldn't find *Tom Bowling*. And it didn't occur to him that he knew the song by heart, anyway.

"Of course, that would be most suitable. Rise to the occasion, Mitchell." Then the headmaster told everyone that Mitchell wanted to sing *The Ash Grove* instead. And Peter turned into the sea of faces. Feeling exposed, naked, and desperately hoping his flies were not undone, he nevertheless sang beautifully, like he had never sang before, with Mr Binstead stroking the keys of the piano in near-orgasmic delight. During the rapturous, rather overdone applause, Peter was proud to notice that the teachers as well were applauding him. After 2A accompanied him with the other two songs and they all rejoined the assembly, Peter found he was shaking so much that he had to put his hands in his pockets to hide their trembling, although to do so was forbidden. A covert peep also told him that, in fact, his trousers were quite secure.

On the stage of the recreation hall at Smithfield Hostel, a couple of women sang *How Much Is That Doggie In The Window*, and on cue some of the adults, already tipsy, were yelling out "bow-wow" — something considered far too childish for the teenagers to even contemplate. The master of ceremonies, a small, neatly dressed Londoner who earlier gave a rendition of a Mario Lanza-like *Bridge Of Sighs*, had now taken over the piano and was actively encouraging this outlandish behaviour. The teenagers were seated at a table near the stage. The girls attracted the attention of Dave Connor, who hailed from Plymouth, and Roger Brampton, a Londoner. The two were a few years older than Peter and he saw little of them other than to say "hello" occasionally in the recreation hall. The girls appeared to welcome the attention of the two older boys, but

Peter wished they would go away. They made him too aware of his own youthfulness and inadequacy. At the next table a group of Welsh and Scottish people, who started out in a convivial mood, became more and more homesick and were now at the point of being downright maudling about how they missed the folks back home. One woman burst into tears because her parents were back in Glasgow and she would never see them again and her husband told her to hush and not make a scene.

Peter hated to see people sad like that, especially when he was trying to enjoy himself and forget about his old friends and Margie and England for a few hours. He preferred the "brave front". He would keep as his secret forever the number of times he had cried into his pillow since arriving in Australia.

So far that evening he had danced three times with Pauline and won from her the promise of the last dance. He danced twice with Veronica, so she wouldn't feel left out and once with Shirley. He asked Lisa up to dance but she giggled and hid her face, so Jim dragged her on to the floor instead and forced her to do a high-stepping comic number which brought applause from everyone and so cured the astonished Lisa of her shyness that afterwards she went around getting boys and men up to dance. But Peter was mostly on the floor by this time so he escaped giving her a second chance to partner him.

He sat at the table and joined in the singing of *Land Of My Father* and *When Irish Eyes Are Smiling* and many others. The stage acts were degenerating into a general singsong which itself was fast breaking down into a rabble as pockets on different tables began singing their own favourite numbers. In the cacophony of noise he was suddenly aware of Veronica smiling broadly at him. She spoke but her words were lost in the din. Seeing his puzzled look she pointed towards the stage where Donna and Shirley were talking to the master of ceremonies. At first he thought they were offering to put on an act themselves. Then Pauline leaned closer to him and half-shouted: "They want you to get up and sing."

The familiar panic rose inside him. "I can't sing," he said desperately, "and I don't know any songs."

"For Pauline's birthday," Veronica shouted at him,

"She's had her birthday," he cried back ungraciously. Then he grinned: "What about next year?"

"Now," called the impish Veronica.

Temporarily, Peter went right off Veronica. He wished she and Lisa had not been allowed out to the dance. They were too young, anyway. Kids could be a nuisance at times.

"I can't sing," he repeated breathlessly, "I'm not doing it."

Donna returned to the table: "For Pauline's birthday — she's only sixteen once, you know."

He could have throttled Donna and was surprised at Shirley who was laughing at the stunned expression on his face. He looked round to his parents' table hoping to escape there but it was crowded with adults and George and he fancied that they were already beginning to look his way. Then came that appalling sound of the microphone being blown into. "Ladies and gentlemen," Peter made himself invisible, "before we start dancing again, and I should say we will be starting with a spot waltz, but just before we restart the dancing . . . we have a special request for one of our young people to sing. Now I want you all to give him a big hand because I'm told he is very shy . . . please — a big hand for Peter Mitchell."

"Ff—u—u—u—ck off," said Jim, as the hall erupted in applause. Peter silently agreed and in wild panic thought of making a dash for the door. But the door was at the other end of the hall.

"A little bird tells me that this young fellow can really sing," came the voice, softly now as the applause subsided. Peter reckoned he knew more songs than just about anybody else outside the music business, but as he found himself in front of the microphone to the tinkling of the piano, they all eluded him.

"What are you going to sing Pete?" the man asked, giving him what was supposed to be a disarming smile.

No one breathed. Peter could hear the grass swishing in the breeze outside. He looked at the man helplessly. "I can't think of anything."

The man began rippling the keys, and still the rest of the hall was silent and still the grass swished outside.

"Do you know the *Ash Grove*," he asked, hoping the man didn't.

The man played a couple of bars to show that indeed he did know it. Then he leaned to the microphone: "Ladies and gentlemen, Peter Mitchell with the *Ash Grove*."

Peter took hold of the microphone and fancied he heard Jim say, "Fuck off" again. There were a lot of people staring his way, but he didn't see a single face, not even Pauline's as he said, shyly, "This is for Pauline, whose birthday was in the week." And then he wasn't at Smithfield Hostel any more — he was on the stage at Rookery Road and Lenny was sneakily pulling his tongue out at him and he was about to sing before his friends and fellow pupils:

The Ash Grove how graceful
How plainly 'tis speaking The harp through it playing
Has language for me

He felt the first warm tear trickle down his cheek.

Whenever the light through Its branches is breaking
A host of kind faces is gazing on me.

More tears now and he had to let them flow if they were going to or stop singing.

The friends of my childhood
Again are before me
Each wakes a memory
As freely I roam

He saw but tried not to think of the flutter of handkerchiefs in the hall. Why were the boys fluttering handkerchiefs?

With soft whispers laden
Its leaves rustle o'er me, The Ash Grove, the Ash Grove
Alone is my home. Margie, dear Margie so loved this song.
My lips smile no more My heart loses its lightness,
No dream of the future My spirit can cheer.

Could he hang on at Rookery Road and keep the tears and
that tremor he felt from overpowering the words? Not long to go
now. Only an eternity.

I can only brood on
The past and its brightness

The last word almost choked in his throat and Peter suddenly
stopped singing, but the pianist gave him a smile and a nod of
encouragement.

The dead I have mourned
Are again living here.
From every dark nook
They press forward
To meet me,
I lift up my eyes
To the broad leafy dawn.
And others are there
Looking downward
To greet me,
The Ash Grove, the Ash Grove
Alone is my home.

The grass still swished outside as he walked, head bowed,
back to his seat. The silence in the hall weighed oppressively.
"Well, what can I say?" the master of ceremonies' voice
burst into the microphone and the hall was suddenly filled
with tumultuous cheering and clapping. Peter had never felt so
stupid in his life. Pauline was blowing her nose while Veronica
stared into space. The others at the table gazed on him with a
mixture of amusement and admiration.

"There's more to you than meets the eye," Shirley said.

"What do you do for an encore," Donna asked pleasantly. Then she clapped her hands over her mouth and leaned towards him: "I shouldn't say that — I know what you do for an encore, don't I?"

"That was beautiful," Pauline said, taking his hand gently. "You have been hiding your light under a bushel, haven't you?"

And a peck, no doubt, Peter thought. The hall was very warm and he needed fresh air.

The night breeze cooled and relaxed him. He hadn't realised how tense he was until he let his shoulders droop and gulped fresh air into his lungs.

The orange lights hung high along the camp roadway, casting an eerie glow into the blackness and haunting the shadows that lurked beside the huts. He shivered and pressed close to the hall doorway, comforted by the noise from inside. The lights were aloof and electric, not romantic. Not like the quaintly fashioned gaslights of Handsworth which a boy could shin up to light a cigarette or, if he dared, a cracker. Yet hadn't just a few electric lights begun to spring up in the main streets back home? It was a bit sad, really. The gas lamps were a link with the past. The new lamps in Birmingham threw a cold, blue, impersonal light.

He was back on the Soho Road, walking home from St John cadets. The snow was new, thick and crunchy under his feet. A scarf wrapped round his face and a beret pulled down as far as it would go to his ears helped to keep out the bitter cold. There was no wind, just the still, frozen air crackling on what skin he still had exposed. He turned into Thornhill Road, almost home, and came to a spellbound halt at the scene before him. The road was carpeted in thick, white wool braided in purest gold at the footpaths and right up to the dark privet hedges behind which the staid brick homes snuggled. Along the outstretched arms of the lampposts sat puffs of glittering orange candyfloss. And on the cotton-wool pavements there were no footprints, not a dog, not a cat's paw, and no car had ventured into the road since this latest snowfall. He stepped ankle-deep into the gutter to continue his journey through this silent, magical world and, once outside his home, stepped two long steps to reach the gate, lest he be the first to spoil the virginal sight.

"What the fuck are you doing?"

Peter jumped, startled, realising he was craning his neck up at the lights.

"Have you got somebody hiding up there?" Jim looked up in mock interest.

"Not hiding." Peter said, obscurely. "I . . . I was just daydreaming. I came for some fresh air." He wished Jim wouldn't swear so much, especially when the girls might be around.

"Here," Jim proffered a half-drunk bottle of beer, "wrap your mouth round this."

Peter had never actually drunk alcohol before, though often in his childhood he had walked past the Frighted Horse at night and smelled the strong yeasty aroma mingled with tobacco smoke. And he had occasionally sneaked the merest dregs from his father's empties at home. He took the bottle from Jim, wiped the top, and took a couple of tentative swigs. It was cold and bitter on his throat and he coughed.

"You can finish that off," Jim said importantly, "there's plenty more inside."

"Didn't they ask how old you were?"

"No, they all think that if you're eighteen you should be able to drink."

"Are you eighteen?" Peter asked incredulously.

"No, but they don't know that, do they?" Jim gave a light shrug: "The guy at the bar just serves you — probably so long as you behave and don't look ridiculously young. My old man's in there, anyway."

"So is my father," Peter said. "That's the trouble, there's little chance of him letting me drink."

"You should leave home — there's room in my paddock if you want."

"Aren't you cold some nights out here?"

"Naw, am I heck — well, not usually. I've got a big sleeping bag and piles of clothes. I'll tell you what, though, one night it was a bit nippy and I slipped back to the boilerhouse and slept in there."

"You must have a lot of fun living in the outdoors," Peter's voice was filled with admiration.

"It's all right, but I'm not staying there in the summer. The fuckin' mosquitoes will eat me alive, the men reckon."

"I might ask my parents if I can stay out with you," Peter said, feeling the thrill of adventure. "They might let me."

"Ask your parents? Gerroff . . . get off! You don't ask — you just do it."

"It's not that easy," Peter said, "not for me, not with my parents."

"Gerroff — what are yer, a fuckin' nancy?"

"No," Peter replied sharply, miffed at the youth's putdown, "I'm not."

"You act like one sometimes."

"By the way," Peter said, ignoring the comment, "could you watch your language when the girls are around?"

"I always do," Jim sniffed. "Am I making you hot under the collar?"

"It doesn't worry me," Peter felt silly, "it's just that the girls don't really like it."

"Yerr all right, if I swear when the girls are around give me a reminder," Jim's tone was pleasant. "In fact, tell me off whenever I swear, I might be able to break the habit." He lifted his hands in exasperation: "I can't stop fuckin' swearing."

Peter lifted the bottle to his mouth to hide his grin and gulped down the last few drops, almost choked and then belched loudly.

"Pardon me."

"Are you all right?" Jim gave him a concerned look. "Is it too strong for you? Can I get you a glass of milk?"

"I'm fine — went the wrong way and I swallowed some air."

"It's all that singing you've been doing. Bloody *Ash Grove* . . . I ask you — who sings that?"

"Me?" Peter asked, laughing.

"You should sing something popular, like *Under the Bridges of Paris* or *A Blossom Fell*. That school stuff just isn't popular."

"Have you got a cigarette?" Peter asked.

Jim produced a pack of tobacco. "I'll roll one for you, seeing as you're a bit simple."

"Thanks," Peter said.

The cigarette and the cold air made Peter feel dizzy.

"I've got the last dance with Pauline so I'd better watch the time," he told Jim, who was blowing smoke rings into the air.

"You fancy her, don't you," Jim said.

"Not like that — just friends. I like her."

"Bullshit," said Jim.

"True," Peter insisted.

"I'm going back home tonight," Jim said. "The thought of you sharing a paddock with me is too much. Anyway, I've got to work on my car."

"You have a car?"

"Well, it doesn't go yet, but it will."

"Where is it?"

"Round the back of our hut, sorry, our mansion. The old man said he might help me with it if I settle down. Which is a big setback, because he doesn't know anything about cars."

"Are you old enough to drive?"

"Who's to fuckin' know?"

"Can I see it?"

"In the morning — I don't know what I've done with my torch."

To have the last dance with a girl had been quickly recognised by Peter as having special, romantic significance. Most girls did not like to keep the last waltz for just anyone. So if they saved it for you it usually meant they felt something for you. That was Peter's reasoning. He also knew that sometimes they saved the last dance for a person merely to keep at bay some boy they didn't like. But that hardly was the case in Peter's situation. He would have noticed had there been anybody pestering Pauline. For that matter, the entire hall would have noticed. Pauline wouldn't be slow in letting any annoyance be known. No, she had definitely kept the last dance for him because he was a bit special to her.

She was dancing with her father when they re-entered the hall. Veronica was dancing with Dave Connor, and Peter wasn't very happy about that. Connor was much too old for her. He hoped her father was keeping an eye on things. Peter couldn't be expected to watch her all the time. Jim handed him a piece of chewing gum, "in case the girls smell the beer".

Peter and Pauline danced in perfect unison together — in perfect rhythm and step. She always allowed him to hold her reasonably close, too. Not like some girls who danced with boys at virtual arm's length as though they were frightened of catching dandruff or something. Sometimes he wished he were bold enough, ungallant enough, to steal a kiss from her while they danced. That was when he felt the most romantic, felt the most in love. Perhaps that was why some girls danced at arm's length.

When the quickstep came on, preceding the last waltz, Peter stuck his chewing gum across a tooth with his tongue and got Veronica on to the floor. He always felt a bit uncomfortable dancing with her because she was so young. But she was also very pretty. She would be a smasher when she was older and less gawky. A wave of possessiveness swept over him.

"That guy you were dancing with is quite a bit older than me," he told her, trying not to sound too scolding.

Veronica cheekily fluttered her eyelashes at him, "I'll be careful."

He escorted her back to the table after and pulled a chair out for her. She gave him a laughing smile and then blushed as she sat down.

He took the chewing gum out of his mouth and stuck it into a bit of paper in his pocket before getting Pauline up. He wouldn't expect her to be thrilled about dancing with a boy who had chewing gum in his mouth. As usual, he made sure they were not the first couple on the floor.

"You sang beautifully tonight," she said.

"The song was a bit silly, I suppose," he replied, thinking of what Jim had said, but also wanting to be modest.

"At least everyone knows it. Thank you for singing it for my birthday."

"I didn't have much option," Peter said, and wished he hadn't said that.

"You didn't mind?"

"No, I was happy to do it; a bit nervous, though."

"And a bit sad."

"Yes, I suppose I was. I get a bit homesick sometimes." Then, to change the subject, "What's your favourite song?"

She leaned her head lightly on his shoulder, "My favourite song, let me see . . . *The Ash Grove* . . . no, not quite . . . *I See the Moon* . . . I don't know — I like most songs."

Peter knew that the secret to unlocking a girl's heart was subtle, gentle and patient wooing. Peter's wooing was unfortunately so subtle it was usually completely lost on girls. He relied heavily on thought transference and so far girls had proved to be poor receptors. Yet now, dancing so close to Pauline and being so utterly in love with her, surely she must know, at least sense, his feelings? He wished he could be bold.

After the dance they helped the adults clean up and move the trestles and chairs to the storeroom.

Then Pauline and Veronica wanted him to go for a walk with them because they were feeling wide awake.

They headed north, through the gates of the hostel and past the railway station. The girls each took one of his arms and he felt important and wanted. Much of the way was lit by the orange glow of the lamps. There was no moon, but in patches they could see a few stars. Pauline talked of home, of Liverpool, and the beautifully furnished if ancient house in which she and Veronica had been brought up. She told him they moved to Australia only because of the promise of permanent work for their father.

"People have to work," Peter observed. "Everyone has to feel useful."

"My father is a good worker and a top tradesman," Pauline said. "But there just wasn't any work for him. We could have gone to Canada, but the literature they sent about Australia sold my parents on this place."

"I know what you mean," Peter said. "Long, golden beaches and bronzed people soaking up the sun. Yachts gliding on azure blue seas . . ."

"Where did you learn to talk like that?"

"I just get carried away sometimes," he replied. "Perhaps I should become a poet."

Darkness enveloped them as they turned at the station to head towards the Main North Road and the 24-hour Roadhouse. The crickets and locusts burst into their eternal love songs, broken intermittently by the deep croaking of bullfrogs. They walked under a conjuror's black cloak awaiting what tricks they knew not.

Peter found himself thinking about the brochures on Australia. They didn't give the real picture. They didn't say the migrant hostels were cardboard-thin, mosquito-infested huts. Oven-hot in summer, he would bet, and freezing cold in winter. A medical examination was compulsory, the brochures said. The medical had been among the most embarrassing experiences of his life. After listening to his heart and tapping his chest and looking into his eyes with a pencil-thin torch, the doctor had looked down Peter's trousers to make sure he had the required equipment. His penis must have deliberately waited for that moment to shrivel to its tiniest ever. But he passed muster. He became just one of a large number of breeding stock, being shipped like cattle to a far distant port.

Veronica shivered and clung more tightly to his arm.

"It's getting near spring," he observed. "All that noise — they're love calls."

"There's one you don't hear," Veronica said.

He didn't know what she meant.

"I miss the woods and parks," Pauline sounded wistful.

"Me too," Peter agreed. "Did you have bluebell woods, as well?"

Veronica put in, forlornly: "We used to pick bluebells and take them home to put in a vase, but by the time we got them home they were all droopy."

"So did I," Peter was surprised. "I wonder if all English kids did that." Pauline sighed, "Who cares."

"They still do that," Veronica said. "England hasn't stopped just because we're over here."

"Yes she has," Peter said, smiling in the darkness. "How could she possibly carry on without us?"

Pauline sighed.

They each bought a packet of crisps and a creaming soda at the Roadhouse and their mood lightened on the walk back to the camp. They sang *Side By Side* and *Danny Boy* and the conjuror lifted his cloak so the cold moon could look down on them.

Chapter 6

Crook As a Dog

Jim's life took a turn for the better. He returned home and was to be given the right to find his own destiny. He wasn't sure whether to sign on for a plastering apprenticeship. He told Peter he might wait a year, "Just in case I want to move on".

He said he would still live at his hideaway sometimes so he could "get away from it all. It apparently consisted of two gum trees sprouting from a patch of long grass. Peter could go there, too, whenever he wanted. Peter felt honoured.

Sunday dawned warm and sunny. Peter rose early and actually coincided his arrival at breakfast with that of his family, so he ate with them while keeping the occasional eye on Pauline across the canteen. Sundays were days for exploring or playing cricket or soccer in Handsworth, more so when you became too old for Sunday school. But if the weather was bad, Sunday could be a long, boring day — a day to watch the raindrops spatter on the windows and to dream child dreams with only the promise of school awaiting the next day. Sometimes Peter was able to pester his mother enough to go out in the rain or the fog or blizzard, if he wrapped up well in case of "catching cold". Peter couldn't see how you could catch a cold from the rain or snow if colds were caused by germs. But adults always thought they knew better. He was even spanked once for eating a handful of snow.

The range of brown hills to the east of the hostel, the other side of the main highway, had beckoned Peter since his arrival that first day when he pointed to them and made some of his fellow passengers on the coach laugh by observing: "There's gold in them thar hills". This morning, while on his way to breakfast, he was entranced that they were suddenly bathed in purple and gold.

Before leaving the canteen he suggested to Pauline and Veronica that they should go up the hills for a picnic. The idea caught fire and by 11 o'clock that morning a crowd of teenagers set forth armed with an apple each and pack lunches made by the canteen staff. A couple of the girls were thoughtful enough to change into shorts and old blouses, while others, Pauline and Veronica included, clung to their skirts and dresses.

All the girls wore identical white ankle socks and all had tied a ribbon in their hair. Pauline and Veronica wore starch-white blouses with frilly collars. Veronica's light-grey pleated skirt fell almost to her ankles and Peter wondered if it was a hand-me-down from her sister. Pauline looked chic in a straw hat and a red ribbon to tie back her hair, with a bow at the nape of her neck. Her skirt, a mixture of dark and light autumn browns, finished about two inches below the knee. Both Shirley and Donna wore shorts, showing off long, well-shaped legs. But it was Pauline, allowing the barest glimpse of white petticoat when she walked, who still attracted Peter the most — she looked so delightfully feminine. He thought he might pick some of the wildflowers for her when they got into the hills.

Once over the main highway, they headed up a grey-white gravel and dirt road that reached forever into the hills. Peter led them at first in songs like the *Happy Wanderer* and *In a Tiny House*. Then they sang *The Story of Tina*, until Peter noticed belatedly that Lisa was with them so he changed the song to *The Story of Lisa*, which made the young girl blush and run on ahead.

Lately, Peter's voice had been croaking on him. The night before it performed well because he had been on guard for it, but now it started breaking again. His voice was taking its time to break fully. Not like Pearson at school who, last year, had come back from the August holidays with a gruff, man's voice. It had happened so suddenly that one of Peter's friends said Pearson's balls must have dropped into his socks.

They walked for more than an hour under the beating sun and still the parched road stretched endlessly before them. They tired of singing so swapped a few jokes and then the boys turned to teasing the girls until they were rebuked by Pauline.

Peter and Jim had a competition to see who could throw a stone the farthest up the road. It ended in argument when Jim said he had thrown one so far no one had seen where it went and Peter said that was because he hadn't really thrown a stone at all.

"You know what our trouble is?" Jim said, after another hour had passed and they were all stopped outside an old farmhouse, "We aren't actually going anywhere."

"We aren't getting anywhere, either," Pauline said, "and I'm thirsty and starving."

Everybody agreed they were thirsty and hungry, but although they had sandwiches and fruit, no one thought to bring water. Peter felt a bit seedy and wished he had worn a hat. He changed his mind about picking the flowers, it would have only embarrassed Pauline, anyway. A woman at a farmhouse said they could help themselves from a water bag hanging near the house but not to forget to clip the long nozzle back in an upright position afterwards. The girls drank first, long and thirstily and it took ages for Peter to get a drink, by which time he was feeling quite ill. He took a few gulps of water hoping it would help, but his legs weakened under him even as he drank. He made it to the partial privacy of a hedge at the farm gate before throwing up violently and then falling into an ungracious heap on the roadway gravel. Jim and Pauline lifted him up and supported him between them on the way back to the hostel, with Shirley and Donna taking turns now and then. He felt much too ill to be embarrassed when Jim said, "You look fuckin' terrible"; and when Pauline said, "How many times have I got to pick you up out of the gravel?" He couldn't manage even a sickly grin. The journey back was slow, with Peter stopping many times to put his head down as waves of nausea threatened to engulf him.

The doctor took ages to arrive at the hostel but he gave Peter a thorough examination. "You have sunstroke," he said, handing the boy some salt tablets. "Rest up for a couple of days and you'll be fine."

Peter wanted to tell him about the room being tilted on its axis but could barely get the words 'thank you' out.

He lay in bed for three days except for occasionally staggering to the toilet. His mother came regularly with a cold, wet flannel for his forehead. He ate virtually nothing but drank copious amounts of brown tap water. When night came, he fancied Margie, Jim, Pauline and Donna came to visit him in strange, ethereal relays. He suffered nightmares and felt drained of energy when he awoke. He got up on the fourth morning and ate a large breakfast at the canteen, arriving when everyone else had gone.

Jim called for him that night, seeking help to fix his car. Peter was only too glad to get out of the hut, even if his "help" proved to be merely shining the torch on various parts under the hood at Jim's bidding. The car was a 1939 Austin convertible, in good condition bodywise and, Jim said, needing only minor but fiddly attention on the engine. It cost £23 and was the result of a surprise gift of money Jim received from an aunt in England. Peter wished one of his aunts would send him money so he could buy a car.

Holding the torch was about the extent of Peter's ability to help with the car. Had it been a steam engine, he reasoned, he could have been much more useful, having built a mini-version of Stevenson's Rocket for the school science exhibition, where it earned a pride of place. He pointed this out to Jim, who told him, "Shut your fuckin' head and hold the torch still".

The next day, a Friday, he felt well enough to go to work. The temperature plummeted and he was pleased his mother made him wear a jumper.

The car took up much of their spare time over the next couple of weeks and became the meeting point for the teenagers. The girls brought a blanket so they could sit and talk — their interest mostly confined to the fact that something different was happening. Several times Jim got the car going, only to have it stop before reaching the camp gates. On one occasion it went as far as the station before spluttering and dying. The carburretor was the focus of much of Jim's attention, but Peter couldn't help wondering after the first few days whether something else might be wrong. Several nights of poking and blowing and cleaning with petrol, had surely left Jim with the cleanest carburretor it was possible to have. But one evening Jim revved the engine for a while and drove it as far as the Roadhouse, where he got the petrol tank cleaned out. Then he took the car to Salisbury and back without even the faintest splutter from the engine and declared the car "fixed up".

On the Saturday morning they jammed three of the girls in the back and took the car on its first spin to Gawler, about 10 miles to the north of Smithfield. Gawler was straight out of the American wild west. It had one main street and more hotels than might be found in some major cities. It had a seemingly small population — you had to really look for the homes, most of them scattered over a wide area back and beyond the town centre. But it had a trotting track and large park, and dozens of small shops, as well as a picture theatre advertising *The Phantom of the Rue Morgue*. They discovered Redbanks — a large swimming hole nestled among reeds and bullrushes. It reminded Peter of some of the large ponds in Birmingham where he used to catch tadpoles, frogs and newts and watch the dragonflies hovering in the sun. It was a warm day and there were several children swimming at Redbanks when they arrived, so they guessed it was safe and vowed to come back soon with their togs.

The morning of Saturday, November 5, 1955, one day before Peter's sixteenth birthday, brought a small parcel from Margie. Inside was a "pure buckskin" wallet with P.J.M. inscribed in gold on the front and a sealed envelope, across the back of which was written in Margie's neat hand the legend "SWALK" — sealed with a loving kiss. Peter felt almost guilty opening it:

Dear Peter,

Thank you for the letter. It was fun in Gloucester but I felt very sad to come home and find you really had gone to Australia. All the kids in the street miss you, we have to find a new leader now. Arthur and Roger and me went to the pictures last Saturday morning, but it wasn't the same without you. We had no one to make us laugh. I told them you were saving to come back and I think that cheered them up a bit. Derek, John, Chrissie and Maureen send their regards, too. We think Donny might grow up to be a you-know-what, because he was caught wearing Chrissie's clothes again the other day. I hope you like the wallet, I got it engraved in the city. Some more coloured families have moved into the street. We called for that dark boy again like we did when you were here. Well, his father told us to clear off again. We all feel sorry for him, not being allowed to play with us. When you come back you can stay with one of your sisters. I saw them shopping on the Soho Road and said hello. They really miss you all and one of them had toothache. They said none of the letters from your mother had mentioned you were returning. They didn't think you would be allowed to come back on your own. Perhaps you should find out. You might have to wait a couple of years. You asked me if I will wait for you — of course I will. I had better close now. Mom wants me to run an errand and I can post this letter while I'm out. Happy birthday and lots of love,

Margie.

PS: Derek asked me to go around with him, and I said I couldn't because I was waiting for you. He said that was silly because you would never be back, so I said I might if you don't come back. But I didn't mean it because I know you'll be back one day.

There were sixteen kisses at the bottom of the letter.

Peter didn't know whether to laugh or cry. Bloody Derek wouldn't have dared ask Margie out had he been there. Everybody knew who Margie belonged to.

The small children were treated to a fireworks display before the dance that evening and most of the teenagers, including Peter, went to the back of the camp to watch. Camp regulations forbade a bonfire.

They announced his sixteenth birthday at the dance and everyone sang *Happy Birthday*, which was a bit much for Peter. Pauline told him, "welcome to the club", Veronica pulled faces at him and he pulled them back at her until Jim, who had turned up dressed as Guy Fawkes, poured a glass of Coke over his head and told him not to be so "fuckin' stupid", which upset Shirley a bit because it was her Coke. Peter was dragged up to the stage towards the end of the evening and meant to sing *I See the*

Moon but his mind went blank and he ended up singing *There Must Be a Reason.*

Light rain fell as they came out of the hall after the dance, so they went to the boilerhouse instead of going for a walk. Donna wouldn't leave him alone in the boilerhouse, brushing lightly against him at first and then resting her weight against him when he failed to respond. Not that he needed any desire awakened within, it never seemed to sleep, but he was too interested in the slow build-up of his relationship with Pauline to have time for Donna. He was getting somewhere with Pauline, there was an even stronger bond of friendship between them, but he wasn't sure how to turn that friendship into love. Love and friendship could be two very different things, he knew that much. And then there was Margie's letter adding confusion to his feelings. No, he really didn't think he could risk having a relationship with Donna, even if she was offering him sex on a plate and even if his body was crying out for it.

His birthday brought fine, calm weather. His mother presented him with a shirt and a £1 note. His father gave him five shillings and George tried to cuff his ears. He put the money in his tin box beside the bed. He had already saved some money in the box, but resisted the temptation to count it, hoping that one day it would surprise him. But he knew that in total it was still probably less than £4 and as he reckoned on needing between £200 and £300 to get back to England and manage until he got a job, he had a long way to go.

Feeling the need to be alone after breakfast he took a walk along his path at the back of the hostel. He used it twice a day now, as did others from the hostel, to get to and from work, but at weekends it remained barely used. The sun was warm so he wore his St John beret, one of the few remnants of his life in England. He walked only a little way before spotting the hare and froze in his tracks. It was sitting bolt-upright, its ears pricked to the sky in acute awareness of his presence. He called to it softly, "chee-chee-chee", and it jerked its head in alarm but stayed its ground. It must have been almost 50 yards away, yet Peter could see the rapid twitching of its nose and the brightness of its bulging eyes. Peter called again, "chee-chee-chee", and from somewhere in that sparse land a bird took up his call, "chee-chee-chee, chee-chee-chee, chee-chee-chee". They must have stayed fully 10 minutes like that, sizing each other up, before Peter took a careful step forward. The hare didn't move. He took another step and still the creature stood its ground. Then another step and another, Peter hardly dared to breathe. He took more steps until less than 10 yards separated them, the hare now sitting right back on its haunches. It must be tame, Peter thought, but stayed his distance, uncertain. The hare, too, seemed uncertain. The sun beat its rays through Peter's hat and the whole world held its breath.

"Chee-chee-chee . . . come on . . . I'm your friend. I won't hurt you. Chee-chee-chee, chee-chee-chee." Peter slowly bent his knees and tugged up some grass. Reaching his hand forward, ever so slowly, he proffered it to the creature. Its nose stopped twitching and it seemed to blend into the brown grass. It was pretending to be invisible, just like Peter did sometimes. He could recognise that and respect it and suddenly he didn't want to lure the hare any more. But he didn't want to scare it away either. He wondered if he was holding it up from some important task like gathering food for its family or spying out the territory so its young could come out for a romp. Peter stepped back, leaving the hare victorious. He walked past the building sites to the newly completed houses, but dared not look inside them in case he was caught for trespassing. Some of the roads had been tar-sealed and the footpaths paved and a few small trees planted on the verges from which seed was just germinating tiny blades of green grass. A police car went by in a scattering of loose metal and Peter was glad he hadn't looked inside the houses.

It was early afternoon when he returned to the camp, there was no sign of the hare on the way back. Through one of the laundry windows he saw Shirley ironing and went to the doorway.

"There wasn't anyone around this morning," he said.

"Some of us have chores," she replied, "and if you got up earlier you would find us all in the canteen." She gave him a friendly smile and looked very attractive in an old green jumper, brown skirt and sandals. "What have you been doing?" she upended the hissing iron.

"Just messing around — I almost caught a hare down the paddock. Yourself?"

"Washing and ironing, almost finished. Have you seen Pauline or Donna yet?"

"I haven't seen anybody," he said.

"We're all going to Donna's tonight to listen to the hit parade and play records — are you coming?"

"There's nothing else to do unless Jim is going anywhere."

"Jim's going to Donna's."

"I'll be there then."

She looked into his eyes and smiled and Peter swore she was trying to tell him more than simple friendliness. "By the way," she said, "many happy returns."

"Thanks . . . see you tonight."

"Around seven," she smiled again.

Peter walked to his hut wishing he could look and be as happy as Shirley and wondered whether people would think he had gone crazy if he wandered around smiling all the time. Some people could laugh and smile all the time and appear perfectly natural. But some people couldn't. Imagine if Jim walked around smiling and laughing at everyone . . . no, he couldn't imagine that.

He stood in front of the mirror practising laughing and smiling and trying to make his eyes sparkle like Shirley's did. Somehow, though, it just didn't look right. In fact, he thought he looked positively deranged. Perhaps he was overdoing it for his type of face. Shirley had one of those naturally happy faces. So he toned it right down, to a thin, half-Errol Flynn-type smile. That was better, he liked that, kind of gentle and mysterious. Yes, that was a happy Peter Mitchell without the crazed look. He went into the living room and casually tried the smile on George, who was reading the *Sunday Mail* and didn't look up.

"Hello George," Peter stood looking at his brother, who didn't even glance up. "How are things, George?"

"Sod off," said George.

"Where's Mom and Dad?"

"Out."

"There's nowhere for them to go."

"Visiting."

Peter stayed deliberately in front of George, wearing his special smile, knowing that if he stood there long enough his brother would eventually have to look at him.

"If you don't sod off I'll kick your arse," George said without looking at him.

Peter left the hut and wandered over to Jim's, but the car wasn't there. He was about to call on Pauline when she came out of the back door of her hut carrying a pile of washing and heading for the laundry.

"Hi," he called cheerily, quickly wearing his special smile. "Hi," she said grumpily, not looking at him.

He went back to his hut and wrote a letter to Margie.

Dearest Margie,

Thanks for your letter and the lovely wallet. I'll treasure it always. The camp seems pretty deserted at the moment and as I have finished my chores I thought it was a good time to write.

They held a big dance in the recreation hall last night and sort of combined it with my birthday party, so I had a really good time, despite being so far away from you and the crowd. Tell them all I miss them, too. If you see my sisters say I hope to be home in a year. I'll write to them anyway.

I had so many things to tell you and now I can't think of anything. I almost caught a hare this morning. It was running really fast, but you know how fast I can run. I was so close to catching it you wouldn't have believed it. Thanks for not going out with Derek. Say hello to him for me and please tell him I'll be back in a year and let me know what he says. I've changed my job. I'm working on a building site at a new town near the hostel. My arms are getting really strong. We are building our own houses in a way. It's called satellite town at the moment and it's due to open soon. But we won't be going there just yet, I don't think. If we do I'll send you my new address. Did I tell you about Jim? He's a friend of mine. I met him when I first came here. He was pointing a gun at me and I wrestled it off him.

We had a really long fight and it was pretty close but I won. It was almost a draw. Anyway, we're the best of friends now and I've just finished helping him to fix his car, one of those nice convertibles. I can't write for long because we are expecting a tribe of Aborigines through the camp and I want to take some photographs. I'll send you a picture of them and the hostel gang.

> Cheerio for now,
> All my love,
> Peter.

PS. Please write soon.

He put a row of kisses at the end of the letter and sealed it in an air mail envelope and wrote SWALK on the back. He felt much better for writing to Margie, though just a little bit sad. He really must start saving more money.

He sat with his parents for dinner that evening, because he was still a bit nervous about his new-found freedom. He could have sat with Pauline and the crowd and his parents probably wouldn't have told him off. But he didn't want to push his luck too far. He couldn't stand the prospect of curfews or not being able to see any of the girls. From where he sat he had a better view of Shirley than of Pauline, so he was careful not to gaze across the canteen too much. He didn't want to put Shirley off or upset Pauline. He could quite easily fall for Shirley if things didn't work out between him and Pauline. Shirley had poise and personality — lots and lots of personality. He remembered his special smile and wore it through dinner, hoping that the girls looked his way now and then.

When Peter left the canteen his Dad asked George if he thought his brother had malaria.

Before going out that evening Peter asked his father if he could have £100 to go back to England. His father told him that if he had even £20 he could think of better things to spend it on. His mother told him that if he wanted to go back to England he would have to save his own money, adding the legend "penny wise, pound foolish", and then gave him a severe look and said, "I hope you are behaving yourself these days."

"Of course I am," Peter blushingly assured her, wondering what she would think if she knew some of the thoughts that went through his head, let alone the things he had "got up to". Like the first time he had masturbated in his bedroom all that time ago when his parents were out — an act done in breathless fear of discovery by one of his sisters or even George and in the fervent hope that God was looking somewhere else. Or playing spin the bottle and postman's knock with Margie and the others on a Saturday night when Derek's parents went out. Or his episode with Donna.

Peter was delighted to get out that night to give his face a chance to cool down. It was dusk when he knocked on the flyscreen door at Donna's hut. The place seemed deserted and he wondered if they had all gone to Pauline's instead. But suddenly both doors opened and Donna stood before him in the darkness. She wore a red and white party dress and white blouse with the two top buttons undone. She had put make-up on her face and wore large gold earrings. Inside, the hut was inky blackness, the blinds pulled down and the lights extinguished. The thought occurred to him that he had fallen into an elaborate trap set by Donna to have her way with him. It also crossed his mind that his sixteenth birthday was as good a time as any to taste the fruits of Donna's passion — and he would try to oblige fully this time.

"Come in, darling," she said, "come and see what I've got for you." Come into my parlour said the spider to the fly.

Peter tried to think of something provocative to say but words eluded him. He stepped inside and Donna closed the doors behind him. She reached for him in the darkness and kissed his lips hard and long. He kissed her back and placed his hands on her breasts but she shrugged them away so he held her around the waist, realising that he might have been going too fast even for Donna. But she had saved him from the most embarrassing of all embarrassing situations that Peter could possibly think of, because the lights suddenly all flashed on and there was the crowd yelling "surprise, surprise" and "happy birthday".

He stood gazing at them with a sickly grin.

"You've got lipstick all over your mouth," Pauline said, fussily taking out a small, lacy handkerchief and wiping it off for him. He felt mothered. "I had no option," he explained, with a lack of grace towards Donna, "she caught me by surprise."

"We all caught you by surprise," Jim observed, handing him a cup of beer and adding "cheers".

"Cheers," Peter answered, shakily raising the cup to his lips. Donna and Shirley drank a small amount of port but Pauline and Veronica sipped lemonade. They threw the rug back and danced, even Jim getting up for an embarrassed shuffle with each of the girls, leaving them on the floor every now and then for a quick gulp of his beer and occasionally proclaiming how "bloody awful" it tasted from a cup, which didn't stop him drinking it.

They sang along with the tunes as they danced — *Unchained Melody*, *Stranger In Paradise*, *Drinking Song* and *Cool Water*. The girls supplied plenty of potato crisps and sandwiches, for which Peter was grateful because the cups of beer were going to his head. He danced more than his fair share with Shirley, who kept getting the giggles, but Pauline didn't seem to mind.

The evening ended perfectly, with Pauline sitting beside him while he sang by request *I Believe* and *Softly, Softly* and all joining in for *Hernando's Hideaway* and *A Blossom Fell*. Yet Pauline didn't kiss him for his birthday, and he couldn't summon up the courage to kiss her.

Chapter 7

A Beautiful Girl

November dreamed itself away with mostly sunny weather. On the 16th of that month the satellite town was officially opened by the Premier, Sir Thomas Playford, in a boring ceremony attended by state dignitaries. An Australian family was the first to move in. The royalty-loving South Australians named the town Elizabeth, after the Queen, which delighted the British immigrants but bemused the New Australians.

As December edged towards Christmas, Clive told Peter that he would end his settling-in period in the New Year and do some real work with the carpentry gang. "So make the most of your holidays."

He caught a double-dose of the homesickness galloping round the camp at Christmas. He had known the festive season would be bad. He heard it in the washrooms, in the canteen, the recreation hall, in the weeks leading up to the 25th. He saw it in the eyes of the women and heard it in the voices of the men. Christmas was going to tug at the hearts of the camp people. But Peter would hide as best he could the overwhelming sadness that was even now descending on him. He tried not to think of home or of past Christmases, lest a tear at breakfast betrayed his feelings. At dinner, he could pass off any glum look as being tiredness from work. Crying when you were sixteen was unthinkable. Thursday the 22nd was break-up day on the building site. Peter was given his wages and holiday pay at around 1pm and Clive reminded him to buy some decent tools for the return to work in mid-January.

Before going home Peter wandered over to investigate the noise from the truck compound, where a large group of men had gathered in a circle. "They're playing two-up," Ronnie told him.

"Some of these stupid bastards will have no money by the time they get home."

The men had their pay packets out and had placed large sums of money on the ground. Someone called "come in spinner" and coins hit the ground, followed by cheers and cries of both mock and genuine anguish.

"Some of them will win a lot of money," Peter observed, fingering the pay packet in his shirt pocket.

"Don't you get into that," Clive told him sternly "These stupid fucking galahs have to go home to face their wives yet. You hang on to your money." Peter reddened, he had never heard Clive quite so angry. But as the men from his gang made their departure, he told the boy to have a good Christmas and not eat too much "pud".

Peter walked to the camp wondering how much money the winners would make at two-up. He had nearly £14 in his pocket. He would bet that had he thrown it into the circle, it would be worth £200 now. And then he could sail back to England and marry Margie — when she was old enough, of course. He supposed that one day they could become really important people, like Lord Mayor and Lady Mayoress of Birmingham or even of London. Or perhaps Adelaide? Lord Peter Mitchell would have lots of important guests popping in to see him, even the Queen when she was in the neighbourhood. Peter had to suddenly stop those thoughts and think of brown grass and gum trees instead, because they were all racing around too much and threatening to spill out of his head. He arrived at the camp composed and calm and people didn't see any secret dreams written on his face or flying around his head.

Jim's legs were sticking out from beneath his car so Peter waited patiently and silently beside them until eventually the other boy emerged and flicked a cigarette butt at him.

"You'll blow yourself up smoking under a car," he said.

"How will I do that?"

"It's obvious," Peter said. "There's a petrol tank under there."

"Do you think I'm fuckin' stupid?"

"Just trying to be helpful."

"The cigarette went out before I went under the car, drongo."

"Sorry," Peter murmured. "What time did you finish work?"

"Midday."

"I've just finished for three weeks," Peter told him, "three glorious weeks."

"Lucky bastard," Jim growled, "I'm going back on the third."

"Short holiday," Peter sympathised, "how come?"

"We're behind, not enough men. I'm getting paid extra for it, though."

"What's wrong with the car?"

"Not a lot. Hey, have you seen the new girl?"

"No," Peter hadn't. "Has she just arrived?"

"Well, I said she was new didn't I? She's been here about a week, apparently. You like the girls — how come you haven't seen her?"

Peter shrugged, "I don't know."

"She is bloody beautiful," Jim said deliberately, "bloody beautiful. That's why I'm making sure the car's going all right."

Peter couldn't keep the surprise from his voice, "Are you taking her out?"

"I will be, so you keep your little eyes off her — she's mine." Jim waved a spanner at him, "Just remember who saw her first."

"What's her name?"

"Wendy something. She's got a brother too — John something."

"How do you know she'll go out with you?"

"Because I've got style — just ask any of the girls. They'll tell you who the stylish guy around here is."

They both laughed. "What's Father Christmas bringing you?" Jim changed the subject.

"I don't know . . . we haven't got much money. Perhaps he'll bring me Wendy — after all, my name is Peter."

"What the fuck's that got to do with it?"

"Peter Pan and Wendy."

"Fuck off," said Jim.

Peter was lying on his bed reading a Carter Brown thriller when Jim knocked and entered carrying a bottle of beer.

"I'm not allowed beer in here," he said, in mild panic. "Fifty lashes on the eyeballs at least for that."

"Let's go to my place then," Jim said, unperturbed, "I have something important to discuss and they've locked up the hall."

Peter felt a mixture of unease and delight when Jim told him what he wanted.

"I've never bothered much with girls — not like you, sniffing around them all the time. I've never bothered with them because I've had better things to do, haven't I? But I've really fallen for this Wendy. You have to help me get to know her."

"But I've never even met her," Peter protested. "You know her, I don't, so how can I help you to get to know her?"

"Shut your face and have a swig of this," Jim handed him the bottle and Peter took a drink.

"You have a way with girls . . . they listen to you. You know words . . . you know what to say to them. I'll only end up swearing or something if I try to make myself known to her. I mean really known, like asking her to go out with me."

"I'll help," Peter said, "but I'm not sure what to do." He thought deeply for a moment. Not only would he have to pretend that he actually knew something about asking girls out, but he would have to actually do something to help his friend.

"Well, for a start," he said importantly, "the ice has been broken. You have already met this girl, so she knows who you are. That's a major hurdle overcome, right?"

Jim nodded.

"Right!" Peter wondered where he should go from there. "Right, so girls have to trust you and like you before they will go out with you, right?"

Jim nodded.

"You must realise that it's all in the timing. I mean, you might knock on her door tonight and find she's in the mood for a bit of fun so she hops into your car just like that. But, if she happens to be in a bad mood, you could spoil your chances forever."

"Is this getting us anywhere?" Jim sounded bored.

"No," Peter admitted, "except that you need to realise the dangers." He was really struggling now and he certainly wasn't impressing Jim. He reached for the bottle of beer and took a couple of large swigs. "I think in this instance . . . boldness is the best way of going about things, so long as you're subtle with it."

"What shall I do then?"

"Just drive up to her in the car and ask her politely if she wants to go for a drive."

"No, I can't do that — what if she says 'no'?"

"What if she does?"

"It would be bloody embarrassing, wouldn't it?"

"That's what holds me back," Peter sighed, "the thought of them saying 'no'. . . What if I arrange a date for you through one of the other girls?"

"No, I don't want that, because if she found out she would just think I was a twit like you."

"All right . . . what if we get one of the girls to come with us and call for her tonight and I stay in the background just to give you moral support. By the way, we had better not smell of beer."

"She might not even be allowed out," Jim sniffed.

But it was an idea worth mulling over.

The problem then was to decide which one of the girls to ask for help. They couldn't ask them all, because Jim didn't want his interest in Wendy broadcast around the camp just yet. Pauline was likely to tell them to not be such cowards and do it themselves. Donna would probably blab about it to Wendy and Veronica would be too shy and was too young to be calling for Wendy anyway. The others, except Shirley, were even younger than Veronica.

"I knew Shirley would come in useful one day," Jim joked.

"I don't know, "Peter said, "Shirley doesn't seem, well, you know she might be sort of too honest to want to do it."

"What an idiot!" Jim suddenly exclaimed. "Why didn't I think of it?"

"What?"

"We'll call on her brother, instead."

"Brilliant idea," Peter agreed. "Why didn't you remind me she had a brother?"

"We can sort of accidentally ask her out as well then," Jim said.

"Sort of incidentally," Peter said.

"Fuck off," said Jim. "No, we'll do that, and while we're asking him out — I'm sure his name is John — I can sort of notice Wendy and say, 'Hey, do you want to come with us?' See how brilliant I am? 'with us' not with just me." Jim gave a dirty laugh as though overwhelmed by his own cunning. "But what can I say to her once we've got her out?"

"Tell her some poetry," Peter said, "The girls like that, a bit of poetry.

"What, like 'the boy stood on the burning deck'?"

"No, not exactly. What about 'Shall I compare thee to a summer's day'?"

"Shall I what?"

"It's Shakespeare . . . just say, at the right time, "Shall I compare thee to a summer's day? Thou art more lovely and more temperate."

"That's quite good," Jim said. "I might try that. Here, have another drink."

Despite a hearty meal that night, both were still feeling a bit tiddly when they arrived at the door of Wendy's hut. Jim knocked too loudly and Peter thought briefly of making a run for it. Their plans were dealt a major blow when a stunningly beautiful Wendy herself opened the door. "Is your brother coming out?" Peter gasped, after a long pause.

"Shall I comfort you in the summer hay?" Jim said.

"Pardon?"

"It's all right," Peter explained, wanting to strangle Jim, "we're learning parts for a play."

"It's Shakespeare," Jim said.

"You've been drinking," she said, with the faintest semblance of a smile.

"Just a Christmas drink with my parents; they're very homesick," Jim lied glibly.

"I can't think why anyone would be homesick," she said ungraciously, but then allowing a broad smile, "Do you want John?"

"We thought you both might like to come out and meet the gang," said Jim.

"That makes a change," she said. "Back home boys only ever call for John."

"Oh, we're not like that," Peter said, awkwardly. "Please feel very welcome to come out with us." He was rewarded with a captivating smile which made him wish he had seen her before Jim had.

John Radcliffe was a tall, angular youth with dark, short-back-and-sides hair and a wave combed up from the front. He dressed super-neat, with a red and blue striped tie, sparkling clean white shirt and expensive, well-pressed grey flannels.

"Are you going to the office?" Jim asked him.

But John looked straight through him. Peter suspected he was, in the modern idiom, totally up himself, but for the 50s, Jim's description of him didn't lack colour: "What a toffee-nosed fuckin' prick".

Peter said he would bet a million pounds that he was ex-grammar school, allowing his secondary modern prejudices to show.

So they saw little of John after that first night. He was studying to become a draughtsman, which was to keep him indoors most nights, anyway, and they didn't make a point of chasing him up. John's main problem was that, like Peter, he hadn't wanted to come to Australia in the first place, but no one had bothered to ask him. Unlike Peter, John had no intention of keeping his feelings mostly to himself and took his unhappiness out on those around him with put-downs and snide remarks. Also, he was seventeen and a half, and probably felt superior on that account. Peter remembered Wendy's words and couldn't help wondering why John would have so many boys call for him back home.

Wendy proved to be the opposite of her brother, describing England as a "3D society — dirty, dingy and dull." And if her brother had made a vow not to enjoy himself in Australia, Wendy looked as though she could indulge in enough enjoyment for the two of them. Her problem might be coming to terms with the fact that sitting huddled and chatting in the boilerhouse at night was a major event for the camp teenagers.

Peter really fancied her. She had a happy, vibrant personality rivalling Shirley's, her hair, very fair rather than very blond, hung almost to her shoulders and framed a Doris Day-shaped face with a perfectly proportioned nose, pale-blue eyes and long, dark lashes. She looked very much the quintessential American film star, despite having the barest of North Country accents. There was not a hint of snobbishness about her and she hit it off with Peter and Jim immediately. Peter wished Jim hadn't staked a claim for her. He had no intention of doing the dishonourable thing by Jim or by Pauline for that matter, but Peter was a bit wistful about it, because he felt Wendy was obviously attracted to him. She was sixteen — two months older than Peter and, it turned out when they finally learned his age, about eight months younger than Jim.

If Jim had any inhibitions in Wendy's company, he certainly didn't show them. That first night he was his normal, bluff self, kidding Wendy the way he would the other girls. Peter just couldn't compete, couldn't even think of anything interesting to say to her.

Chapter 8

Sad Eyes

The adults had put up a large Christmas tree in the recreation hall and decorated it with baubles, silver cones and tiny candles in fairy holders and tied bonbons with blue ribbon to its branches. Trimmings of many colours were draped beneath the hall ceiling and paper bells pinned high on the walls. Someone put up a large banner proclaiming in green paint and gold glitter "Goodwill to All Men", and on strings across one whole side of the hall, were arranged everybody's greetings cards from overseas, which had begun flooding into the camp up to a couple of weeks before. And as the cheerful look of the place increased, so the despondency among the residents deepened. Christmas had arrived.

Only Jim's eyes, flickering from one teenager to the next, told of his embarrassment the next night, when he turned up to the dance with Wendy on his arm. They were all surprised at the speed with which Jim must have wooed her.

The evening was strangely subdued at times. There would be periods of dancing and singing followed by a hush over the hall — an almost expectant hush, as though no one could quite believe that the people they were subconsciously waiting for would not arrive.

George sat with his and Jim's parents at the other end of the hall. Peter went over to chat with them early so that later he might dodge having to talk to them with the smell of beer on his breath.

Jim had placed some bottles of beer on the teenagers' table, but the girls stuck mainly to the fruit punch, which they ladled sparingly into their glasses from a large silver bowl on a nearby table. Some of the older people gave them funny looks and one of the Welshmen told them not to get drunk or they would get the barman into trouble. He was, in fact, looking after the bar himself and was smiling as he spoke, no doubt remembering his own youth.

Jim poured Peter's drinks for him throughout the night, sliding the glass over to him when he thought parental eyes were looking elsewhere. Peter felt a bit of a twit at having to sneak drinks when his parents weren't looking, but the alternative could be even more embarrassing. The last thing he wanted was either parent coming over to the table and making a scene or even cuffing his ears. Such things could happen.

They sang mostly Christmas carols, which made some people cry and others drink too much. Peter felt happy-sad through the evening while Jim, Wendy and Pauline were definitely just plain happy. Veronica stared into space a lot or sometimes pulled faces at Peter, who pulled them back at her. Shirley made constant trips over to her mother who kept bursting into tears, and Donna disappeared out of the hall early with Roger Brampton. When they weren't dancing, Jim and Wendy sat very close and held hands under the table. Peter would have dearly loved to hold Pauline's hand but still she gave no suggestion of having any romantic inclination. Later in the evening Donna returned without Roger and surprised those who were noticing by getting George up to dance. Jim had stopped drinking long before Peter and had begun developing a posh undertone to his accent. Peter was feeling tipsy, having consumed nearly two bottles of beer and a glass of punch and he forgot to book the last dance with Pauline — realising this when she was asked up by Dave Connor. Miffed, Peter asked Veronica up and danced with her at almost arm's length until she suddenly pulled him closer to her and nestled her head against his chest, bringing an embarrassed flush to his cheeks.

He walked Pauline and Veronica the few yards home afterwards and then went straight to bed. The room spun too fast and too many thoughts filled his head for sleep to come easily. He remembered the white Christmas all those years ago when he was about six and confined to bed with the measles. He had sneaked to the window before dark that Christmas Eve, excited despite being unwell that the snow had come so early.

The sight enthralled him; once bare trees now shimmered with white lace while drifts of sparkling diamonds hung against the back fences. Even the disused air-raid shelter, the few electric power lines and the fewer telephone lines were topped with white fleece and everything was so very still — suspended in time, Peter was to think years later. And as he watched this wondrous scene, a robin redbreast settled on a tree below the upstairs window and bobbed its head to look at the small, pale face pressed against the glass. The creature chirped querulously for several seconds before flying off, leaving the boy convinced that it had been trying to pass a message on to him, and leaving him in fear that the message might be from Santa Claus himself to say that he couldn't make it to Handsworth this year. But Christmas had come, if only with an orange and a few nuts and a little picture book.

Now, at the age of sixteen on another Christmas Eve, Peter, with his eyes open to stop the ceiling spinning, lay in bed and thought about that loyal, redbreasted robin and wondered whether it could have known who would stay in England no matter what, and who would one day leave its war-weary shores. Then he thought about the war and about his Mickey Mouse gasmask, which he could remember because of the number of times he had been told about it, and wondered what would have happened to England had the Germans won the war. And he wondered what would have happened to the robin. That was the only white Christmas he could remember . . . North winds doth blow, and we shall have snow . . . and what will the robin do then, poor thing?

Peter loved the snow in an English winter, snowballs and snowmen, iced-up ponds and sledging down the slopes at Handsworth Park, and he loved the fly-a-kite-blow-a-boy-over winds of March, the fine, cleansing showers and pot-of-gold rainbows of April, the swirling hide-and-go-seek fogs of November, the colours and smells of woodsmoked autumns and the magical rebirth of every spring. But most of all, he loved the warm, sunny, salad-crunching days and balmy, busy nights of summer.

The room wasn't spinning quite so much now, but Peter thought he might try going to sleep with his eyes open. Though he had to close them for just a little while as he placed his hands together beneath his chin:

Matthew, Mark, Luke and John,
Bless the bed that I lay on.
May four angels round my bed,
Trap my heels, trap my head.

God bless Mom and Dad and George. Please God bless my sisters and their husbands and Margie and ... He fell asleep with the thought that he was madly in love with about six girls and as just a few crystal tears squeezed through his eyelashes.

He awoke to the warm sun streaming through his window and a second-hand bicycle with gift wrapping paper round the handlebars propped against his bed.

Christmas Day brought a bike ride to Elizabeth South and back and skidding around the camp at breakneck speed. It brought turkey and plum pudding for lunch and a choice of stuffed chicken or lamb in mint sauce with roast potatoes, cauliflower and peas for dinner.

Peter found a wishbone in his chicken and, before either of his parents or George could offer to break it with him, he took it over to Pauline, making sure she got the largest end so her wish would be more likely to come true. Scarlet-faced but committed to his foolhardy act under the eyes of her parents, he broke the bone with her, making his wish. He didn't tell her what he had wished for and she didn't tell him what she had wished for, either.

An hour or so after dinner they went for a walk — Peter, Pauline, Veronica, Donna, Shirley, Jim and Wendy. John had returned to his hut looking glum and the other older boys were in the rec playing badminton. Peter resisted the temptation to take his bike — he would have had to ride it too slowly, or even push it, so the others could keep up. He was more content to have Pauline and Veronica on each arm, especially when George saw the girls clinging to him and gave his kid brother an admiring look. Peter walked back to him and whispered urgently for him not to tell. Darkness lit the sky with stars and a threequarter moon. Around them the crickets and locusts gathered forces to celebrate the warmer nights and the bullfrogs grumpily bemoaned the receding waters of their ponds. The air was electric with romance which tingled through the bodies of the teenagers. The others were now a way ahead of Peter and talking flippantly of something. Pauline stopped, allowing Peter to catch up. She laid her head against his shoulder and, surprised, he almost took her tightly to him, but was afraid at the last second. He didn't know what to do then, so he placed his hands tenderly around her, thinking she had experienced a spasm of homesickness.

"Some girls would do it," she said, "but only with one of those things." So they had been laughing and talking about sex, Peter realised. The rest of the gang had stopped and were looking back at them. He knew they couldn't hear what was being said.

"I've never bought any of those . . . I wasn't thinking of going that far. You can trust me."

"It's not you I don't trust," she said. "Anyway, I didn't say it applied to me."

"Can I kiss you?" He was suddenly emboldened.

"Perhaps not, perhaps we had better join the others."

Girls were bloody hard to understand sometimes.

They sat in the tiny shed at the railway station. Peter fanned away mosquitoes and watched giant moths flickering in and out of the light above, wondering if anyone else in the world was spending Christmas Day in quite such a way. Pauline sat next to him and he was conscious of the pressing together of their bodies, yet he knew she wasn't doing it deliberately. He forced his leg not to jiggle against her.

They talked about their presents. Pauline had been given a purse and clothes, as had Veronica. Donna received money from England and clothes from her parents and Shirley, some records and a bicycle. Wendy showed them her nice Swiss watch and Jim said he had been given a kick up the arse, which brought him an elbow in the ribs from Wendy.

New Year's Eve was virtually a repetition of the Christmas celebrations, except that the Scottish people took over the dance arrangements. A Scotsman in full regalia played the bagpipes and everybody sang Scottish songs, though there was a feeling of relief when the bagpipe player finally put his pipes away and allowed the piano to be played. The teenagers sneaked beer and punch again and the adults, especially the Scottish ones, drank whisky and some of them got paralytic.

Shirley asked Peter if he would get up on the stage to sing with her. He was surprised to hear himself say "yes". They sang *No Place Like Home*, which made the handkerchiefs flutter again. Then Peter gave a startling impression of Johnny Ray singing *Cry* while Shirley stood silently beside him at the microphone until he grabbed at his shirt collar in mock frenzy and she dashed from the stage. Then three women got up and did a few medleys, allowing Peter to escape back to the table.

Auld Lang Syne came all too quickly for the teenagers, though Jim and Wendy had eyes only for each other during the evening and probably barely noticed the event. Peter kissed Donna three times and wished her a happy new year. She dragged him around the floor despite his efforts to get to Pauline. Donna finally spied George and headed off in his direction. Peter then shook hands awkwardly with Shirley, who grabbed him and kissed him passionately on the lips, before running off with peals of laughter. He kissed Veronica on the cheek and then patted her on the head, meaning to be nice but regretting it, hoping he hadn't made her feel like a child. Then some of the married women took hold of him and he had to extricate himself from them before he could get to Pauline. When he did get to her, he said "happy new year" and meant to kiss her on the lips, but somehow it ended up with her kissing him on the cheek and he feeling only her hair against his lips. They shook hands and he wandered around afterwards feeling silly until Wendy grabbed him and said: "You're not escaping, either." And she kissed him long and tenderly, which made Peter look round afterwards to see if Jim had been watching but he hadn't.

He realised for the first time that night just how popular he was, and felt pleased and humbled by the discovery. He didn't know what it was about him that people seemed to like, and was afraid to think that it might be his boyish looks. After all, he was grown up now.

Peter was a bit upset at not kissing Pauline on the lips and at completely muffing his efforts to show her how much he cared when he had the ideal opportunity. Surely, as pure as the driven snow that she undoubtedly was, she had intimated a possible sexual liaison with him. He couldn't have made a mistake about that, could he? Yet he couldn't even kiss her properly. In fact, he hadn't kissed her at all. He touched his cheek where her lips had brushed him and wondered how long it would take for them to become lovers. He could be patient, he decided, he could wait with his dreams until the day she made them come true. In the meantime, he would have to be satisfied with being her friend and confidant.

He thought of Jim and Wendy and the speed at which they had become a wooing twosome, and he supposed that some couples just took longer to find romance. One day, the magic of true love would weave its spell over Peter and Pauline, Peter was certain of that, and as for sex, well, he wanted to marry a virgin anyway. Who didn't? Girls, he thought, behind that capable and practical exterior, might well suffer the same turmoils, the same feelings of inadequacy, the same hopes and dreams that haunted him. It was obvious that Pauline felt the same way about him as he did about her, and was tormented by the same inability to show it.

It was so obvious, Peter thought in bed that night, that he should have realised it, and he felt much happier, and fell asleep with his hands tucked comfortingly between his legs and smiling a satisfied smile.

He spent much of the holidays riding around on his bike, sometimes in the company of Shirley, with whom he felt awkward, despite her friendliness and outgoing nature. He never knew what to say to her, so their bike rides were usually undertaken with Shirley doing the chatting and Peter merely answering now and then in monosyllables. Jim and Wendy went off in the car early most mornings and weren't seen until the evenings, when they managed to arrive back just before dinner had finished. Pauline's father bought a car and took the family out regularly to one of the beaches. With Lisa accompanying Veronica and Pauline and their parents, there was no room for anybody else.

Peter realised that the holidays were going to be a crashing bore. He was left often to his own thoughts. Even at night, when he saw more of Pauline, there was a strange standoffishness between them, which Peter suspected was really his own doing. He decided not to look directly at her quite so much, in case she got annoyed with him for ogling all the time. But the result was that she stayed on the periphery of his vision and he found himself looking too much at Donna and Shirley instead. He was given scant chance to woo her.

Chapter 9

Flare-Up at Work

The day before Jim went back to work, everyone piled into his car and went swimming at Henley Beach, the other side of Adelaide. It was the first time Peter had swum in the sea, but he was a good swimmer having spent many a summer day at the indoor pools in Handsworth. The seawater was much saltier than he expected and as there was a surf he had plenty of it to taste. When he bought a car, he decided, he would bring Pauline to the beach every night for a swim.

Friday, January 13, brought a seamail-posted Christmas card from Margie. On the front were woodland animals skating on a frozen pond and inside she had written, "Have a lovely Christmas and a wonderful new year, love Margie" followed by 16 kisses. Homesickness engulfed him again and he realised that one day he might have to choose between Margie and Pauline. But he didn't want to think about that — at this stage in his life he was quite content romantically to believe that both were his girlfriends, as were, for that matter, Shirley and possibly Donna if he wanted them to be. He fantasised having sex with a girl that night before going to sleep, but not with Pauline or Margie — usually his erotica was with someone he didn't know, a completely imagined girl.

The next morning Pauline knocked on his bedroom door and they went to breakfast together. Was his patience already being rewarded?

Thanks to money from his parents and a dip into the tin box, Peter fronted up to work on his bicycle with the best Swedish tools available and a brand new, all-leather nailbag at his side. The men inspected the tools approvingly and told him he was "almost a carpenter". But disappointment awaited — he would not be using his tools for a while yet. His first major task was dipping into an arsenic-borax bath the long, heavy jarrah beams on to which the floor boards would eventually be nailed. They had yet to be cut to undercarriage size and were up to 16 feet long. Peter struggled even to pick one up. He was given rubber gloves to protect his skin from the poisonous dip and they helped to guard his hands from the hard timber and sharp splinters. However, they also made the job very slippery and many times he almost smashed an ankle when a beam eluded his grasp and crashed to the ground.

The beams rubbed his shoulder raw and he had to pack his nailbag over it to bear the pain of carrying any more of them. But the bag helped only a little. As his shoulder became more painful, he tried just picking up the beams and walking while holding them sideways with both hands, but they were too heavy and cumbersome. Old Charlie came by and said they were all a pack of bastards for giving him that task. "That's a job for a man," he said. Smarting at the remark, Peter grimly vowed not to give in.

His shoulder afire with pain, he tried dragging the lengths of timber to the dip, but one of the men yelled out to him that he would "fuck up" the timber doing that. Peter didn't agree, but he couldn't argue. He switched to using his left shoulder for a while, but that was too awkward and the beams kept bouncing against his neck.

He dabbed copious quantities of calamine lotion on his shoulder that night but his skin still burned with pain and his right arm became stiff and sore. He was exhausted by bedtime, yet slept badly, trying to lie on his stomach and then his left-hand side and finally propping himself almost upright against the pillow.

The next day he took a towel to work which he folded and draped over his shoulder and tied bulkily under his armpit, but he was still so sore that he thought of going home a number of times and when he had to swing the billies round he was almost in tears. The afternoon brought overbearing heat and despite many trips to the waterbag he felt dizzy and sick by home time. And the week became worse as each day passed — the temperature rising and the floor joists feeling heavier and heavier and his shoulder, neck and arm more and more painful, with sunburn adding to his woes. He spent the weekend mostly indoors, using up the calamine, too sore and anguished to take any interest in what the other young people were doing.

On the Monday morning he glumly set off for work, knowing that the same dreaded task awaited him. He had told George how impossible the job was and his brother had said: "You're British — you can do it." But George was also a big fan of the *Goon Show* and Peter wished, if only the floor joists were cardboard replicas.

Peter nearly collapsed at work on the Wednesday and one of the men took him home, throwing his bicycle in the back of the ute. He had suffered sunstroke again and was delirious for two days and at night shivered in a cold, saturating sweat. But he felt much better by the weekend. The wounds to his shoulder were healing and the stiffness in his arm had disappeared. Nevertheless, he had decided to call it quits and fronted up to work on Monday ready to hand in his notice. He would tell his parents that he had been put off because they needed somebody with more experience. However, before he had the chance to tell Dave he was leaving, he found that Ronnie had been assigned to help him with the carrying and dipping.

Life became much easier. Peter enjoyed the tall youth's chatty company and he even heard how Ronnie and his girlfriend had made love the night before — on her back porch, only feet from where her father was listening to the radio in the kitchen. Peter laughed and told him he would get caught one day. Ronnie asked him if he had a girlfriend and raised his eyebrows when Peter answered "yes, several". Ronnie knew a lot of pop songs and when he wasn't talking would burst into song which would be echoed by the men on the roofs, but Peter was too shy to join in.

One morning at smoko, Mush produced even thicker sandwiches than usual, crammed with layers of strange meats and oozing with butter and garlic which became smeared all over his moustache and his chin and then on to his bib-fronted overalls. Peter normally tried not to look at Mush while the big man was eating, the smell of garlic permeating the shed being enough to make the boy feel green around the gills. But the mammoth task facing the man in trying to open his mouth over the sheer bulk of the sandwiches fascinated the boy. It fascinated the men, too, though they watched in open distaste. At lunchtime Mush, who despite his bulk sat on an upturned nailbox, was about to repeat his revolting exhibition of the morning when he was grabbed by three of the men, nailbox and all, and unceremoniously dumped outside the shed. They told the astonished Greek that he could return to the shed when his eating habits improved.

Mush didn't speak to anyone for weeks after, though he did manage a guttural grunt to Peter's breezy greeting each morning. Peter felt sorry for the man and made a point of letting him know, with the regular greeting, that he still liked him and he wasn't completely ostracised. Not long after the incident with Mush, Peter was alone in the shed putting on a pair of new rubber gloves when a shadow fell across the doorway and in stepped Helmut. The German stood there for a moment, blocking the sun and plunging the shed into darkness. For no apparent reason, a thrill of terror ran through Peter, who tried to ignore the silent presence of the man and attend to his gloves. Suddenly the German moved to the boy and took hold of his hands.

"I like you very much," Helmut said, speaking softly. "You know? Very much."

Stark terror froze Peter to the spot. He nodded, praying the man would leave as quickly as he had arrived.

"You are so good looking," Helmut said, gazing at Peter with his searching light-blue eyes. "We shall be close friends, you and me, but it will be our secret. All right, boy?"

Peter nodded, in breathless fear, then managed desperately to extricate his hands and flee from the shed, gasping out that Ronnie would be waiting for him. He told no one of the incident, but avoided Helmut from then on, and sometimes a tremor of fear would run through him as he felt those pale-blue eyes searching him out on the building site.

Peter took raspberry jam sandwiches to work one day and found they were crawling with ants when he unwrapped them at morning tea. He tried to pick the ants out of the jam but there were too many and it became difficult to tell which were bits of ants and which were raspberry pips. He was so hungry he ate the sandwiches ants and all.

February brought a heat so oppressive that Peter wondered whether he could survive. The evenings gave no respite from the searing days and he lay in bed late at night, bathed in sweat, listening to and swatting uselessly at wave after wave of divebombing mosquitoes. He went to work one morning covered in so many bites that the men thought he had "shingles or something". When he told them about the mosquitoes they didn't laugh, but expressed concern over conditions at the camp. None of the Australians ever seemed to get bitten by the insects and Peter wondered why the creatures were so fond of fresh English blood, especially his.

A new task came his way in late February. He was to plug and line the windows and doorways in readiness for the architraves of the second-fixing gang. At last, he was able to use his tools and his own initiative. He worked alone — most of the gang were now a paddock in front of him, pushing on with the roofing. The second-fixers were still a few houses away, so he wasn't too pressed for time. He liked the solitude and sang as he worked, though quietly.

Occasionally, one of the men would drop in for a quick chat and to check his work. His most regular visitor, though, was Dopples, who popped in for a "spell" and to talk of his native land and his dreams in this new country and to roll a cigarette, or a quirly, as some of the Australians would say. Peter learned many Cypriot Greek phrases from Dopples, who told the boy that he was speaking Greek without any discernible accent: kale mere, kale spera and kale nichta — good morning, good day and good night · were among the phrases he learned and Dopples wrote them down for him so he wouldn't forget.

Sometimes they spent too much time talking, with Dopples telling Peter about his home city of Famagusta and all the troubles there, but they kept an eye out for Clive and when they saw him heading their way, Dopples would sneak out the opposite side of the house and Peter would begin banging his hammer as though he had been working all the time. Peter actually got to the stage, anyway, where he could work and listen to the Cypriot, though he banged his thumb more than once through not concentrating. He knew that Dopples was a very hard and fast worker and wasn't bludging - just desperate for company and someone to talk to. They got on so well that Peter looked forward each day to the man's visits and sat beside him, with old Charlie on the other side, at tea and lunch. This prompted Dave to warn Dopples, and Charlie for the umpteenth time, not to fill the boy's head with any "crap", which was exactly what Charlie always did, having found a patient and willing ear in Peter. But the boy never let the old man know that he didn't believe a single word he was being told.

One morning Dopples drove to work in a brand new, shiny red Holden stationwagon and proudly showed it off to the other men. But for some reason which escaped Peter the Australians weren't happy about it and gave Dopples an even harder time, with sarcastic comments about the car and how it was probably on time payment, which went way beyond friendly leg-pulling.

Dopples flew into an ungovernable rage one day after being goaded and went for one of the men with his side-axe. He didn't cause any actual injury but was fired by the site foreman. Jobs were hard enough to find for the Australians, let alone foreigners, so more than a few dreams had suddenly crashed for Dopples. Peter felt angry and sad about the incident, but he could do nothing to help the Cypriot. He would have fired the men doing the goading rather than see Dopples lose his job. The boy had an affinity with anyone who dared to dream.

On his journeys with the lunches, Peter walked by the brickies, usually calling "hello" or waving to Charlie. One morning as he was on his way to gather the morning tea orders, he found the old man sitting on a pile of bricks, beside a full barrow of cement, having a brief spell and smoking a quirly. One of the men was yelling at Charlie, though in mock anger, to get his "lazy arse into gear". Feeling helpful, Peter offered to push the wheelbarrow up to the men.

"Along there, up the plank, and be careful not to spill any," Charlie said, giving the boy a toothless grin.

Peter hadn't realised how heavy the barrow was and could barely lift the handles at first attempt. Keeping it balanced and the contents intact was going to be an even more difficult task. He should have made a joke of it and told Charlie that he was saving his strength for his girlfriend, but, not wishing to lose face, he instead mustered what for him was a superhuman effort to get the load to the plank, pushed it halfway up, lost the battle for control, and dismally watched the barrow handles wrench themselves from his grasp and crash on to the paddock, spilling all the cement in a thick, grey, gooey mess. The brickies told him to "fuck off out of here" and Peter went, feeling stupid.

"Never mind young feller, you meant well," Charlie told him at morning tea.

At around 2 o'clock that afternoon, Clive came by the house in which a still embarrassed Peter was working and told him the brickies wanted him to help Charlie for the rest of the day. Gratified at being needed by the brickies and at being given the chance to show he could do the work, he reported immediately to their foreman, who was built like a "brick shithouse" and who looked at the boy in astonishment and asked him if he had had his first fuck yet. Peter walked back to his own job as nonchalantly as he could amid the jeers and guffaws from around the site. The men often played poker at lunchtime, putting in a few pence each for interest. Peter wasn't allowed to play because Clive didn't want him to learn bad habits. Sometimes he would watch, though, sneaking a look at the hands each of the men held and knowing who was likely to win.

He had thought once of eating his lunch in whichever house he was working on, but discovered that the bits of paper lying several feet beneath the joists contained fly-blown turds where some worker before him had emptied his bowels.

He told Clive, who reacted with the words "dirty fucking bastards", but nothing was done about it.

February gave way to March and the weather changed from scorching heat to very warm. Some days there was a cooling breeze instead of one from the ovens of hell, and Peter stopped wearing his hat quite so much at work, having heard his father say that a hat could make you go bald.

Peter usually did a satisfactory job on the plugging and lining and received few complaints from Clive or the second-fixers. However, he was starting to believe himself better at the job than he really was. He came back to earth with a visit from Dave, who told him he would have to redo round the window in a couple of houses because the plugs were too loose. The job involved having to bash out with his coal chisel about one to two inches of cement at the edges of the top, middle and bottom of the window frames and doorways. Sometimes, large chunks of cement came away or the corner of a brick would break, requiring a much larger wooden plug to be hammered in to keep it firmly embedded. Where too much of a brick had broken off, he would have to go to the plasterers or brickies for a handful of cement to do a patch repair job. All things being equal, though, the work was easy. Once he made the holes he had only to chop plugs from scraps of timber, hammer them in and, when all the plugs were tightly level with the brickwork, nail the lining over them, top, bottom and sides for the windows, top and sides for the doorways.

By the time he finished patching up the faulty work, the flooring gang had moved to only a few houses from him. Peter was fascinated by the speed at which the floorers worked, rat-tat-tatting a handful of nails across the boards once they were tongued and grooved together. In no time at all they transformed a skeletal shell into the beginnings of a room. He had just about finished the plugging and lining, so he asked Dave if he could move to flooring work next, but Clive intervened, saying he had other ideas for him. Next week, he could join the roofing gang, which was the job Peter wanted least of all. He had often watched the men carrying long beams of timber in precarious balancing acts along the roof joists, his heart in his mouth lest one of them should slip. But he could hardly tell them he was too scared to go on the roofs. Foreboding filled him for the rest of that week, though Friday evening brought a decision, and with it nervousness of a very different nature.

Chapter 10

A Scary Purchase

A problem at the back of Peter's mind for some time had been how to get hold of a packet of french letters. He was fully aware of the youthfulness of his looks and, as with most situations, was haunted by the fear of rejection as well as the fear of actually asking for the forbidden things. Nevertheless, he set off on his bicycle to nearby Salisbury in the hope that courage would come to him, on the way furiously trying to think what it was he should ask for. He thought the term french letters was obviously slang and, anyway, might be too bold. He mustn't overdo it. He must be calm and relaxed. And what if the chemist or an assistant wasn't familiar with the term? How would he explain what it was he wanted? He thought the other name for them might be condoms, but he wasn't sure. There was another name - the correct name for them. But what the devil was it? By the time he reached Salisbury he was certain the name he wanted was prodilactics. He spent a long time outside the chemist, picking tiny, imaginary stones out of the treads of his bicycle tyres, until finally the shop had emptied of customers. Peter entered the shop followed by an elderly woman who seemed to appear from nowhere. The girl shop assistant was about eighteen and looked bored. The chemist was middle-aged, thin-faced, and severe-looking. He wouldn't have been out of place teaching at Rookery Road Secondary Modern. He wasn't a bit like the friendly, balding apothecary of Grove Lane, in Handsworth, who had kept Peter supplied with so many different kinds of chemicals for all those once so important and exciting experiments. Peter stared blankly at the man for several seconds, bought a comb and walked out of the shop.

But he knew where else the small, mysterious packets might be purchased, because he had often glanced discreetly at them stacked in rows behind the counters of barbers' shops. And he really did need a haircut. Peter hated the barbers. He hated the white cover which wrapped him and trapped him claustrophobically in the chair, and the jiggling of his knee in protest at his being so constrained. He loathed the buzz of the electric clippers vibrating through his head and the threatening snip-snip-I'll-cut-your-skin-if-you-flinch of the scissors which would bring him an inch off the chair, and he detested the gagging smell of human hair and the way the barbers always stood so close to his elbows that he could feel their groin pressing against him.

Once back outside the hairdressers, he breathed deeply the cooling fresh air and tried to appear nonchalant as he swung his leg over the bicycle. The small packet of three french letters was tucked securely into Margie's wallet, deep in his hip pocket. It had been so easy. "And one packet of those, please," he said to the barber as he was paying for the haircut. And the barber automatically, almost absent-mindedly, reached round, picked up one of the packets and dropped it onto the counter in front of Peter. It was almost as if the man sold a thousand packets a day and no longer realised what they were. Peter accidentally rang the bell on his handlebars as he rode off.

He felt strangely elated through dinner, yet only picked at his food. The mood stayed with him while he readied for the dance, helped not only by the forbidden goods tucked in his wallet, but also by what he had perceived to be the very light-hearted and devil-may-care behaviour of the girls, especially Pauline, at dinner. It was almost as if it were spring and not nudging into autumn. Jim and Wendy helped with the illusion. About the only time they didn't hold hands was while they were eating. Shirley was as cheerful as ever, particularly, Peter fancied, towards him. Veronica pulled more faces than usual his way and he pulled them back at her until he was assailed by guilt when he remembered the french letters. He would swear that Donna had poked him more than usual with her elbows as she ate, something which Pauline, who sat the other side of him, never did. And he was always careful not to jostle Pauline, or Donna, for that matter, which led to some discomfort at times sandwiched between the two of them. But he was willing to put up with that. Pauline was in such a mood at dinner that could only suggest she was in love. She wasn't a giggler like some of the girls, yet she laughed and joked all the time and went into an almost hysterical fit when the top fell off the salt shaker and ruined Shirley's dinner so she had to go and get another meal. Admittedly, everyone else saw the humour of it as well.

Peter scrutinised his face in the mirror, George's shaver poised at the ready. There was the faintest hint of blond down on his upper lip, which he could just see if the light fell at the right angle. But he wasn't searching for that which couldn't be shaved. He was looking for any single hairs which might be protruding from his face. Many of the boys who did not yet shave regularly, nevertheless had ugly, stray tufts of soft hair on their faces. And Peter thought it likely that girls found the pubescent growths objectionable. But he couldn't find any on his own face.

Nevertheless, he was grown up now, he decided. He had a packet of condoms in his wallet. He had a good job with future prospects, a girlfriend he was sure he was in love with and who, time would prove, was in love with him. She had openly asked him to have sex with her and at the age of sixteen, Peter reckoned, that wasn't bad going. And she certainly wasn't the type to mention sex to just any boy. She had recognised the bond between them and acknowledged his maturity. He had definitely left his childhood behind him. When they eventually got married, he reasoned, they could still visit their friends and have them round to the sumptuous Mitchell estate. They could still go to the dance on a Saturday night and he would still be able to dance with Shirley or Wendy or Donna. Peter stretched himself up to his fullest height and flexed his arm muscles in the mirror. Yes, he would definitely be able to fend for and provide for Pauline and, of course, the children. A strange calm and happiness fell over him. For the first time since leaving England, he didn't feel a bit homesick.

They gathered in the boiler house later. Pauline and Veronica leaned against the opposite side of the small, dark shed, talking to Wendy and Donna about the dance the next night. Peter didn't know how to get Pauline away from everybody else, but he looked her way a lot in the gloom and sent many messages of love by thought transference, until Jim told him he looked constipated.

He lay in bed excitedly anticipating the dance, turning over in his mind dozens of times how he would take Pauline for a walk after the last waltz and somewhere where the bullfrogs croaked and the crickets sang, would seal his love for her in splendid, all-consuming passion.

The letter from Margie reignited the turmoil within him. She wrote of the thick snow blanketing the ground and how they had been out throwing snowballs and sledging. Peter took a deep breath and forced back the tears stinging his eyes.

North winds doth blow . . .

Had it been only a couple of years before when they had all raced to see who could make the most snowballs and he won and rashly challenged the rest of them to a snowball fight? He more than held his own against the other six at first, but eventually, worn down by sheer weight of numbers, had tried to surrender. Yet still the snowballs had rained at him, hard and icy into his face, until he burst into tears and Margie made them all stop. As the leader of the gang he pretended that a chunk of ice had hit him in the eye because he couldn't bear the thought of their knowing he had cried. And then he punched Denny on the nose and threw him into the snow, blaming him for keeping up the barrage of missiles, but really doing it so they wouldn't even start thinking that he was a sissy.

North winds doth blow . . . and we shall have snow . . . and what will the robin do then, poor thing?

The shame hadn't quite left him after dealing with Denny, so he told Margie that King Richard the Lionheart had instructed him to bestow on her the title of Dame Maid Marian. She seemed so pleased by this that he had then bestowed knighthoods on the rest of them and made Denny the Black Knight and chief tax collector and reminded him that none of the knights had to pay taxes. And he reminded them all that their foes must be given the right to surrender. Peter spent much of his life rescuing damsels in distress, both in Sherwood Forest in his role of Robin Hood, or the Earl of Locksley as he preferred to be known, and throughout the land as the gallant Sir Lancelot.

So the letter and its accompanying flood of memories brought sadness. A sadness and pain not eased by the knowledge that his tin box contained little money, and saving anything that week was unlikely following the added expense of a haircut and a packet of french letters. He wrote straight away to Margie that morning and told her he expected to have the photographs of the Aborigines developed soon, and that his mother had assured him he could return to England as soon as he had saved the money. He almost told her about the condoms, but thought better of it when he realised that she might not even know what they were. He didn't mention Pauline, either, though he touched on the hostel gang, saying he was still meeting more and more kids from all over Britain and that the girls were nice, but not as nice, nor as good looking as she was. He didn't want her to think she was losing him. There was always the dream that one day he would knock on Margie's front door and sweep her into his arms. He must protect that dream, as he must stand guardian over his other hopes and dreams. The only dream dimming slightly at times was becoming Lord Mayor of Birmingham. Wouldn't that be a little boring? What would his hero William Brown have thought of becoming a Lord Mayor? Why hadn't Richmal Crompton allowed William to grow up so Peter could find out?

When he called for Pauline that night, Margie was temporarily forgotten. Peter wanted desperately to show Jim the small packet in his wallet, just to let the other boy know that he had been brave enough to buy them. And there was always a chance that Jim would want one of them, the way he and Wendy were carrying on together. But he wasn't sure that he could trust him to keep his mouth shut. Any other embarrassment Peter could think of paled at the thought of having his prized secret bandied around the camp by a tipsy Jim. And imagine what that might do to Pauline's reputation.

Everyone knew they always went around together. Her parents would likely forbid him ever to see her again. His parents . . . there went his mind, racing around inside his head again.

He danced with Pauline immediately the music started. There were only two other couples on the floor, but he didn't feel a bit shy. He held her as tightly as he dared, glancing despite his efforts not to at her parents over in the corner by the entrance. But they were just settling in and were not looking Peter's way. They trusted their daughter.

He tried to think of something really intelligent to say and told her England was covered in thick snow. She said she already knew that and was glad she wasn't in it. He said he missed the snow and she pulled at his arm and he felt a shiver run through her.

Jim often placed his arms round Wendy's neck when they danced, pulling her tightly to him. But that was too bold a style for Peter. Nevertheless, dancing as he was, he could feel Pauline's soft body pressing against his chest and smell her perfume. She didn't seem to be at all affected by their closeness. She smiled and sang or hummed to the dance tune and . . . just danced.

Among the tales he had heard about having sex was the cautionary one of girls losing interest if you took too long to put on a condom. Peter could imagine that if you had worked a girl up to a fever pitch of passion so she was willing to have sex with you, it must be a cooling experience having to wait for you to put one of the things on. It also gave girls time to decide they were being too hasty. He thought about that problem as he danced. Peter could sometimes come up with good ideas, though at other times his ideas were not so good.

Midway through the evening, he stepped nervously into one of the cubicles in the gents, locked the door, and opened the packet of condoms. They were individually seal-wrapped inside, the smaller packets more difficult to open, especially when you were fumbling in haste lest anyone enter the toilets. By the time he had the small balloon-like thing out, his mouth was dry with fear of discovery. The thin-rubber sheath slipped easily and sensuously over his penis, which had been erect all night and which now was bursting with the hardness of desire. It seemed to fit perfectly. At least he knew he was normal in that respect. He had fervently hoped it wasn't going to be baggy.

He returned to the table and asked Pauline if she wanted to go outside for some fresh air, pretending that he was feeling too hot by loosening his tie and running his fingers around the inside of his shirt collar. Surprisingly, she did.

They took deep breaths of the sweet, cleansing air.

"Cleaner than Liverpool," she said.

"And Birmingham," he added.

She took his arm and pulled him close to her and for the second time that evening he felt her shiver.

"Are you cold?"

"No," she said, giving another little shiver. Or was it a tremble?

"I had a letter from home today," he said, and could have bitten his tongue off, "from a friend."

"We had a letter from our sister the other day," she said distantly.

"I didn't know you had another sister."

"She's only been married a year. It was a lovely wedding. Veronica and I were the bridesmaids. She looked so lovely . . . so lovely all in white." She shivered again, and this time Peter took off his jacket and wrapped it round her shoulders.

"Oh, Peter," she turned to him, "Oh . . . I want so much to have a big, fancy wedding and to walk down the aisle in the most gorgeous, sweeping white dress with a train so long that it trails the length of the church. Oh, that's what I want." Suddenly, beside herself with excitement, she jumped up and down, landing on Peter's toe.

"If that's what you want," he said, wincing at the pain, "if that's what you want — that's what you'll get."

"And a tall, handsome groom waiting for me at the end of the aisle. Tall, dark and handsome. And strong and rich, but it doesn't matter if he's not rich. Just so long as he is strong, tall, dark and handsome."

"What if he were tall, blond and handsome?" Peter asked.

She punched his arm. "Don't be stupid."

He shrugged. "You can have anything you want. You and only you can make it happen."

"Do you think so?"

"Of course," he said, "the world's your oyster." He hoped he wasn't getting carried away. A strange, vanquished feeling came over him, which could be why he had dredged up one of his mother's rarer sayings. Pauline had put his jacket on and was facing him. He could again smell the subtle fragrance of her perfume.

"L—l—look," he stammered, "if I look after you until you meet your tall, dark and handsome stranger, will you stick with me? Will you go out with me?"

"Where to?"

He didn't see that her eyes were smiling.

"I don't mean go out with me to anywhere in particular. I mean knock around together." He was making a mess of it, but couldn't quite bring himself to say 'let's go steady' or 'I love you so please go out with me and me alone'. "I just wanted you to know that you had a friend," he finished, lamely.

"You're sweet sometimes," she said, smiling up at him, "sincere."

He shrugged, "I don't know."

"You are," she said. "Is there anything else you want to say?"

"Like what?"

"Oh, Peter," she tugged at his arm impatiently, "come on — let's go in." Pauline's father took hold of her for a dance as they re-entered, so he asked Veronica up. It was a quickstep, which neither of them liked very much so they jived to it instead. He felt embarrassed when her handkerchief dropped on the floor and he thought about picking it up for her, like they did in the olden days. But he relaxed when she bent quickly, retrieved it herself and stuffed it into her pocket. He felt sorry for her and pretended not to notice what happened. His mind was too preoccupied with wondering what it was Pauline had wanted him to say and wondering whether he said things in a peculiar way so that people never really understood what he was trying to tell them.

"Mitchell!" his teacher thundered at him across the classroom. "Explain briefly what we have been discussing about the convict settlement of New South Wales."

"Er. . . umm . . . I don't know, sir."

"A hundred lines," Peter mused aloud, now dancing the last waltz with Pauline.

"Pardon?"

"A hundred lines for stepping on my foot."

"I didn't step on your foot."

"True," he said, "but write them anyway."

"I'll give you a belt in a minute," she warned.

"That's what they used to say," he replied.

Pauline laughed, "Whatever are you talking about?"

Chapter 11

An Emergency

He leaped out of bed panic-stricken the next morning. What had happened to the french letter? He certainly wasn't wearing it. It wasn't in his underwear. He checked and rechecked his socks and then his shoes. Mortified he scoured the bedroom floor. He stripped the bed and searched the sheets and looked under his pillow. Then he separated the two blankets and shook them out. There was no sign of it. He dressed quickly and retraced his steps of the night before, first to the recreation hall, then to the front door of Pauline's hut. The toilets at the hall similarly yielded nothing. He remembered going to the toilet before turning in for the night. He hadn't been wearing it then, either, come to think of it. So it must have fallen off into his underpants. He went back to his bedroom, latched the door, stripped naked and searched his clothing and his socks and shoes again. It wasn't there. He dressed and went back to the hall.

"Excuse me, sir," he said to the man sweeping the floor, "I lost my badge somewhere in here last night — is it all right if I look for it?"

"What kind of badge would that be, then?" the man asked in a thick, Scottish accent.

Peter thought quickly, "It's like a small, errmm . . . St John Ambulance badge."

"Would that be a round, brass-coloured badge with a fancy cross on it?" Peter's mouth opened in amazement, "Yes, that's it."

"I had one of those when I was a wee man," the Scotsman said. "I wonder now what happened to it? It was so dear ta me."

To Peter's astonishment the man suddenly burst into song: "Sa dear ta me, 'tis aye sa dear ta me; Scotland, Scotland, Scotland aye sae braw left my heart in Scotland, though I'm sa far awah . . . have a look for your badge. Better still, grab a broom and give me a hand — you might find it that way."

Peter helped to sweep the hall, checking carefully under the chairs that had been piled up near the stage. After the first few minutes he had to go back over the places he had swept when he realised he had been absentmindedly looking for his St John badge. When the cleaning-up was done, the man thanked him for his help and said he wished more people were as considerate. But there was no sign of the french letter.

He returned to the hut and made one last desperate search of his bed, then tidied the covers and tucked them in carefully so there was no need for his mother to pull back the bedclothes. It must be somewhere, he reasoned, and it would be just his luck for his mother to find it. But pangs of hunger told him he had to give up.

He ate breakfast pensively, going over in his mind the events of the night before, in the hope that he could track the whereabouts of the embarrassing item. Pauline asked him why he was so quiet and he told her he was tired. "I slept like a log," she said, "and I left the radio going and got into trouble this morning. Dad said the BBC had kept him awake all night. But I told him the BBC was only on for an hour and he said that wasn't the point.

Peter hadn't a clue what she was talking about. He glanced down to his shoes to make sure there was no strip of pink rubber hanging out from the top of either of them.

Pauline ironed her underskirt with meticulous care. Like most girls of her age, she wore only white under her dress, and that white had to be always spotlessly clean and perfectly ironed. Veronica sat on the wooden bench of the wash-house, catching up on homework and awaiting her turn with the iron. Beside her was a small pile of underwear, which she had covered with a gym slip in case any of the boys walked in. The radio was giving a crackling rendition of Frankie Laine singing *Humming Bird.* The crackling would stop when the iron was turned off. Apart from the radio, it was peaceful for once in the washroom. There were three ironing boards and three power outlets. People supplied their own iron, by courtesy of the enterprising never-never salesman who left in each empty hut, for each new immigrant family, an electric jug, a toaster and an iron and a note that said to try the goods out for a week with "no obligation to buy" but if you wanted to you could purchase on the never-never. He reputedly never lost a sale. Frankie Laine gave way to Nat King Cole crooning *A Blossom Fell*. Pauline switched off the iron.

"Some nice songs this morning" she said, "nice and romantic."

Veronica looked up from her exercise book: "How are you getting on with Peter Mitchell?"

"Fine, Peter's all right, except for when I'm in a romantic mood. Then, I could strangle him."

"Why?"

"Well," Pauline frowned at her sister, "well . . . I don't know."

"Doesn't he get romantic?" Veronica pushed eagerly.

"I think he's romantic all the time. It's not that — it's sort of different with him." She switched the iron on again and threw a crackle through *Suddenly There's a Valley*. "I mean, I keep expecting him to grab hold of me and kiss me and all he does is look at me and smile and send a thrill right through me. Mind you, when I'm not in a romantic mood, his manner really pleases me."

"He's a gentleman," Veronica said. "And he's probably too young for you, even if he has got a man's body."

"He's quite grown up mentally," Pauline said defensively.

"He's cute," Veronica said, smiling wickedly.

"Don't you start having any thoughts about Peter . . . you're too young anyway."

"But he is cute," Veronica grinned.

"Yes," Pauline sighed, "he is cute." But cuteness had never entered her dream of walking up the aisle with a tall, dark and handsome man.

"He's really good looking," Veronica said dreamily. "He's really good looking and cute."

Pauline laughed. "He put his coat round me last night because I was shivery and he had his shirt sleeves rolled up. When we got back inside his arms were covered in goose pimples. But he didn't say anything about being cold." She sighed again, "He's so distant sometimes. You can talk to him and he hasn't got any idea what you're saying."

"Perhaps he's wondering how to make a gentlemanly pass at you," Veronica joked.

"Nobody makes a pass at me," Pauline snapped, "not unless they want a black eye."

"Keep your hair on, I was only kidding. You went outside with him, not me."

"We just talked. He told me he was my friend. I was feeling a bit sad and sentimental. And, and he wanted to make sure I would carry on going around with him."

"Did he ask you to go steady?"

"I don't think he meant it like that," Pauline frowned. "No, I'm certain he didn't mean it like that. He just means knocking around together until the right person comes along. That's the trouble with Peter — if you go out with him for some fresh air, that's what you get."

"But you said no one could make a pass at you anyway."

"Stop talking about things like that," Pauline said irritably. "If you don't know what I mean, then you're probably too young yet."

"You're lucky or you're not lucky he's a gentleman," Veronica said, and before her sister could reply, "I think he fancies me. He's always pulling faces at me."

"You pull them at him," Pauline said. "You shouldn't confuse friendliness with anything romantic. He just likes you."

"How do you know?"

"Look," Pauline said patiently, "I don't want to hurt your feelings, but you're too young for boys. You aren't even fifteen yet. You'll find plenty of boyfriends when you're older — and break a few hearts, no doubt. But you're too young for boys at the moment. You've got to know how to keep them at bay when need be."

"You don't have to keep Peter at bay," Veronica grinned.

"Pauline was exasperated, "That's the bloody trouble!" In a flurry of impatience, she picked up the pile of ironed clothes and flounced out of the washroom.

There were too many things going through Pauline's head these days. It seemed to her that she might have found her very first real boyfriend if she wanted him. She was fond of Peter. True, he was a few weeks younger than her, but he didn't act stupid like some of the boys. And he had lovely, fine features — a perfectly shaped nose and long, dark eyelashes under blond eyebrows and even blonder hair. And he was tall and strong-looking and quite gorgeous. The trouble was that sometimes she felt she might have acquired a long sought-after brother, and how could she contemplate romance with someone she might look upon as a brother? Pauline's romantic moods had become stronger with desire over the past few months. She had to hold off. Waiting was everything to her. And, with Peter, she knew she could wait. He was easy to handle. He was too easy to handle. There was no pressure from Peter Mitchell. And when her thoughts went back to that balmy night when she had told him that some girls might have sex but only with one of those things, she would wonder what she could have been thinking of even mentioning sex. Not that she had said she would do it — and she wouldn't have done it, anyway. Just as well, though, that Peter wasn't the pushy kind. Perhaps he was a bit young for her. But she really did trust Peter and she really did feel safe with him, and she really did want to be a virgin on her wedding night. And if it ever became difficult to see that dream through, then she would call on her resolve, and she would remember what she had to lose.

Chapter 12

Sad News

Jim's car was outside his hut, but Jim wasn't home. Peter had seen the girls go into the washhouse but decided not to pester them. He knew they could well be washing or ironing their under garments and wouldn't want him around. So he went for a bike ride along the usual path that led to the mushrooming township where he worked.

He scanned the paddocks as he rode, in the vague hope of seeing Jim. It was all very well for Wendy to go out with Jim, but Peter didn't see why he should lose a friend in the process. He rode for a couple of miles, almost to the main construction site, before he saw them — Jim, Wendy and Shirley, standing at the edge of the eastern-most paddock, almost beside the main highway. He sensed all was not well. Shirley came towards him as he approached. She looked troubled.

"What's wrong?"

"It's Wendy. Her parents are going back to England, and she has to go with them."

He glanced fearfully at Jim who was standing defiantly with hand on hip. "I'm sorry to hear that," Peter said, awkwardly to Wendy, "we'll miss you."

"She wants to stay here with me," Jim put in. "And I keep telling her there's no problem - she can stay here with me."

Peter knew Wendy couldn't stay in Australia without her parents' permission - she was too young. And she certainly couldn't stay with Jim unless they got married.

"You could get married," he said.

"Yuh wot - with her father. He'd rather boil me in oil."

"You could go to court and get permission," Shirley said. Then, turning to Peter, "That's what I've been telling them. That's right, isn't it?" Peter nodded: "I think so."

"Thanks," Jim said, "I know you're only trying to help, but I haven't even got round to proposing yet."

"When are you going?" Peter asked Wendy.

"July . . . that's when my parents and brother are going." She gave him a look of defiance to match Jim's mood, and she looked particularly beautiful when she did that.

"Is it possible your parents will relent and let you stay?"

"I don't know, but I want to — there's nothing back there for me." Peter noticed Shirley's bicycle propped against an old fence post. "Should we go for a ride, Shirley, I think Jim might have something to say to Wendy."

The two of them rode off, heading in a circuitous route back to the camp. "What do you think?" Shirley asked, as they rode side-by-side.

"There're only two ways Wendy can stay here," he said knowledgeably, "and that's for her to get married or her parents decide she can stay with some responsible adult."

"It is possible to leave home when you're sixteen," Shirley said. "But I think you might have to convince the police you have a bad home life. And Wendy wouldn't be able to do that."

"No, she has a good home life, good parents," Peter agreed.

"A girl can get permission to marry if she's pregnant," Shirley said.

"She's not . . ."

"No, I shouldn't think so," Shirley laughed. "I was just saying, if."

"I think they could get permission anyway," Peter said, "that's why I left them to it. Perhaps Jim will propose."

"They've only known each other for a few weeks," Shirley said. "But I suppose they know whether they are in love."

Peter felt much more comfortable with Shirley now. It was as if a thin veneer of ice separating them had melted. Shirley, he realised, despite her outgoing nature, had either an inborn mistrust of the opposite sex, or an aloofness disguised by her bubbling personality.

They jumped off their bicycles upon reaching the camp and, as if by mental telepathy, both headed for the boilerhouse. They sat there in the gloom for a couple of hours, Peter keeping a respectable distance, chatting and waiting for Jim and Wendy.

Shirley wore denim short-shorts, with the mainly red plaid turn-ups becoming fashionable with the girls for casual wear. He gave them only a glance in case she thought he was looking at her legs. She had beautiful, long, shapely legs, almost always bare, even of ankle socks, and he wouldn't have minded risking her wrath by looking at them. But the fear of being considered a pervert was enough to keep him in check. Had he not met Pauline, Shirley would have been a very nice girlfriend to have. He could very easily have fallen in love with Shirley, but he didn't know how she thought of him. And he suspected she was good at hiding her thoughts, just as he was good at hiding his. He never really thought of girls as people. Did he think of them as sex symbols? He put girls on a pedestal and honoured and respected them and enjoyed their company, often more than he did the company of other boys. But why did he always think about sex when he was with them?

"Have you heard the latest song?" She broke into his thoughts.

"Probably — which one?"

"*It's Almost Tomorrow* . . . it's really nice."

"It's been rocketing up the hit parade," Peter said. "Yes, it is nice. The Dream Weavers sing it." The thought occurred to Peter that he wasn't very keen on thinking about tomorrow. He had managed to forget that he was to join the roofing gang and would be walking rooftops that weren't even there. "They are very good," he said, determined not to think about work. "I like Nat King Cole, Johnnie Ray, David Whitfield . . . and Ruby Murray and Jo Stafford . . . and Petula Clark - I love *The Little Shoemaker* . , . and I like Frankie Laine . . . and Doris Day and the Crew Cuts, especially *Earth Angel* . . ."

"I like most of those, too," Shirley said. "And I like Bing Crosby and Lonnie Donegan."

"What does he sing?"

"*Rock Island Line*."

"Oh, I know. That's really good to jive to."

"I haven't got any of his records," she said. "I don't think you can buy *Rock Island Line* yet. It's not in the shops."

"It should be," Peter said. "Perhaps they've sold out and are waiting for new stocks."

"A shop in Rundle Street said they hadn't got it yet. Mind you - it's very new and perhaps they have to import records."

"I shouldn't think so," Peter said. "They must have their own record-making facilities here. A population of nine million — I mean to say!" It was important to Peter that Australia should have its own record-making industry. He wanted to write his own song — a big song that would be on everybody's lips. And just in case he never got back to England, he could sell it here and let it find its own way across the world. And then he would have enough money to go and see Margie and ask her to come back to Australia with him. Or would he stay in England with her? He wasn't too sure about that. He had some good friends here, and he had good friends over there. How could he live in both places? If only the two countries weren't so far apart. If it came down to a choice, he supposed it would have to be England. He didn't even want to think about choosing between Pauline and Margie. It was all very confusing. And now he was going to have problems keeping his mind off Shirley.

Sometimes he wished he could talk to somebody about his problems. About all the strange thoughts which ran through his head and about how he couldn't keep his mind off sex and how he felt inadequate in not knowing what girls thought of him, especially Pauline, and whether Margie would still love him in a couple of years when she was old enough to go dating boys. And sometimes he wished he could talk to somebody about the terrible rent that had taken place in his life when his parents decided to follow one last dream of their own and head for the other side of the world. And he wanted so dearly to tell of how he wished everything could be back where it was before they had left England. And he knew that was an impossible wish, but he wished it anyway.

"You're not the eternal chatterbox," Shirley said. "Shall we go? It's getting a bit chilly."

"It doesn't look like we're going to see Jim and Wendy for a while," he replied, absently. "I'd better go. I'll see you tonight."

"See you tonight," Shirley echoed. "At my place, I think."

Peter rode to his hut in a light-hearted mood. No matter what his problems, he could always push them to a corner of his mind where they couldn't keep annoying him.

He sat between Pauline and Donna at dinner, where it was established that they would all go to Shirley's to listen to records. Jim and Wendy sat at the end of the table and Jim kept glancing across the cafeteria at Wendy's parents as though he had something to say to them. But he didn't go over.

They all liked Shirley's records. She had *Unchained Melody, I Believe, Answer Me,* and *Little Things Mean A Lot* and many more top hits. Jim took Peter outside early in the evening, where they shared a bottle of beer on Shirley's back steps, from under which Jim had magically produced the forbidden brew.

"Do you have bottles of beer hidden everywhere?"

"Not at your place," Jim said, "you would only drink it."

They swigged the beer as Dean Martin began *Memories Are Made of This.*

"What's happening?" Peter asked.

"I proposed," Jim said with an edge of excitement, "and she accepted."

"Congratulations," Peter was formal. "So what's happening?"

"That's a good question. It depends on her old man."

"Do you think he'll let you get married?"

"Naaah — he's too protective. He doesn't realise his daughter is grown up now. He wants to hang on to her forever."

"You'll have to ask his permission to marry Wendy," Peter reminded him.

"That should be interesting," Jim groaned, "I suspect he hates my guts."

They sat in silence then, Peter allowing Jim his own thoughts and wondering himself about marriage proposals. He supposed they should be made in the most romantic of ways — soft lights, violins, a hand pressed tenderly in love . . . or under a full moon on a warm night in August. No, not August, not here — it would have to be a warm night in January or February . . . or perhaps you should propose in a lush green meadow, sparkling with wildflowers and heady with the fragrance of a spring morning. Would he ever have the courage to propose to Pauline or Margie? It wouldn't be so difficult with Margie, who must surely realise that he had arrived to marry her if she ever opened her front door to see him standing there. But with Pauline . . . well, that could be awkward. She hardly struck him as the soft violin-type. Perhaps green fields and wildflowers would be more her forte . . . no, he wasn't sure about that, either. Perhaps Pauline was a full-moon, romantic night person. Then it could happen by chance, by magic. He wouldn't be able to deliberately trick Pauline, he suspected. He suspected she would always be a step ahead of him.

"What did you say to her? When you asked her to marry you, what did you say?"

"I said, 'shall we get married, then?' and she said 'all right, then'."

So it was as simple as that. Probably they were standing in the middle of a brown paddock under this alien sky · too early for the moon, too cloudy for the sun, cowpats for wildflowers and the squawking of some Murray magpie for a violin. Peter suddenly felt sorry for Jim and Wendy.

"Do you want me to come with you when you ask her father?"

"Course not — that's something I have to do myself, fucknuckle."

"Just trying to help," Peter said, in a singsong voice.

"Thanks, anyway, but I'm not scared of him. I just don't quite know what to say. One thing's for sure — I'd better not go to him smelling of beer."

"You better not," Peter agreed.

"The other problem," Jim said, "will be finding somewhere to live and enough money to keep us both. I earn sweet fuck all."

"Wendy works, though," Peter pointed out. "You should get by."

"Oh, yeah — get by," Jim spat into the darkness. "She earns four fuckin' pounds a week and ten shillings of that goes on fares."

Peter groaned. "They pay girls disgusting wages — I don't know how they get away with it."

"They pay us disgusting wages as well," Jim added. "How can you live on what we get?" He took a large gulp of beer, "What can we do about it? Sweet fanny nothing, that's what!" He leaned heavily against Peter and nudged him with his elbow. "Hey . . . what do you think of little old Jimmy boy scoring Wendy, then?"

"I think it's marvellous," Peter said, "I'm really happy for both of you."

"You talk quite fuckin' queer sometimes," Jim observed. And then, "I love her you know. I would do anything for her. By the way, you must tell me off every time you hear me fuckin' swear. I must stop fuckin' swearing."

"I'll do that," Peter promised.

Jim clung to the bottle with one hand and gestured with the other, "You know, she's got a lot of class has my Wendy — I've got to show I'm worthy of her."

This, Peter thought, was strange talk coming from Jim. But he understood. Jim was overwhelmed both by Wendy's beauty and the fact that she had chosen him from all the other males in the world. Peter couldn't help feeling wonderment · what could Wendy possibly see in Jim? He pushed the thought away. Jim was his friend, and he mustn't harbour disparaging thoughts about his friends.

"When will you ask her father?"

"She wants me to ask tonight, to get it over with. But I might wait a while seeing as I've been drinking."

"A good idea," Peter said.

They finished their bottle and went back inside. Everybody looked up at them briefly as they re-entered the lounge, but then went back to their conversations. Peter's stomach felt a bit bloated from the beer, which he had swigged rather quickly. He sat away from Pauline, in case she smelled it on his breath. But after a short time she came over and plonked herself on his knee.

"I've just had a few swigs of beer," he was apologetic.

"It doesn't matter," she said, leaning back and resting her hand on the chair, behind his head. She didn't ask about Jim.

Perhaps the girls had already discussed the matter while he and Jim were outside.

There was nowhere else for Peter's arm to go but round Pauline's waist. So that was where he put it and he felt very happy about that. Marriage was already in the air between Jim and Wendy. What if he were to suddenly stand up and announce that he and Pauline were getting engaged and everybody was invited to the party? If he had the courage, he would propose there and then. But what an utter idiot he would feel if he were to propose in front of all his friends only to have Pauline burst into hysterical laughter. For that matter, what an idiot he would feel if she merely politely declined. And what an idiot he would feel if she accepted but told him he had to ask her father, because she wasn't going to. And then he would go home and tell his mother he was getting married and she would ground him for a year. Would he ever come out of his dream world long enough to actually do anything of consequence in the real one? Long enough even to propose marriage, or to make a positive move to be sure of winning Pauline's affection or to find out whether he had already won it?

Pauline shifted slightly, taking some of her weight off one of his legs so it was more evenly dispersed. Unlike some girls, who probably didn't realise what they were doing, Pauline didn't sit right into a boy's lap, squashing his testicles. She had a finesse about her at times which belied her outwardly brash manner.

He put both arms round her waist, holding her gently, but there was nowhere to put his hands without taking hold of a small piece of her dress between his fingers or letting his wrists fall on to her lap. He didn't feel he could do either of those things. He couldn't physically hold her waist for long either, without actually squeezing it or gripping it more tightly. He felt the same discomfort that visited upon him when his knee began to shake while sitting next to a girl. And he had to use mind control to keep his hands poised at her waist, actually touching her, but so gently that she could not take offence nor believe that he might start to get fresh. Thus, he sat — bolt upright and with a half-terrified look on his face. Eventually, he removed his arms from round her, which made things worse, because he had absolutely nowhere to put them then and he didn't like to put them back around her just like that.

Tony Bennett began singing *Stranger in Paradise* when Peter asked her to let him up to get a drink. He went to the tap and took a glass of cold, brown water and drank it thirstily. Jim threw him a look of distaste from across the room. But Peter barely noticed · the song had sent his mind wandering off to when he would be a pop singer like Tony Bennett and Dean Martin.

He must do something about his song. If only he could apply himself. But there was so much happening, both in his mind and in his day-to-day practical existence. There was so much to experience in life. He was too green, too virginal to the world to write songs with any real meaning. Nevertheless, he would write a song as soon as he found the time. Perhaps Pauline and the others would like it and then it wouldn't matter quite so much if it was never recorded. But it would be wonderful to write a popular song, to hear the men at work singing it and to sit here among his friends and hear it come on the radio.

Suddenly he began whistling *Mocking Bird Hill* and won a smile from Veronica, who had been a bit quiet most of the night. And then for some reason he remembered the missing condom and felt his face turning red.

He burst in on his parents and George. His mother was knitting; his father had dozed off in the armchair and George was listening to the radio while reading a book, which was a favourite double pastime of his.

Peter would brazen it out. He would deny the offending item was his and claim angrily that one of the other teenagers had probably planted it in his room for a joke. His mother wouldn't see the joke, but she could hardly blame him, could she? His ploy was a waste of time because obviously none of his family had found the condom. All he got was a growl from his father for entering the room so noisily and waking him, a consequent frown from his mother and a glare from George.

"I've lost my badge," he said in a loud voice to his mother. "You haven't found a badge in my room?"

"Keep your voice down," she said sternly, "you'll have the entire camp out looking for it."

"Did you find it?" he whispered.

"No," she whispered back. "You must have lost it somewhere else."

"Make a pot of tea," George whispered.

"All right," Peter whispered.

"Not too strong," his father whispered.

"And then get to bed," his mother whispered.

So he never did find the missing condom. And the only person who knew what happened to it, never told. And it wasn't until years later, while he was lying in bed one night — a time when strange thoughts and scenarios popped into his head — that he realised somebody must have deliberately rescued him from a most appalling embarrassment. And he had the good grace to blush that night, too.

Matthew, Mark, Luke and John
Bless the bed that I lay on.
May four angels round my bed,
Trap my heels, trap my head.

Dear God, please let Wendy's father allow Jim and Wendy to get married so she doesn't have to go back to England. And please God let me be able to go back to England soon to sort out with Margie what we are going to do about our romance and that. And let me be able to decide between Pauline and Margie. And, by the way, it's no good sending me back to England just yet, because Margie is too young to talk about marriage. Perhaps when she leaves school would be a good time. Please God bless everybody I know and everybody I don't know and forgive me for my sins and I'm very sorry about the condom and it won't happen again. And please God don't let me fall off the roof tomorrow.

Chapter 13

Giddy Heights

Of course, Peter thought bitterly the next morning while fighting a gusty wind on his way to work. Of course it would be windy today. It would have to be windy if he was going to join the roofing gang. What did he expect? Perfect calm and sunshine? No, he should have realised it would be windy. Not that he could do anything about it, but he should have realised. He had nurtured the faint hope that Clive would change his mind and put him on second-fixing or even send him genuinely to help the brickies. But no such luck.

Climbing the ladder with the wind tugging at him was bad enough. Now, standing knees-bent and precariously on top of the framing waiting for Clive to slide the first length of timber to him was terrifying. He felt much safer with his knees bent. It was tough on his legs, keeping his knees bent like that. But his legs shook when he tried straightening them.

"Make sure you nail them good and sturdy," Clive warned him. "We don't want them turning over under anyone's feet."

A long way beneath him gaped the hard jarrah undercarriages and Peter wondered what sort of mess they would make of his body if he fell on to them and what his chances would be of surviving such a fall.

Clive slid the first heavy beam to him and Peter found that gripping it gave him extra balance. So he was able to straighten his knees most of the time and do the nailing quite comfortably, considering where he was. He adopted an almost nonchalant air, though his legs still shook and every now and then he had to bend his knees slightly in a bid to ease the ache in them. But he didn't bend his knees as often as he bent some of the nails.

"One nail on each side and one for luck," Clive had said. "And don't put them in line or you'll split the timber."

Peter wasn't sure whether he was expected to walk on the ceiling joists to nail the beams for the hip into place, because the joists didn't look at all safe and they didn't feel safe when he gingerly tested a couple with his foot. He watched Clive and was grateful to see the big man step cautiously over the joists while holding on to the hip beam. Peter didn't have to put on any big show of being a circus trapeze artist. But he did have to step across what seemed to him a yawning chasm, with his heart in his throat.

Clive asked him if he was all right. "You look a bit peaky."

"I'll get used to it," Peter forced a grin. "Just nervous to start with. I'm not sure I like heights."

"You'll get used to it," Clive agreed. "Just be careful, but do it as though you're walking on a footpath - not the high wires. Just take it easy, mate. She'll be right."

So now, at least temporarily, he was "mate". He had graduated from "boy" or "lad" and "laddie", to "mate". Peter wasn't going to let his mate Clive down.

They worked steadily until morning tea, with Peter gaining just a little bit more nerve as each minute ticked by. Clive would burst into song every now and then, but Peter wasn't confident enough to follow suit. He was content with his daydreams into which he had escaped to shield his fear, manifested when the wind whipped through his shirt and pulled at his trousers and made banging noises with loose battens below. Despite the trauma, Peter was able to bang the nails in almost as fast as Clive did and although he bent more of them and had to pull these out and bang new ones in, he hardly ever kept his boss waiting too long.

Unbeknown to Peter, Old Charlie was making the tea that morning, to enable Clive to have more time to teach the boy. So when Clive yelled "smoko in ten minutes" and disappeared off the roof, Peter, who had no idea of the time and was expecting to be called on to make the tea, was caught by surprise. He hadn't noticed how Clive had got off the roof. And he hadn't been told how to get off, either. Climbing up to the roof had been simple enough: climb almost to the top of the ladder, grab hold of a joist, and hoist yourself up. Getting down wasn't going to be as easy. How could he swivel himself round to get his feet on the ladder? What if the ladder decided to fall backwards? Peter's stomach told him he was panicking. He must stay calm. When he thought about it, he was sure Clive must have merely walked to the ladder, gripped the top, and swung himself around and on to it, before descending safely. Peter decided to try that, but the ladder wasn't where it had been and he almost plunged headlong to the ground. Only by quickly bending his knees and grabbing hold of the brick walling did he save himself.

He sat on top of the walling and thought the matter out, feeling surprisingly calm. He could work through his tea break, pretending to be conscientious. The trouble was, he had no idea what work to do without Clive being there. Roofing was usually done by a three- or four-man gang and you certainly couldn't manage on your own. Across the site he saw a large crowd of men, including the brickies, around the carpenters' shed. He wondered what was going on, but was grateful that no one seemed to be looking his way. He had a bit of time yet before anyone noticed that he was too scared to get down.

While gathering his nerve, remembering George's oft-spoken phrases "you can do it because you're British" or "You mustn't do that because you're British", depending on what they were talking about, he heard an urgent "Hey!" from below and looked down to see Ronnie about to place a long ladder against the inside of the house. Then he put a finger to his lips beseeching the boy to silence.

It was much easier getting down on the inside of the house, even when your knees were shaking.

"Don't say a word about this to anyone," Ronnie warned a grateful Peter. "Clive will cut off your balls if the brickies find out."

"What's going on?" Peter asked, still shaken but pretending not to be.

"We've taken the brickies for a ride. They bet good money that you wouldn't make it down for morning tea."

Peter never said a word to anyone about the incident except to casually mention that he had climbed down the inside framing. Nevertheless, some hint of what had taken place may have found its way to the brickies. About a week later while Ronnie was sitting in the dunny, four of them marched up to it, lifted the little shed high into the air and placed it carefully down on the paddock about 10 yards away. Ronnie was brilliant — he just sat there reading the morning paper as though nothing had happened, and eventually wiped his bottom seemingly oblivious to the yahoos and catcalls from around the site. Peter made sure he was regulated enough not to have to use the dunny after that. He didn't like the little shed anyway — it was supposed to be a favourite meeting place for poisonous redback spiders and of course it stank to high heaven and buzzed with flies on a warm day.

Chapter 14

Donna in Hysterics

Jim's car proved to be of little benefit to the camp teenagers, because he and Wendy were always out in it. The other young people still went to the boilerhouse or hung around the camp shop or walked up to the Roadhouse for a Coke or a Cottee's lime and perhaps a Chiko roll.

Peter missed the activities of life in Handsworth, like mixing up stink bombs with his chemistry set, attending the YMCA, St John cadets, or playing tracking through the streets at night. And he missed the bluebell woods where games were limited only by a boy's imagination. He didn't realise that, anyway, the time for childish things had ended forever.

The temperature varied widely through March — sometimes pleasantly cool and at other times uncomfortably warm. But the searing heat of February had abated. Most nights he was comfortable in his shirt, but now and then wore his jacket, only to take it off and put it round the shoulders of Pauline or Veronica should they start to feel cold in the night breeze. In his wallet, he still carried hopefully the two french letters. But at the back of his mind was the philosophy that his bride should be a virgin on her wedding night. Also on the back of his mind hung a wisp of fear that he might spoil things like he did during his sexual encounter with Donna.

The following Saturday, Jim went to Wendy's father and asked for permission to marry his daughter. Permission was declined, leaving Peter with a very angry Jim to contend with for the rest of the weekend.

"He reckons we're too young," Jim explained bitterly. "Why can't he realise that his daughter has grown up? Does he want to keep her with him forever?"

They were sitting outside the camp shop, Peter eating a Violet Crumble bar and Jim sucking noisily at a bottle of Coke.

"It's ridiculous," Peter said, sympathetically.

"What the fuck am I supposed to do if she goes back to England? It's fuckin' ridiculous."

"It really is ridiculous," Peter said, "it's not as if you can't look after her." He thought it could be a bad time to remind Jim about his swearing. "You could go to court and get permission," he pointed out. "You're bound to get it."

"That's what we're going to do," Jim said. "I told him that, I told him he was only putting off the inevitable. I said it politely, of course. I was very polite." He squirted a fine spray of Coke through his front teeth into the grass. "Then he got angry and said perhaps I shouldn't see her any more. Then Wendy started on to him and he walked out on us. Now Wendy's locked herself in her bedroom and says she's never coming out."

"What about your parents?" Peter asked gently. "Can you get their permission?"

"They don't mind - they're probably glad to get rid of me."

"It's different with a girl, though," Peter said. "Parents tend to be more protective with girls."

"I'm going to the welfare department on Monday to find out about getting permission. I'll probably need a lawyer and have to fill in all sorts of papers, which I'm no good at. And then I'll have to go and stand before some beak in Salisbury or Adelaide." Jim whistled lightly through his teeth, which was his way of sighing. "My parents weren't all that happy," he conceded, "but they like Wendy and eventually came round to seeing the problem we're up against."

Peter thought he had a brilliant idea. "Couldn't your parents look after Wendy until she's old enough to get married?"

"Shit, no — her parents wouldn't allow that. You're talking about nearly five fuckin' years until she's twenty-one."

"I don't see why girls can't get married when they're sixteen if they want to," Peter was genuinely puzzled. "I mean, they can have sex without permission at that age . . . it doesn't make sense, does it?"

"Nothing makes sense," Jim said, managing a smile. "The old man threatened to punch my head in if I stuffed up my trade by getting married. I told him to fuckin' try it and he burst out laughing and gave me a pat on the back. Nothing makes fuckin' sense, I can tell you that much. I mean, who would have thought a couple of months ago that I would even be interested in girls yet . . . there's so much to see and do, and here I am talking about marriage. So much to see and do . . . I've done fuckin' nothin' yet."

"You can see and do it together," Peter said. "You and Wendy, together — and I hope you'll visit me and the gang sometimes."

"Of course we will. Do you think we'll get permission to marry, then?"

Peter had thought about this. In Britain, young lovers always seemed to be eloping to Gretna Green or somewhere to get married, so the Sunday papers said. And if they had to elope, didn't that mean they couldn't get permission to wed? But he wasn't going to upset Jim any further. Hope sprang eternal.

"I don't really see why not," he said. "It must depend, though, on just how much opposition you get from her parents once you're in court."

"I'll get plenty of that," Jim groaned. "A fuckin' barrowload."

Peter had just finished his crumble bar when Veronica rushed up to them. "Come quick — it's Donna, she's having a fit in the boilerhouse."

"What do you mean?" Peter gasped. "What's she doing?"

"She can't stop laughing," Veronica said, bursting into tears, "and she's turning blue in the face."

Peter doubted that he had ever run so fast in his life. Donna was lying on the floor, her breath coming in short, desperate gasps.

St John had never taught Peter how to deal with someone who couldn't stop laughing, but it had taught him commonsense, "Get some cold water, quick," he cried to Pauline, while giving Donna a resounding slap across the face. Pauline threw the cold water into the girl's face and it dribbled down her neck and soaked her dress. It worked instantly. She lay there sighing loudly.

"Vuggin' bashtards," she gasped, sitting up.

"Don't laugh, whatever you do," Jim said.

Peter glared at him.

"Thanks," Donna said, breathing easily now and fast recovering her composure. "That was scary. I thought I had grown out of that." She clutched the front of her dress, "God, that water's cold."

"Take your dress off and I'll give you a rub down," Jim said, earning glares from everybody.

"How did it happen?" Peter asked.

Shirley answered, "We were just talking and I said something funny and everybody started laughing, only . . . Donna couldn't stop."

"How long since this last happened to you," Peter asked, importantly.

"A couple of years," she said.

"Mention it to your parents, in case they want you to see a doctor. A doctor might give you something to take or tell you what to do if it happens again. Not that you can actually take anything while you're like that, I shouldn't think."

"You're all right now," Jim said. "I would go and see a doctor, though."

Peter looked round at the white faces and realised that everyone was suffering a bit from shock.

"If you've got any brandy at home," he said to Donna, "Give everyone a tot or even a cup of sweet tea or coffee."

"Shit," Jim said, once they were outside, "what was all that about?"

"I don't know — I haven't seen anything quite like it before," Peter said. "I suspect she'll grow out of it eventually, though."

Wendy turned up at the dance that night, but Donna didn't appear. Pauline told them all the girl was "fine", just a bit embarrassed.

April came and went, leaving little for Peter to remember it by. There was the showery weather he expected for such a month, even if April was falling in the wrong hemisphere for its true romanticism, and some warmth still clung to the air. He had lost much of his timidity on the roofing work and been told by Clive that he was doing well. He still had trouble negotiating the ladder to get off the roofs, but he took his time, believing in having a "safety first" attitude. Better that than tumbling head-first to the ground.

A couple of families with small children moved from the camp into houses in the new town. But Peter's parents heard from the Housing Trust of South Australia that they could expect a wait of a few more months yet before being given a house. Peter guessed, as did everyone else, that the authorities wanted to move mostly Australians into the town first, to appease a population angry that the new town was going to be made up of nearly sixty per cent British immigrants and more than twenty per cent New Australians. Peter's family were told, though, that when they did move into a house, it would be in Elizabeth South — three miles from the camp. He could easily cycle up to see Pauline and the others if they were still at the camp.

It was sunny and warm through the first week of May, and a letter from Margie made Peter think of the swelling buds on the trees and the activities of the birds in the hedgerows back home. Many wildflowers would already be in bloom and there would be just a hint of that wondrous smell of spring in the air. And he thought of how even more beautiful it would be away from the big, industrial city, away to places such as Blackwell and Bromsgrove. The ache in his heart, never really far away, gripped him through his working week and brought back sleepless nights. Only when he was with Pauline and the others did the homesickness leave him. But his tin box still held only a few pounds and England was still so very far away. Would he ever save enough to visit his beloved country, and his darling Margie?

On Tuesday the eighth of May, 1956, Jim and Wendy went to the state magistrate's court to seek permission to marry. That night Peter and Jim walked up to the station so Jim could explain the events of the day. Jim was in good spirits. Things had gone well.

"They interviewed us separately. Asked me if I realised the responsibility I was undertaking. Then they asked me if I thought she might be pregnant. They seemed pleased when I said there was no way she could be, because she was a virgin. I got asked how much I was earning and stuff like that. I told them I was earning more than I really was. Let's hope they don't check with my boss, though I only put my wages up by two pounds. They asked Wendy similar stuff. They've got a bloody cheek when you think about it."

"You should have told the truth about your earnings," Peter interrupted. "They will probably get read out in court. You could be up for contempt or something."

"Fuck them," Jim said. "All's fair in love and war. Anyway, I'll just say I made a mistake."

"One thing in your favour," Peter said, "is that they probably don't like bringing people all the way out here, only to have them pack up and go back."

"And the fact that she's a virgin," Jim added, "I bet her old man's pleased about that."

"I'll bet he is, too," Peter agreed.

"Funny, they didn't ask me if I was a virgin," Jim guffawed.

"Neither will I," Peter said, "that's your business."

"It's her business, too, whether she is one."

"I agree," Peter said, "they've got a bloody cheek."

"A what?"

"A bloody cheek."

"Fuck me — you swore," Jim said. "You'd better watch that, it can be habit-forming." He took hold of Peter's sleeve, "Hey, let's go and get a beer to celebrate."

Peter couldn't help marvelling at Jim's seemingly inexhaustible supply of beer. There were several bottles of the brew under his friend's bed, but they shared only one bottle between them. Peter was still wary of breathing beer fumes near his parents or over Pauline for that matter, and Jim said he was seeing Wendy later that evening. "Even if only for a quick kiss through the window," he added, with an exaggerated, maniacal giggle.

What a pity, Peter thought, that Wendy couldn't talk her parents into letting her stay. They could save a lot of money by letting her stay, because they would have to repay the Australian Government their original fare if they hadn't stayed here for the obligatory two years. He understood her parents wanting to go back to England, after all, that was what he dreamed of doing most of the time. But he would miss seeing Wendy around. One day, like Pauline and Margie, and perhaps Shirley and Donna and cute little Veronica, Wendy might inspire Peter to write that love song. He hoped somebody would inspire him.

Wendy turned up at Jim's place before they had finished their beer. She looked radiantly happy and even more lovely than usual. Peter lingered long enough to establish, though, that there had been no change in her father's attitude. He said "cheerio" and that he would see them later.

He went to his hut and shut himself in his bedroom. Pen and paper ready, he waited for inspiration - the flow of poetry which would enable him to begin his song. But inspiration deserted him. Perhaps if he could think of a title for the song, the rest would follow. What could he call it? How could he call it anything if he didn't know what it was going to be about? Peter's mind had done something so rare that he couldn't remember it ever happening before, it had gone completely blank. He tried to think of the pop songs that had already been written, his mind eventually finding them and going over the words of those which spoke mostly of love. But how do you catch hold of something new, something no other songwriter has thought of? With extreme difficulty, Peter guessed. He spent more than an hour trying to think of a title, then he went to call on Pauline. Perhaps she would inspire at least a start to his great undertaking.

Pauline had intended to have an early night, her mother having pointed out to her that she had been "staying out till all hours and you need your beauty sleep". Her father had then stated that he wanted Veronica in earlier in future as well. "I don't mind you both having a late night a couple of times a week, but Veronica is too young to be staying out so late all the time. And her school work will suffer."

Pauline appreciated their concern, though she was sure she didn't really need any more sleep than she was already getting. Being a teenager she was possessed of boundless energy and the ability to bounce back under the most exhausting of circumstances. But if her parents were going to get worried about it, then she would have an early night and head off any trouble. The last thing Pauline wanted was to invite a curfew for herself or for Veronica. Except for the 1 am return home after Saturday night dances, she was in just after 11 o'clock most nights anyway. So when she opened the door to Peter's knock, she almost declined his invitation to go for a walk. Her mother's attitude, when she was a bit grumpy, always changed for the better when Peter was around. Both her parents liked having him call.

It was too hard not to go out. Being out was much better than being in. So she put on her blue coat - the nights had a distinct chill about them now - and accompanied him on a walk to the Roadhouse.

"I don't want to be late tonight," she told him, "say, about nine."

"Fine," Peter agreed, pulling up the collar of his jacket. They walked in the usual fashion, arm-in-arm, with one of Pauline's hands nestled in his jacket pocket. He never held her hand when she placed it like that. He didn't know why. He wanted to hold it, but for some reason, he never did. Perhaps he thought that she put her hand in his pocket to keep it warm and so she would have somewhere to keep it. She didn't put it there for him to hold.

He felt detached, not really belonging anywhere, as they walked beside the huts, from which glimmers of light peeped out in places and comfortable noises sounded of people living their family lives. What was he doing night after night with his friends that was so important it kept him from his family? They would be sitting in the lounge now - Mom and Dad and George - sitting beside the kerosene heater, listening to the radio or swapping anecdotes or worrying about paying the bills or when they would be moving into their new house. And they would be enjoying their togetherness, without actually knowing it.

That was how it had been in Thornhill Road, too. Why had his life changed so much? Or was he in love with a few special memories. As he had grown older in Handsworth, he had spent fewer cosy evenings at home, preferring to go out into the dark, mysterious nights, whether they be warm or cold.

But evenings at home with a good book or listening to the radio round the family hearth in the depths of winter were still worth remembering, even if you couldn't spend all your life indulging in such homebody things.

"Have you ever roasted chestnuts in a coal fire?" He asked Pauline.

"Of course I have — who hasn't?"

"And did you toast bread at the fire on a long fork? And did you listen to Dick Barton and the Goon Show on the radio?"

"Sometimes," she said, stopping. "Listen, you shouldn't dwell so much in the past. This is now, not then. There's a different future for us out here — for better or worse, that's where you should be looking. You've got to make the best of it." She smiled up at him and he felt suddenly very young and inadequate.

He put his arm awkwardly round her shoulder as they continued their walk, and Margie and the Handsworth gang and the warm, cosy sitting room at Thornhill Road were on another planet.

"One thing's for sure," he said, looking up into the darkness of the night where a few bright stars lay revealed by patches in the clouds, "I will never know the answers to everything. There are some things mankind will never know the answers to."

"What sort of things?"

"Well, have you ever wondered what lies beyond the stars?"

"No," she said. "More stars, I suppose."

"I mean when there are no more stars. When you go so far that stars no longer exist."

"Perhaps there is never a point where stars don't exist. Perhaps stars go on and on and on forever. To infinity," she said, looking up into the sky.

"I don't think that's possible," he said, patiently. There must come a stage where there is absolutely nothing — just billions of light years of nothingness."

"Well, what if that were true? So what?"

"I just wonder who made that nothingness. Where did it come from?"

"Don't be silly, Peter. Nothing is nothing, so it doesn't have to come from anywhere or anything or anyone."

"Of course it does," he replied, but feeling himself struggling to explain. "It has to come from somewhere or something, because even nothing is something. There's no such thing as nothing. What about the very beginning of anything that ever was. What about the time before there was any matter . . . what about then?"

"You've lost me," she said, "and you're giving me the creeps." He shook his head and pulled her gently closer. He was starting to frighten himself. "Forget about distance," he continued. "Think about time. What if you were to go back in time to before there were any stars or planets — way back, before there was anything whatsoever. When there was just "nothing". What I'm wondering is, where did that nothing come from?"

"Another thing," she said, "if there was nothing, how did all the stars and planets form? How did the gases form, let alone explode and cause suns and planets and things?"

"Exactly," he said, "that's another thing."

She turned her pale face to him: "Can we talk about something else? This is really giving me the creeps."

"Sorry," he muttered. "It's giving me the creeps, too. But I just want to say that there must be a God, because there is no other explanation for how things began, even if you believe in the Big Bang theory."

"I believe in God, too," she said simply.

"I didn't mean to scare you," he said, "I just get carried away sometimes. I suppose it's the wonder of things that I can't grasp. I just get overwhelmed by the wonder of things."

"You're a strange person," Peter. "You're different to the other boys."

"I hope I'm normal," he said, concern in his voice. "I'm not really strange, am I?"

"No," she said, "but you're definitely different. Sometimes, sometimes, I wish . . ."

"Wish what?"

"That you weren't such a gentleman, except I don't really mean that."

"What do you mean?"

She sighed, "Oh, nothing. I don't know what I'm trying to say." She turned to him and clutched at the sleeve of his jacket. "If you want something that isn't there for you to have — then sometimes you can get it by just going after it."

"Because then you're creating it, you mean?" Peter asked, puzzled.

"I suppose," she said. "That might be what I mean. But would you go for it?"

He shrugged, "I don't know, it depends on what I'm supposed to be going for."

Me, you fool, her mind screamed at him.

Peter thought he knew how to woo a girl, but he also knew that every girl was different. They had to be wooed differently. With a girl like Pauline, who wore a "Don't Touch" sign around her neck, you had to be subtle with the romance and genuine with the respect. Girls like Pauline could read your mind and interpret your every action. Girls like Pauline were entitled to your every consideration. In fact, they insisted on it. Peter felt that girls with "Don't Touch" signs should make the first move to romance. It fitted into the scheme of things. If he were to lay a wandering hand on her right now, he would expect to get a slap across the face or even a thump in the eye. And even if she didn't hit him, their relationship would never be the same again. For better or for worse, things would never be the same between him and Pauline, if he made one sexual move towards her. And he wasn't sure he liked that idea. He was very happy in some ways with his dream-world romance of Pauline. Of course, there was much more to wooing a girl than touching her body. Touching should perhaps come after the wooing.

But that "Don't Touch" sign made him sometimes almost desperate to try something. But when, and if, he did, he had better do it right. It was all so confusing, really.

They walked almost to the Roadhouse when he stopped and said, thickly, "Are you talking about us?"

"I don't know what I'm talking about," she replied. "What do you think I'm talking about?"

"I don't know."

"I don't know either," she said.

"The only thing I know . . . is that neither of us knows what we're talking about," he said, bursting into laughter.

She dug him in the ribs, "Don't be smart."

"Just joking," he said.

"I don't feel like a Coke," she said, stopping at the side of the highway. "Let's go back — I have to iron my things for the morning."

What Peter needed, Pauline decided, was a few more years to mature. He seemed grown up, he acted mature, but he was not yet a man. He was still too young to win her heart. She had to be swept into the arms of a strong man, held in a loving embrace and then made love to. That was the stuff of her dreams. And it could not be any other way. Pauline was not going to sell her dreams short. She wanted romance and passion and a lasting love · one that would endure through the years. He had to be tall and handsome, and he could be just a little willful and just a little masterful. And in love his boldness would win her completely. She would give herself to him absolutely · there would be no holding back. And it was impossible for her to take the initiative. She had to be wooed, gently and subtly, but surely. She was very fond of Peter, but the magical spark that might be fanned into flaming passion just wasn't there yet. At least with him, she told herself for the umpteenth time, she would have little trouble staying intact for her wedding night.

She sighed deeply and ran the iron over her skirt for a second time. It was just after 9 o'clock and she had made a point of letting her parents know she was home early and was off to the washhouse to iron her things. What did she really want? Who did she really want? Sometimes she wished boys had never been invented. Sometimes she ached for Peter or a boy like him. And then there was that tall, dark man who haunted her dreams. And then there was that dream where Peter had come to her, but she had wakened up before they could make real love. Even in her dreams she must remain a virgin, it seemed, thank goodness. That was what she wanted, wasn't it? But she dared to wonder what it would be like. Was it as deliciously wonderful as those forbidden books told?

"Damn!" Pauline banged the iron down.

Veronica looked up from her comic, "What's up?"

"I've singed my blouse."

"You've been out with Peter," Veronica observed.

"That's very clever of you to work that out · especially as you saw us leave the house . . . the hut."

"My, isn't my sister in a good mood tonight."

"I'm fed up, that's why," Pauline rapped. "I'm sick and tired of . . . of things." She laughed, "I didn't mean to take it out on you."

"People always behave strangely when they're in love," Veronica said, with a wicked grin.

"I'm not in love," Pauline replied quietly.

"Sounds like Peter has made a pass at you."

"You're obsessed about that. He certainly hasn't made a pass at me. I've told you, no one makes a pass at me."

"Then what's the problem?"

"There isn't any problem. For goodness sake . . ."

"I'm only trying to be helpful."

"No you're not, you're being nosy."

"I'm just interested in whether we have a romance in the family or not."

"How the hell should I know," Pauline yelled, and suddenly burst into tears.

Bewildered, Veronica left the washhouse and went to bed.

Peter was in bed by 10 o'clock. He still had no idea how to begin his song, and he had no idea of how he stood with Pauline. But some of her words kept repeating themselves in his mind. Sometimes you can have what you can't have — if you go after it. Was that what she had said? It was something like that. He thought he understood what she meant, when she said it, but now he wasn't so sure. But he was feeling pretty sleepy, too sleepy for heavy thinking. He put his hands together and said his prayers.

Chapter 15

An Angry Jim

Work wasn't bearing the financial fruits Peter hoped for. He was now earning just over £6 a week. Where was the independence in that paltry sum? He was slogging his guts out, as the Australians put it, working a full 40 hours a week and had nothing to show for it but more-muscular arms and a broader chest and patches of painful sunburn in the summer. He enjoyed the company of most of his workmates. He loved the fresh air and the feeling of importance of being one of the work gang building houses for people to live in. But where were the financial rewards?

He took Pauline and Veronica to Adelaide to see a movie and had asked his mother to waive some of his board. True, Pauline and Veronica insisted on paying their own way, but that wasn't the point — he had to have enough money in case they didn't insist on paying. And he had to splash a bit of money around on ice cream or sweets when he was out with the girls. It was only right. He wanted a car, but how could he ever afford to buy one? What was all this about; this slaving day after day for virtually nothing? Every working day now he set off on his bicycle, dreaming of owning a car when he wasn't dreaming of going back to England, yet the money in his tin box was meagre and there was no sign that it would ever turn into even a useful sum. But what could he do about it? What company in the entire country was going to pay an inexperienced sixteen-year-old a decent, livable wage?

At least in England he should have expected disgusting wages, in keeping with what his father would say was that country's self-destructive philosophy of keeping the working class down to as near rock-bottom as possible.

Still, there was no point in complaining. He was trapped here, anyway, wasn't he? He was trapped in his new environment, the promised land. Where was the milk and honey in vast, brown paddocks and even browner tap water? He might as well make the best of things. He could still dream that one day he would be rich and would live in Handsworth and have a weekend cottage in the English countryside. Dreams didn't cost anything, did they? And they were private — the Australians couldn't call you a Pommie whinger if they didn't know what your dreams were. If they didn't know you dreamed of going back home or that you still dreamed of sycamore leaves and mayflower and hawthorn and robins and wildflowers — more wildflowers than they would ever believe existed. Not that most of them wouldn't try to understand, but the arrogant ones, those so quick to condemn even the barest hint of dissatisfaction by any new chum, they would never understand. And they would never know of England. They would never know of England the way Peter Mitchell did.

Within a fortnight of their application to marry, Jim and Wendy learned that permission had been declined. Jim was a wreck.

"Do you know why?" he demanded of Peter. "Do you know what those bastards have dreamed up for a reason?"

"I haven't a clue," Peter said, "how can there be any reason?"

"She's not pregnant. Have you ever heard such a load of fuckin' crap in all your life? They can see no reason why she should be removed from the custody of her parents , as though she's a nine-year-old or something. I mean — what the fuck!" Jim exclaimed, spluttering with rage. "Have you ever heard of anything so daft?"

Peter had to admit that he hadn't. "What are you going to do?"

"I'm going to stowaway on their boat."

"That's a good idea," Peter said, without conviction.

They were sitting behind Jim's car at the back of his hut, facing the railway lines and the highway and hills beyond. It was a very private place. No one could see them swigging beer and, with reasonable care, no one could overhear their conversation.

Peter couldn't help the thought flitting into his head now and then, though, that Jim's parents must be deaf and blind and have no sense of smell.

"I'll probably throw the old man overboard before we get to England," said Jim, who was showing signs of tipsiness. "Mind you, he's a big bugger."

"That's getting a bit extreme anyway," Peter pointed out. "Why not try to save enough money to go over there?"

Jim ignored Peter's suggestion. "Perhaps if I got her pregnant. Not that I would — the chance would be a fine thing. These girls guard their virginity like gold."

Peter thought of Donna, "Not all of them," he said.

"The classy ones do, though," Jim had an edge of triumph in his voice. "The classy ones like Wendy do."

"The classy ones like Pauline do as well," Peter said, not to be outdone. Jim opened another bottle of beer. "They know what they're doing, too. So long as they've got that mystery to taunt you with, they can wrap you round their little finger."

"I don't know whether I'm wrapped round Pauline's finger or not," Peter said, glumly. "I've decided I don't really understand the opposite sex, except my mother. I understand my mother because she takes direct action."

"I don't want to talk about your mother," Jim said, "I've got too many problems to worry about your mother."

"I'm not asking you to talk about my mother," Peter fought and controlled a surge of anger. "We're talking about you and Wendy."

"Another reason they wouldn't let us get married is my wages. They are too low. There's some work available in Whyalla — paying good money. I might see how things go from there."

"So you're not really going to stow away?"

"Am I heck! It's all right to think of those things, but the reality, no; I'll go to fuckin' Whyalla, work my tits off and the rest of the fuckin' world can go and get fucked."

"What about Wendy'?"

"What do you mean, what about Wendy? I've asked her to run away with me to Brisbane or Perth. She's too scared. She said we'd starve to death. Hey," Jim turned, proffering another bottle. "Hey, how much are you earning?"

"About £6 a week."

"That's about what I'm getting. How come they pay a dickhead like you the same money as me?"

"Possibly," Peter grinned, "because they think you're a dickhead as well."

"Watch yourself," Jim said in mock anger. "How can I support Wendy on that sort of money? I can't even support myself on it."

"And girls get about half as much," Peter said, "which seems very unfair."

"They get a bit more than half, I think," Jim said. "But if we're getting peanuts, they're only getting the shells."

"How do they manage to buy records and stockings and make-up and things? That's what I wonder," Peter said. "How can they afford to buy anything?"

"Their parents," Jim spoke knowledgeably. "Their parents buy all those things for them. Parents always look after their daughters like that. Then the daughters find boyfriends or husbands to look after them."

"You rarely see Pauline wearing make-up," Peter thought aloud. "In fact you don't see many of the girls wearing make-up. They look better without it, I reckon. Yep," Peter took a swig of beer, "they look much better without make-up on."

"Have you gone out of your fuckin' tree, or what?" Jim glared at him. "What the fuck are you going on about? You go on and on and on sometimes about the stupidest things. Who cares about fuckin' make-up?"

"I was only saying that girls look better without make-up."

"Sometimes they do and sometimes they don't," Jim said.

"True," Peter relented, "when they dress up really nice and put not-too-much make-up on, they look beautiful."

"How much money have you got?" Jim asked, suddenly.

"About £3 or so, I think," Peter said, "That's including £2 or so in my tin, why?"

"I need to borrow some money — I'm off to Whyalla on Monday and I don't know if I can get a job straight away."

"I'll lend you some," Peter said. "I'll get a pay before then, so I could stretch it to about . . . maybe £5?"

"Fuckin' good on yer," Jim said.

"You needn't worry about paying me back," Peter said.

"You'll get it back."

"I didn't realise you were planning on going to Whyalla so quickly."

"I've just decided."

Peter frowned, "Will your car get there?"

"I won't know until I try," Jim said. "If you give me £5, that means I'll have about £12, plus what I can beg off my darling parents. That's heaps of money to get by on. I can sleep in the car."

"Will your parents mind you going?"

"Yes, but they won't stop me."

"You should get some holiday pay when you finish up," Peter reminded him. "Every little bit helps."

"I'm working for a subcontractor, so I might not. He's a tight bastard."

"We'll all miss you," Peter said. Then wistfully, "I wish I could come with you."

"No one would employ me if they saw you with me," Jim said.

The Saturday night dance was more subdued than usual for the young people. Both Peter and Jim drank more than they should have. Jim danced with Wendy, despite the presence of her parents. At first, she had to return to her parents' table after each dance, but later she must have convinced them that she wouldn't suddenly elope with Jim, because she joined the rest of the teenagers. Wendy's father looked sour about it, though, and Peter hoped for Jim and Wendy's sake there wasn't going to be a scene.

Jim told Peter and Pauline that he intended to put up his age when he got to Whyalla, so he could earn a decent wage. Peter thought he might like to do that himself if he ever changed jobs, though the prospect of being found out was a bit scary. It was probably against the law to lie about your age to an employer so you could earn more money. He knew his mother lied about her age, because she had been 39 for as long as he could remember. He smiled at that and glanced quickly round at his parents' table, feeling a spasm of guilt to find they were looking his way.

Peter and the others were ready to steer Jim out of the hall after the dance, just in case he was tempted to say anything to Wendy's parents. But they and Wendy and John left before the last dance. Anyway, Jim had drunk himself into a happy mood.

Peter and Jim ambled unsteadily up to the railway station long after the hall had closed and the girls had reluctantly decided to call it a night. Most of the camp lights were out and a quiet calm had settled over Smithfield. Jim still clung to a bottle of beer, but Peter had cried enough. The liquid swam, swished and gurgled in his stomach as he walked. As they neared the station they burst into song, with noisy renditions of *Walking My Baby Back Home* and *The Loveliest Night of the Year*. On the station platform, they sang *Rock Island Line* and Jim drank a toast into the darkness. There was a bravado within them that night and on the way back to the camp, Jim began a slow drum march while chanting: r-r-r-root, r-r-r-root, root-me-boot, root-me-boot, r-r-r-root, r-r-r-root, root-me-boot, root-me-boot. Peter soon joined in and they marched through the hostel joyously chanting their made-up song: r-r-r-root, r-r-r-root, root-me-boot, root-me-boot, r-r-r-root, r-r-r-root, root-me-boot, root-me-boot, r-r-r-root, r-r-r-root, root-me-boot, root-me-boot, until suddenly they were confronted by a woman about half their size and clad in a dressing gown. With arms folded, she meant business.

"What the devil do you think you're doing?"

They gazed at her silently as though she were some strange apparition.

"Are you trying to wake up all the bairns in the hostel? Don't you know that it's 3 o'clock in the morning? And you, Peter Mitchell, I'm very surprised at you. I thought you would have known better.

Peter groaned inwardly, it would have to be Mrs McAllister, a friend of his mother's.

"We're sorry — we didn't think," he mumbled.

Jim spat on the roadway and took another swig of beer.

"And where did you get that drink from at your age?"

"What the fuck's a bairn?" Jim asked.

"Don't be cheeky or I'll call my husband." She peered at him in the darkness, "I know you've had problems, but don't take it out on us." With that she turned on her heels and stalked back inside.

Peter saw Jim home without further incident, despite his cries of "send ya fuckin' husband out, then."

The next day Peter's mother informed him that he was grounded for three weeks, and that if he were ever caught behaving like a hooligan or drinking alcohol again he could expect even bigger trouble. Peter had it in mind to put all the blame on Jim — after all, it was really Jim who had been caught with the bottle of beer, but he bit back any excuses, knowing that he had misbehaved and deserved to be punished.

Jim almost broke down the door to Peter's bedroom early on the Monday morning to say cheerio. "See you again someday," he said simply.

Peter grabbed the money from his tin box and handed it to him. "There's £5," he said, handing it to the other youth. "You should have waited until I got my next pay and I could've given you a bit more. Good luck and don't forget to visit us." Peter wondered whether he should dress and see Jim off outside. But Jim probably wouldn't want that. They were British, they couldn't get too close. Even a handshake was embarrassing.

"I'll write with my address as soon as I've found somewhere," Jim said. "Give it to Wendy so she can write, only don't let her old man see you." And he was gone.

A great emptiness welled up in Peter as the roar of Jim's car became fainter and fainter as it ate up the miles away from the camp. It was not yet dawn but there was no point in going back to bed. He dressed and went to the canteen, which was just opening. He was halfway through a cooked breakfast and dawn was breaking when George entered the canteen and asked him if he had fallen out of bed.

Peter hadn't actually witnessed an Australian dawn breaking before and was struck by its suddenness, as was a Murray magpie somewhere, which squawked out its welcome as though it was suffering a hangover. It was going to be a beautiful day.

He had only work and meals in the canteen to look forward to for three weeks and the time stretched interminably. He wrote to Margie twice and to each of his sisters once, which would have been a major surprise for them, and he worked on his song. He became more homesick and missed Margie desperately. The words wouldn't come the way he wanted for his song, but at least he made some progress:

I'm lonely without you, so lonely
I write and you don't reply
That's why I'm lonely without you
That's why.
I catch a glimpse of your face
In every secret place
But shadows fall and hide you
In every secret place
That's why I'm lonely without you
That's why.

He could go no further, but kept the verse in the hope that one day he might finish it. He ran the words round in his mind constantly, searching for a suitable tune. He didn't think they were very good. He didn't think they would get the whole world singing, and George agreed.

"What a load of rubbish," he said. "It doesn't make sense, does it? Mind you . . . that might be to its advantage."

"Thanks for your encouragement," Peter said.

Towards the end of the first week of his grounding, the weather changed and it poured with rain. The building site gangs used up their eight hours' rain money time and lost almost a day's pay. Some of the men switched to second-fixing so they could work under cover, but Clive explained to Peter that there was not enough work indoors for everyone and that the married men had to get preference because they had mouths to feed. That was fair enough, but Peter's wages took a hammering. He took home just over three pounds and hoped his mother would waive board, but she didn't. He wasn't allowed out, anyway, she reminded him, so he didn't really need any money. But she gave him ten shillings back nevertheless, so Peter was able to sneak out now and then for a Cottee's lime or a Coke at the camp shop.

He did his punishment hard. The extra freedom allowed since his arrival in Australia had spoiled him. But he dare not fully break his curfew. He felt stupid in the canteen when telling his friends that he wasn't allowed out and Pauline tutted at him and called him a naughty boy, which made him blush, which made Donna point a finger at him and say, "Look who's blushing".

They visited him a few times, though it was awkward crowding into the kitchen, especially with George deliberately asking the girls stupid questions, like saying to Wendy: "What made you decide to come to Australia?" Or he would raise his eyebrows at one of them and mouth silently at Peter, 'is that the one you fancy?' They listened to the radio hit parades or just talked, but Peter felt stifled with his parents there most of the time, let alone George. There was no point in asking whether the teenagers could go into Peter's bedroom — his mother would never allow him to take girls into his room. He was surprised that John visited with the rest, the youth explaining the first time that he needed a break from studying before he went mad. Peter, though, couldn't help wondering whether he had been given the task of keeping an eye on his sister. Wendy was mostly bright and bubbly, but now and then her face would slip and betray the turmoil she was going through. Peter told her that Jim was sending his address as soon as he had one and that he would sneak it to her, but she stared at him coldly and then looked away. At first, he wondered whether she blamed him somehow for Jim's departure or whether the thought of their parting was still too unbearable to think about. But then he realised he had spoken in front of John.

Had he been in the army, Peter reckoned, he would probably have to peel potatoes for a couple of days, the punishment at home was much too severe. After all, he had apologised and said it hadn't been all his fault. And his mother had heard of his misdemeanours second-hand. It was hearsay, wasn't it? Circumstantial evidence. Where was the burden of proof? Mind you, they had hanged many a man without real proof. So much for British justice. Often he would shudder when he thought of people being hanged for murder. He would wonder at the callousness of the state and how they could justify murdering someone in the name of justice.

In the year 1956, Peter Mitchell was having grave doubts about the greatness of his country of birth, thoughts brought on by an idle mind and bitterness at being grounded by his mother. Merry Olde England? People use to starve to death and they killed children for stealing loaves. Had the knights in shining armour really rescued damsels in distress? His beliefs were threatening to collapse around him. He wished Margie would hurry up and write.

His punishment came to a shaky end, with Peter reminding his mother that the three weeks were completed and his mother hesitating and not remembering when the grounding had started. But she lifted the ban when he insisted that, indeed, he had been grounded for fully three weeks.

It seemed an age since he had last been in the boilerhouse, still the favourite meeting place for the teenagers. But no one had come along to steal the hearts of his girlfriends. And he hadn't heard from Jim, nor had Wendy.

The letter from Margie brought back his homesickness. She was looking forward to another trip to Gloucestershire. Everybody missed him and they all hoped he would come home soon. How much money had he saved? Had he saved almost enough to pay his fare? She didn't think so, because she had bumped into one of his sisters on the Soho Road and she said he probably hadn't saved anything. Sisters could sometimes be annoying. How could anybody possibly know how much money he had saved? He wrote back to Margie and told her he had saved nearly £40, but had given his friend Jim £20 to start a new life.

He also remembered to mention that the photographs of the Aborigine tribe had failed to reproduce. Once you start telling fibs, you have to have an escape route.

Chapter 16

A Sad Farewell

The day in August they dreaded so much arrived all too quickly. The gang caught a train and a bus to get to Port Adelaide for their tearful farewell to Wendy. Her cabin seemed even smaller than the one Peter and George had shared when heading for Australia on the Orontes. But they all managed to squeeze into it while she deposited her things. Then they retreated to the deck to escape the warm, airlessness of the place.

Peter stared out at the choppy, dark sea. Had he really spent four weeks on such a ship? Had it all been a dream, perhaps? Could it be that he had never left England at all and was asleep in his bed in Thornhill Road, dreaming this vivid dream. How could it all be real? Who would have thought he, Peter Mitchell, the last person even to dream of leaving England, would be here, seeing off a girl — not to Australia, but to England. It was all so crazy. It was all so scary. And where the hell was Jim?

Wendy gave them an aunt's address, where she and her family would stay for a short time once they reached England. She looked long and hard into Peter's eyes while she read it out for them to copy down. He got the message. Jim must write.

The call came over the speakers for visitors to leave the ship. Handkerchiefs fluttered and Peter shook hands with John, stuck his thumb up at Wendy, said gruffly, "Good luck," and walked a short distance away as his eyes threatened tears. But Wendy followed him and took his hand. "Look after them all for me, won't you?" She said quietly. "Tell Jim I understand, and I want him to understand. Tell him I'll be back."

"I'll do that," Peter assured her, before hurriedly descending the gangplank. He waited for the others among the crowd on the wharf. They were just about the last to descend and the gangplank was about to be raised when he saw the fiery mop of hair bearing down on them. Peter searched fruitlessly into the sea of faces gazing from the ship's rail.

"Where is she?" he demanded of Pauline. "Where did she go?"

"I told her to go below because she was so upset. But she probably didn't, why?"

"Jim's here."

"Am I too fuckin' late?" asked a breathless Jim. "Where is she?"

"She'll see you, don't worry," Peter assured him, again looking up to all the faces. "We're trying to find her for you now."

"All those fuckin' people going back to England — must be fuckin' mad," Jim said, making Peter glance hurriedly round to see if anyone had heard the youth swearing.

"Watch your language," he said, "We'll get arrested if a policeman hears you."

"Fuck the cops," Jim growled, "where's Wendy?"

"Wave to her," Peter told him, "she'll see you if you wave."

"How can I, if I can't see her?"

"Wave anyway — just wave."

There she is," Pauline shouted over to them, "she's over the other end there watching you."

"I can fuckin' see her," Jim cried, taking off his scarf and waving it. Peter saw Wendy wave back to Jim, then walked away from his friend.

Sometimes it was good to feel a little bit sad — not to wallow in tears and depression, but sometimes to have a nice happy-sad feeling. Peter felt very sad for Jim, and he felt happy-sad at the thought that Wendy would one day sail back to her loved one. And he felt sad because it was Wendy going back to England and not him. And he felt kind of happy because it meant that he didn't have to say goodbye to all of his new friends on this side of the world. But he couldn't help wondering when that day would come. He hoped he wouldn't have to wave goodbye to Pauline. But if he never said goodbye to her, how could he ever sail away to see Margie? Then Peter felt sad — and it wasn't happy-sad, either.

Jim gave them a lift back to Smithfield in his 1950 Dodge. He also paid Peter the money he borrowed. He explained that he was working on the inside of a ship at Whyalla and was being paid adult wages.

"You've got to work for it, though," he said, remembering briefly not to swear in front of the girls.

A puncture had made him late for Wendy's departure. "There were so many things I wanted to tell her," he said, allowing a dismal note into his voice. "I'm earning enough to get married now — if only that prick of a father would let her . . . bloody ratbag."

"Any vacancies in Whyalla?" Peter couldn't resist asking.

"Are there heck — I was really lucky to get in. I had to really bullshit."

"You'd be really good at that," Pauline piped in.

"Hey, watch your fff — watch yourself," Jim grinned into the rear-vision mirror.

"How did you manage to get another car so quickly?" Peter asked.

"Traded mine in and put myself in hock — how else do you get a car?"

"There's no way I can get a car," Peter said wistfully. "Even if I had the deposit, I wouldn't be able to afford the repayments."

"I'll tell you what, though," Jim said, ignoring Peter's remarks, "it's fuckin' cold in Whyalla at this time of the year, especially right on the sea. The wind comes straight off the water in the mornings. It goes right through you, freezes your bones. Shit, it's cold." He half turned in his seat, "Excuse my language girls."

"No," said Pauline.

"Hey, Pauline, would you like to come to Whyalla with me and keep me warm on cold nights?"

Peter shrivelled up in his seat.

"I beg your pardon?" Pauline said, but she was smiling.

"Just joking," Jim said.

Peter wondered about people like Jim. They could get away with saying just about anything to anyone, whereas if he tried it he would soon get into strife. People like Jim rolled with the good times and the bad times equally well. They could take a big fall and get up with barely a bruise. Jim seemed to be taking the loss of Wendy much better than he, Peter Mitchell, had taken losing Margie. Why couldn't he be like Jim? Why couldn't he go away to find work and end up on adult wages and owning a car? Why couldn't he be positive, assertive and fearless? Why did it have to be only in dreams that his strong character shone through? Peter indulged in a fantasy then, in which he was standing up to Margie's parents and telling them that he was taking their daughter to Australia and that he would prefer to go with their blessings. Her parents had just realised that they couldn't keep her to themselves forever. Her father had laid a gentle hand on Peter's shoulder, when Jim's voice interrupted his thoughts.

"You wouldn't believe it! I followed this dirt road for about 50 miles and it just came to an end. It didn't go anywhere. It just stopped in the middle of nowhere. Who would make a road that didn't go anywhere? Only the Australians. They've got so much room that they don't know what to do with it — so they make roads that don't go anywhere."

"Is that where you got your puncture?" Shirley asked.

"No, luckily I got that near Gawler — close to a garage, too. Good job, because my spare was no fff — bloody good."

"You must have got on to a cockie's road going to a farm," Peter offered.

"What, for 50 fff — bloody miles? How big a fuckin' farm would that be? Anyway, they should warn people. They should put up a sign saying 'this road goes for 50 miles into the middle of a farm which is in the middle of nowhere. Bring plenty of food and water in case no one ever finds you again. That's what they should do."

"That would be a very big sign," Veronica observed, "To have all those words on it, it would have to be very big."

"I think your sister has me on sometimes," Jim said to Pauline. Then, to Veronica, "Look me up when you're sixteen, darling."

"Oh, sure," Veronica said, trying to look serious.

"It's a shame you missed Wendy," Peter said, "but we've got her address, so you can write to her."

"I'll give you my address, too," Jim said, "In case anything crops up and you have to contact me. You never know, she might jump ship at the next port and head back here."

"I don't think she would do that — even if she wanted to," Peter frowned at his friend.

"I was only fff — bloody joking."

Peter's mind went back to dealing with the road to nowhere that Jim had traversed. He couldn't help wondering why it had been made and then whether perhaps they were all on a road to nowhere. Was he on a road to nowhere? This new road in his journey through life — where would it end? Was it a pathway to riches and fulfilment? Or would it lead to emptiness and despair? What riches could he find in his life as a carpenter? Certainly not great riches in a material sense, but perhaps a reasonable standard of living and the satisfaction of a good job well done. If he were on a road to nowhere, he could make it go somewhere. That's what he would do; he would make his road to nowhere go somewhere. And what of the girls? Would they all marry someone rich and handsome and go to lots of garden parties and social gatherings, have lots of children and live happily ever after? No wonder Wendy's parents were against her marrying Jim. They wanted her to marry somebody rich, he would bet. Some rich man who would look after them as well as their daughter.

"Hey, egghead, I'm bloody talking to you."

"What?"

"I was just saying that I'm working about 60 hours a week in Whyalla, that's all."

"You must be filthy rich," Peter observed, "Working those hours, you must make a pile of money."

"I get just over £30 a week in my hand after paying board."

Peter was astonished, "Sheee — that's a fortune."

"I've got to work for it, though, it's fff — bloody hard yacker."

Peter thought of what he could do with £30 a week. He could save up for a year and buy land all over the place. He could go back to England and marry Margie. Or he could buy a house for Pauline in the Adelaide Hills. He saw himself in a brand new Holden or Chrysler, driving around and glancing out at a passing girl, smiling at her. The girl suddenly stops and smiles back at him. He brings his car to a halt, gets out and opens the passenger door for her. Oh boy, what couldn't he do with £30 a week!

"When I've saved enough," Jim was saying, "I might go to Coober Pedy and dig for opals. You only need one decent-sized gem to set you up for life."

Why hadn't Peter thought of that? He could go there — to Coober Pedy. That was the place where dreams came true, wasn't it? Peter saw himself standing in the blazing sun and holding the biggest opal anyone had ever seen. Would he sell it for millions? Would he give it instead to Pauline or Margie as a wedding gift? Better to sell it and buy a house and a car, he decided.

"Hey, fuck-knuckle," Jim broke into his reverie, "I'm talking to you. Are you away with the fairies or something?"

"Sort of," Peter grinned, "just thinking about Coober Pedy."

"You wouldn't be any good there, you're too soft," Jim said, seriously. "You've got to be really tough to work out there."

Peter looked sideways at his friend and wondered how Jim had managed to decide that he was the tougher. Peter doubted that he was. He might look softer than Jim and he might act softer, but Peter knew he wasn't softer. "I'm as tough as you are," he retorted, trying to smile one of George's more deadly smiles.

"That's not what I mean," Jim said. "You've got to know how to get out of scrapes — and you can't go around getting sunstroke out there."

"I'd wear a big hat and sunglasses."

"You're a dreamer, mate."

"I know," Peter said.

"By the way, ladies, pardon my French," Jim said. "I've been trying not to swear, you know."

"I should think so," said Pauline.

"I've never heard anyone swear as much as you do," said Shirley.

"You want to hear some of the Aussies I work with," Jim said. "They swear so much that you feel shocked when they say a non-swear word."

"You should go for elocution lessons," Donna suggested. "Then you might speak nice like Peter."

"Who the fuck wants to speak like him?"

"I do," said Peter.

"He's a fuckin' nancy," Jim said, then put one hand over his mouth and said, "Oops."

Peter turned to the girls, "I'm not," he said. "Whatever a nancy is — a sissy or something — I'm not."

"We know that," Veronica said.

"Hey," said Jim, "how do you know that at your age?"

Veronica blushed and Pauline cuffed Jim across the back of the head.

"So, you're not a nancy, Peter?" It was Donna.

Peter merely shook his head and suddenly wished he had kept his mouth shut.

"Well, well, isn't that interesting, Shirley?"

"Very, very interesting," said Shirley.

"Super interesting," said Pauline.

"Super duper interesting," said Veronica.

"Sod off," said Peter.

"Hey," Jim interrupted, "guess what they all call me at work?"

"Bluey!" everyone yelled together.

"Fff — bloody spoilsports," said Jim.

He dropped them all off outside the camp shop, bringing the car to a long, skidding halt in the gravel. Peter lingered beside the car until the girls had gone into the shop.

"When do you start work again?"

"As soon as I get back." He gave Peter a quick glance, "I love her, you know."

"I know," Peter said, uncomfortably, noticing his friend's eyes were watery. You've told me that before. "I always knew that. We all know you love her and she loves you."

"I won't get over her," Jim said, pulling out a pouch of tobacco. "What will I do?"

"You have to go back," Peter said. "You've talked about doing that and you're on good money now."

"I could save up, go over there, and find she's going out with some other prick."

"You must have faith in her," Peter admonished. "Anyway, you can write to her regularly so she'll know you're going over for her."

"I used to write on walls back home." Jim lit his cigarette, "I'm not sure if I can remember how to write on paper."

"Then send her a brick."

"That's really fuckin' helpful — yuh galah. No, I wouldn't blame her if she met a nice guy over there, what with me being on the other side of the world and she being so bloody attractive. Shit — they'll all be buzzing round her like flies."

"All the boys used to call for John," Peter reminded him. "I remember her telling us."

"Don't be so fuckin' daft, will you?"

"I'm serious," Peter said, "She told me that — and she meant it. She wasn't joking or being smart or anything."

"I know you're serious," Jim waved his cigarette at him, "and that's what worries me about you. You're so fuckin' daft."

Peter shrugged, "I don't know what's daft about it."

"You fuckin' wouldn't! Listen — let's go out in the paddock and have a beer.

They drove out to the back paddocks and leaned against Jim's car each sucking at a bottle of beer, which Jim had produced from under the front seat. It was warm, but somehow refreshing.

"You've got to get away from the girls sometimes," Jim said. "Girls don't understand why we need beer and swearing and stuff."

"Man's talk," Peter agreed. And then, "Did you write to her while you were in Whyalla?"

"Several times, well twice. But I'll bet she never got them. I'll bet her old man kept them from her."

"That would be a mean trick," Peter said with passion.

"Did she say anything to you?"

"She didn't get them." Then he remembered the address Wendy had given him. He pulled out the folded piece of paper and handed it to Jim.

"That's where she'll be staying for a while. She said you must write to her. And she told me to tell you that she will be back and . . . loves you."

Jim pushed the piece of paper, still folded, into his trouser pocket and opened the car door, "I'd better be going — it's a long drive back."

Peter shut the car door for him and waved, "Drop me a line, too," he yelled, as the motor kicked into life. Jim gave him a curt nod of his head, skidded round in a U-turn, and roared off in a cloud of grass and dust.

Chapter 17

New Friends

At the end of August the Mitchell family moved to a house in Elizabeth South. Peter felt mostly neutral about the move, but at least it gave him something to think about other than the loss of Jim and Wendy from his circle of friends. Pauline and her family were not in the lucky batch, nor were Shirley's or Donna's. But Jim's family and Roger Brampton's family moved to Elizabeth at the same time, which pleased Peter because Roger intermittently took an interest in the girls, and Peter didn't like other boys taking an interest in his girls, so he could keep an eye on him.

Peter had roughly the same distance to travel to work — it just meant going in the opposite direction. Each night he would double the journey by cycling to the hostel, cutting through his workplace to get there. And late at night he travelled by memory along the paddock tracks when there was no moon to guide him. He didn't cycle on the Main North Road — nobody cycled on the Main North Road at night. It was dangerous enough in daylight. He sympathised with his friends. It wasn't fair that he should get preference for a house, just because his father worked at Weapons Research. His parents were quite excited about the move, but Peter wasn't. He worked on such houses and, anyway, it was only a single-storey, semi-detached house. Nowhere near as grand as the three-storey home he had left behind in Thornhill Road.

On the first Saturday morning of his arrival in Elizabeth, Peter spied from his lounge window a group of teenagers gathered outside the small block of shops across from his house. He put his jacket on and walked through the little reserve that separated Bubner Street from the shops and bought a milkshake at the delicatessen.

There were four of them — two boys and two girls. One of the girls watched him enter the shop. A radio behind the counter played the Crew Cuts singing *Earth Angel*. The two boys, one dark-haired and the other fair, wore thick woollen jumpers. When he thought about it, fewer and fewer teenagers were wearing jackets. But he liked wearing a jacket. It was easier to put a jacket round a girl's shoulders on a cold night than struggle with a jumper. He stood in the doorway of the shop, looking at the group. The boys stared at him and he held their gaze until the shopkeeper told him to bugger off because the shop bell was driving him mad.

"Hello," he greeted them, stepping outside with his metal milkshake container, risking the shopkeeper's wrath. One of the girls giggled and looked away. The other gave him a friendly smile. 'Here we go again,' Peter thought, Girls, girls, girls. One of the girls was slim and strikingly pretty and wore her dark hair down past her shoulders. She wore a pink T-shirt and white shorts; the other, the one who had giggled, was pleasant-looking but with a more homely, pale face and blond hair that fell just over her ears. She too wore white shorts but with a frilly white blouse. He wondered if they were cold.

"I'm Peter."

"Gidday," said the boys.

"Welcome to Elizabeth," added the dark-haired boy, moving closer to shake his hand. "Welcome to extreme boredom, I'm Chico."

"I'm Bill," said the other boy, also shaking Peter's hand. "This is Debbie," indicating the dark-haired girl, "and this is Gayle."

Peter wanted to shake the girls' hands but instead nodded cheerfully at them.

"Isn't there anything to do around here?"

"There's a church hall where they hope to organise dances," Bill told him, "and they're building a scramble track near the Gluepot Road. We're walking up that way, if you're coming."

"They are also building a big shopping centre way over there," Chico said, pointing vaguely behind the shops.

"It's all happening," said Bill, sarcastically.

"Could have fooled me," said Debbie.

Peter told them he was from Smithfield Hostel. Bill said he was from Gepps Cross Migrant Hostel and Debbie and Gayle from Finsbury Migrant Hostel. Chico was Australian-born. The others were pleased to be out of the huts and into houses.

Though Peter wasn't so sure about that, "At least you met plenty of people in the hostel," he pointed out.

"But you've already met four new people," Bill said. "Or don't we count?"

"Of course," Peter said, laughing. "I didn't think."

'You know what thought did,' his father's voice said.

They headed south on reaching the Gluepot Road, which was soon to be renamed the Prince Philip Highway. There wasn't much to be seen of the scramble track when they got there. The earthworks had barely begun. "I'm going to make a name here," Chico said. "When I get my Velocette — I'll be famous here."

"Are you saving for a motorbike?" Peter asked in surprise.

"I've saved, I've got the money, just have to wait for one more birthday, about four months."

"I prefer four wheels beneath me," Peter told him.

"So do I," Bill agreed, "I'm getting a car soon if my old man forks over the money. And when I'm old enough I'm going to drive a taxi for a living. There should be good money around here for taxi drivers, the way the houses are filling up."

Debbie suddenly slipped her arm through Peter's. He wasn't really surprised. Girls did that to him. But Bill and Chico were a bit taken aback and gently ribbed them both.

"Must be love at first sight," Bill said.

"What's your secret, Pete?" asked Chico.

"He's cute," Debbie said, laughing. "Aren't you, Peter?"

"Anything but cute, please," said Peter, blushing.

"He's going all red," said Bill.

"So would I," Chico said, turning red.

"I think Gayle really fancies you," Debbie told Peter in a hushed tone, but loud enough for the other girl to hear.

"Don't be stupid," Gayle shrieked, hiding her face in her hands.

Peter couldn't help smiling. Oh boy, he thought, here we go again. Girls, girls, girls.

"Let's go to my place," Chico suggested, "we can listen to some records."

Chico lived just off the Gluepot Road, about a third of the way to Salisbury. Peter was walking away from the migrant hostel, literally and figuratively.

Chico's real name was Vincent Leonardo Bagliano, which he hated, especially the Vincent part. Mr and Mrs Bagliano were short in stature, like their son, and, Peter thought, very Italian-looking. Both were friendly and spoke excellent, precise, English. Mr Bagliano was wiry in build and his wife comfortably plump. Their son was a little taller, more thickset, but without an ounce of extra weight. Bill was obviously a regular visitor to the Baglianos, flopping into an armchair as soon as he entered the house. Peter stood uncertainly in the middle of the kitchen until Mrs Bagliano told him and the girls, "You are allowed to sit down if you want to".

He sat next to Gayle, on one of the wooden chairs at the table. Mrs Bagliano fixed her large, brown eyes on him and asked what part of England he was from. He had until then said only "hello" to her, but she explained that anyone would know he was from England, because he looked so English.

"Doesn't he look English, Vincento?"

"Do we look very Italian?" Mr Bagliano replied, gesturing palm-upwards. "She thinks everybody looks like the place they come from, right?"

Peter hesitated, "I think they do, but I'm not sure, because everyone looks different, too."

Mrs Bagliano raised her eyebrows, "Of course everybody looks different, so what do you mean?"

"Well," Peter said, "If I look English and every other English person looks different to me - can we all look English? Strangely, I think we do."

"Does a blond Italian look Italian?" asked Mr Bagliano.

Peter thought for a moment, "I don't know," he grinned.

The man threw his hands in the air in mock victory.

"He still looks English to me," Mrs Bagliano said, and went to the refrigerator and poured them all a glass of fruit juice.

Mr Bagliano winked at Peter, "She is never wrong," he murmured, "so we won't mention that she is half-Spanish."

Peter never really knew why he endeared himself to people. He had obviously won over the Baglianos. Perhaps it was his confusing talk and simple shyness.

During their conversation he had been very aware that he was sitting next to Gayle, and that his knee was pressing hard against the table leg, so it wouldn't touch her leg. It was important that he should appear to be just a little aloof from any female company when in the presence of adults, because adults might easily suspect what you were thinking, even if you weren't thinking it at that particular time. They knew what you were capable of thinking — and that was bad enough. One could not be completely free, uninhibited. One must put on a show of good behaviour in adult and female company. One must be British, he supposed.

When the flyscreen door flew open with a resounding bang, Peter shot from his chair more in shock than politeness as the most beautiful girl in the world entered in a mini-whirlwind, threw a pair of sandals into a corner and yanked open the refrigerator door. He sat down again when he realised she was ignoring the gathering at the table, but he was transfixed by the vestige of utter loveliness before him. Her perfectly formed nose and cheekbones and classically shaped lips were sculpted under long, black eyelashes, dark, slender brows and a broad forehead. Her lithe, shapely figure moved with sublime grace and waist-length raven hair flowed and shone in the pale sunlight. She was, absolutely, the most beautiful girl Peter had ever seen in his life — on or off the screen. When she turned to them, holding a bottle of milk and about to take a drink from it, he realised he had been staring and looked quickly away, only to stare straight into Mrs Bagliano's deep, knowing eyes. He blushed and looked back at the girl. She was drinking thirstily, her long, creamy white throat bobbing in unison with each swallow. Then she lowered the bottle and Peter was looking into rich ebony and humorous eyes. She smiled at him, revealing even, pure white teeth and crinkling her nose, "Hello."

"Hello," he squeaked, hurriedly clearing his throat.

"Hello Bill, Gayle, Debbie. Hello Momma, Poppa."

"This is Pete," Chico said. "Say hello to Caterina, my horrible sister, Pete."

"He just did," Caterina said shortly. "Are you deaf, perhaps?"

Chico grinned at Peter, "She's not really talking to me. I had to throw a cup of water on her this morning. She's very fiery and horrid."

Caterina gave her brother a sinister smile, "You just wait."

Mrs Bagliano lifted her arms in despair, "Sometimes, they are not controllable."

Peter glanced across at Bill. He was watching Caterina. Peter had known he would be. And Mrs Bagliano was watching Peter and he had known she would be. And Caterina kept looking at Peter, and a thrill went through him and he half-wished she would look at Bill instead.

Peter decided to set off early for the hostel that night. He would wait at Pauline's and give her plenty of time to get ready for the dance. He walked across to the shops first, for a small packet of cigarettes.

She was waiting on the bench beside the telephone booth. He looked through the deli window for Chico and Bill and the girls, but they weren't there. Her short, navy-blue skirt was just above her knee. A white cardigan, open most of the way down, revealed a pale-yellow cotton blouse. She wore plain, brown sandals over her bare feet. Her hair hung over her shoulders and flowed on to her lap as she bent to attend to some imaginary bite on her ankle.

"Where's Chico?" he asked, mainly because it was the only thing he could think to say.

"He went mad and they carried him off in a strait-jacket," she said, now attending to a spot on the back of her leg, licking her finger and dabbing at her calf.

"Are you waiting for the girls?"

"No."

"Who are you waiting for?"

"Who says I'm waiting for anybody?"

She sounded like Pauline. Peter felt a stab of guilt, "I assumed you were," he said, "hello, anyway."

"Hi," she smiled and melted his heart completely. "I was waiting for you. Who did you think I was waiting for?"

"Bill," Peter said. "I don't know . . ."

She shook her head slowly, "Bill is too interested in having fun with the guys."

Peter should have been elated, so why did he have a sinking feeling. He should have said there and then, 'Look, I'm already going steady with a girl at the hostel'. But he didn't say that, he said, "Shall we go somewhere tonight?"

"I thought you would never ask," she said.

Peter was surprised he had.

"There's a rock and roll dance on at the Salisbury Hall," she said. "Shall I put on my fine things?"

"You look fine as you are," he said, and then stupidly, "There's a dance at Smithfield Hostel as well . . ."

"Oh, good!" she cried, slapping her hands together, "I've never been there. Salisbury can be a bit boring. They don't serve alcohol, so all the boys gather behind the hall, swigging beer most of the time. You're lucky if you can get a dance."

Surely, he thought, it would be impossible for Caterina to have trouble getting a dance. He was in a fix — he could hardly front up to the hostel with Caterina in tow.

"I wouldn't mind going to the Salisbury dance, come to think of it," he said. "We could dance all night . . . so who cares if the guys are outside drinking? But," he shrugged, "if you want to go to the hostel, that's fine by me."

Caterina grabbed his arm eagerly sending a thrill through his whole body. "Can you get hold of a car?"

"I can't even drive yet," he replied, dismally. "I'm going to learn soon, though. I'm saving up for a car right now."

"How much have you saved?"

"Nearly £50; I had to give a large sum to a friend of mine, though, so he could make a fresh start in Whyalla. It's just set me back a bit."

"I didn't mean to be nosy," she said, "I was just interested."

"What shall we do then? Smithfield or Salisbury — it's up to you."

"Perhaps we shouldn't go to either," she said, "perhaps we should find something else to do."

"We could try the pictures in Adelaide, though they're probably booked out by now."

"I don't feel like the pictures." She leaned her head against his shoulder. He turned and looked into her eyes and she said, "Think of something else."

He wanted to put his arm around her but didn't. He didn't know what to suggest. Was it his imagination, or was she hinting at something more than he would dare to dream of?

The silence became pressing. He would have to speak soon.

"What are you thinking?" she asked.

"Nothing," Peter said.

"You can't be thinking of nothing."

"I'm thinking how beautiful you are."

"Thank you," she bowed her head in a miniature, mock curtsy. "What else are you thinking about?"

She was hot! It dawned fully on Peter at last — unbelievably, she had the hots for him. She wanted him. Desire surged within him and he felt that familiar quickening of his heart, the dryness in his mouth and the painful bursting in his groin.

"We have wine with our Sunday dinner, do you?" she asked, inexplicably. What did she mean by that? Peter wondered.

"Do you have wine?" she prompted.

"Pop," Peter said, "we have pop."

She wrinkled her nose at him, "You mean soft drink."

"Yes," he said, distantly, "soft drink."

"Why won't you tell me what you're thinking?" she purred at him.

"I'm just thinking how beautiful you are."

"You've already said that."

"Secret thoughts," he said, trying to grin. He took a gulp of air and his mind said, silently, 'I was wondering what it would be like to make love to you.' That was what she wanted to hear, wasn't it?

She looked up at the sky, "It would be a nice night for walking. Shall we walk somewhere tonight?"

"All right with me," Peter said, "I like walking." He moved away from her and absently watched Mrs Bagliano walk out of the chemist shop.

"I have to go home first," Caterina said. "I'll meet you here at around eight."

"Around eight," he acknowledged, greeting Caterina's mother with a shy smile.

Chapter 18

Armed and Ready

"Inner peace," George said, waving a book at him as he entered the house.

"Pardon?"

"Inner peace — it's the New Age. Only a few of us know of it yet. It's the pathway to tranquillity and perfection of self.

"I'm going out with the most beautiful girl the world has ever seen," Peter replied. "You won't believe she's real when you see her. I don't believe her myself."

George pointed a finger at him, "Just remember who told you first about inner peace and the New Age."

"How could I ever forget?" Peter said, hurriedly. "You want to see this girl — she's so-o—o·o gorgeous."

"You have to put yourself above the physical plane to find true happiness," George said. "It's written."

Peter shivered, "I'm going in the shower," he said.

"You've only just had a shower," George frowned.

"I'm having another one, in case I've been sweating. Where's . . . Momma and Poppa?"

"Mater and Pater have gone off hobnobbing it with a scientist and his wife from Weapons. They are at an establishment known as the Old Spot — a famed drinking hole of quite adequate repute. They have yet to put material enjoyment behind them. Like yourself, they have not discovered the joy of total spirituality."

"Mom will belt you one if she hears you talking like that," Peter warned him.

"Violence is in direct conflict with the teachings of this book."

"She'll still belt you," Peter said.

He showered until the water turned cold and dried himself vigorously. He sprinkled Johnson's baby powder liberally over himself and dressed in the same clothes he had been wearing, because they were the ones he had changed into to go out in the first place, anyway. He made a mental note to buy a different talcum to use for dates, stole some of George's Brylcreem, and burst into song with the *Loveliest Night of the Year*.

George was sitting cross-legged in a corner of the kitchen, staring into space with a book on his head when Peter finally emerged. Being possessed of a healthy survival instinct, he would not normally bait George. But how could he resist this? He waved his hand in front of his brother's eyes first, but when this elicited no response, he stepped back and pulled the most horrible faces he knew how to pull. Still George did not respond. Peter kneeled so their faces were level, though keeping a healthy distance between them, and tried again, bouncing up and down while pulling faces and making weird grunting noises.

"Sod off or I'll kill you," George muttered.

A surreptitious check told him that the two french letters were snug and safe in his wallet. The evening was clear and crisp, but warm with promise. Peter still couldn't believe his good luck in winning so swiftly Caterina's affections. He looked up at the blaze of stars, the half-moon and took a deep, luxurious breath of air. Yes, the night was ready to keep all of its promise, and he was eager to accept.

The appearance of a large, black tooting Chevrolet containing Bill, Chico, Caterina, Debbie and Gayle placed that promise under immediate threat. Not that Peter wasn't pleased to see them all, but he had to make a rather radical adjustment to his thinking. He crammed in beside her in the back seat, conscious that their legs pressed together. She smiled in the gloom, "Hi! A bit of luck Bill getting his father's car, don't you think?"

"Marvellous," Peter said, unconvincingly. Then to Bill, "How did you manage it?"

"I've borrowed it before. I've taken Caterina out in it a couple of times, haven't I Cat?"

"Meow," Caterina said, making Gayle and Debbie burst into laughter. Peter didn't know what to say. Something had conspired against him. He hoped that same something was not planning more treachery and going to take Caterina away from him completely. He sat with his hands almost demurely in his lap. How could he put his arm round her with her brother in the car? How could he exhibit his feelings for Caterina with Bill sitting in the front seat? Bill could hardly keep his eyes off her at the Baglianos. He must obviously have strong feelings for her. He could be in love with her. He had already taken her out on dates.

The car did a U-turn and Peter realised they were heading for Smithfield Hostel. The dance would have started and the gang would wonder where he was. He felt a stab of guilt when he thought of Pauline. He could have betrayed her . . . He might yet betray her. The night was young and for all he knew, Bill could be going out with Debbie. He ran it through his head, and it made sense: Caterina had told Bill that she was in love with Peter, so Bill had paired up with Debbie; Chico had dated Gayle, leaving Peter and Caterina free to continue their romance. But what about Pauline? What about Pauline!

The early part of the evening was nightmarish for Peter. The storyline, most of which unfolded in Peter's head, would have fully tested the intricacies of Maupassant. He introduced the new crowd to the old one, hardly noticing that Roger had turned up. Peter pretended to be with Pauline while pretending to Caterina that he was with her.

While Peter was worrying about whether he should ask Caterina or Pauline up for the first dance, Bill took Caterina's hand and led her to the floor. Peter was miffed at first but then decided that this was a spot of luck and politely asked Pauline up to dance. Looking over Pauline's shoulder on the dance floor, he strived to catch Caterina's eye and give her a knowing smile. But Bill was taking her round the floor so fast that to begin with he found it impossible to even see her face. Eventually, Peter settled to dancing in a small area of the hall, so Bill and Caterina passed by them several times. He caught her eyes once and his heart leaped with joy when she smiled. But he also felt a pang of jealousy when he noticed how tightly Bill was holding her. It was hardly necessary to squeeze a girl like that. Poor Caterina would be glad to get off the floor.

Peter went for drinks before the second dance and arrived back at the table to find Roger getting Pauline up to dance and

Bill already on the floor with Caterina. He sat next to Chico, opposite Veronica and Shirley, and placed the drinks in the middle of the table, pretending in his usual vague way that none of the beer was for himself.

"I think I'm going out with your sister one night," he said quietly to Chico. "I'm not sure where we're going yet, but she seems to want to go out somewhere." Immediately, he wished he hadn't mentioned Caterina. Now he would be nervous that Chico might say something in front of Pauline. Chico reached for one of the bottles, "You've got some competition — you know that don't you?"

Peter nodded, "I don't want to spoil things for Bill, but it's up to Caterina, I suppose."

The other boy took a long drink of beer and placed his glass very carefully and thoughtfully on to the table. "I don't want to worry you," he said in a low voice, "but you've got much stronger competition than Bill." He glanced over at Shirley and Veronica to make sure they weren't listening, then leaned closer to Peter, "She might not have told you yet, but she is training to be a nun."

"A nun," Peter repeated. "What kind of nun?"

"The kind of nun who has nothing to do with men — what other kind is there?"

"Christ," Peter said, "you should keep an eye on her."

Chico sighed, "I'm trying, but it isn't easy. Mind you, she's pretty strong-willed. We think she will make it all right."

Peter threw a quick glance to the front of the hall to check that his parents weren't looking, realised that neither they nor George were even there because they had no intention of ever coming back to the hostel, and filled himself a glass of beer.

"Are you very religious?" he asked Chico.

"My family are — I am only sort of."

He should have known they would be staunch Catholics, Peter realised. The Baglianos even looked like Catholics. Though he had not fully grasped the implications of what Chico had told him, he knew he could never marry Caterina without at least one almighty row with his parents — staunch Protestants that they were.

"How long does it take to become a nun?" he asked.

Chico shrugged, "It can take years sometimes, why? Are you thinking of becoming one?"

Peter shook his head, "Men can't become nuns. Anyway, I'm Protestant." Chico gave him a sideways glance, like the look George gave him sometimes, and reached quickly for his drink.

Peter drank about three glasses of beer in the time it took for Roger to yet again get Pauline up to dance and for Bill to do likewise with Caterina.

"Does Bill know?" He asked eventually.

"Bill is resigned to it. Mind you, he's more like a brother to her than anything. More like a brother to her than even I am. Their relationship is purely platonic."

Peter looked over his beer glass at Bill and Caterina, still dancing close together on the floor. A lot of people danced quite naturally holding each other tightly. Professional dancers always did, especially for a waltz or a quickstep. It just showed how wrong you could be. He must have a dirty mind to have thought immediately that there were sexual connotations in the way Bill was dancing with Caterina. He went over his meeting with Caterina earlier in the evening. He had been delighted to see her, a vision of utmost beauty smiling at him. She told him she was waiting for him and he naively believed her. Obviously, she was waiting for her mother. And when she said it would be a nice night for walking, she meant exactly that. And when she had tried to wheedle from him what his thoughts were, well, she probably hadn't expected him to have dirty thoughts. Just as well he hadn't told her. What if she had read his thoughts? He would bet she had read his thoughts. She made a good job of covering up her shock, hadn't she? She avoided embarrassing him. No wonder she turned up with Bill and Chico and the others.

Peter felt his face reddening. Why did he have to always think of sex when he was with a girl? If he had looked upon her as a new, lovely and intelligent friend whose company he cherished, none of this embarrassment would be with him. How could he face her now? How could he be her friend now that he had completely misunderstood her attempts at friendship?

Whatever you do girls, don't joke with Peter Mitchell, because he will think you are serious. Peter Mitchell has only three interests — sex, sex and sex.

And yet, he could have sworn she had flirted with him. And girls who wanted to become nuns shouldn't be flirting, should they? And they shouldn't be up dancing with members of the opposite sex, should they? Then again, perhaps she hadn't been flirting with him at all. And perhaps nuns were allowed to dance and enjoy themselves before they actually became proper nuns. You were a long time being a proper nun, weren't you? George would know about all this, and he made a mental note to ask him when he got home.

Roger had turned his attention to Gayle by mid-evening, Chico pounced on Shirley, and Peter asked Pauline up to dance.

"Hello, stranger," she said, once they were on the floor.

"Sorry," Peter said with excessive humbleness, "but I had to make sure all the new people I brought were being looked after all right."

"She's a dish," Pauline said.

"Who?"

"The dark one."

"Oh, that's Caterina — she's Catholic."

"I suspect you wish she were," Pauline said, yanking him closer.

"She is." Peter gave her a puzzled look. "She really is Catholic — anyway, I'm Protestant."

"So am I," Pauline said, looking up into his face, "and don't you ever forget it."

Girls said the strangest things sometimes.

He spent much of the evening wanting to ask Caterina to dance, but not daring to. He found some consolation in dancing with Donna, Veronica and Debbie as well as Pauline. But he was so wrapped up in his own thoughts and problems, he didn't even notice that Chico and Shirley were hitting it off together and that, astonishingly, Roger and Gayle had disappeared outside. The master of ceremonies called on Peter towards the end of the evening to sing. Peter had got over much of his initial stage fright during his stay at the hostel, but he felt it all return now that he had to sing in front of new friends. He wanted to sing something which would tell Caterina that he understood what she was doing, while telling her he was sorry for being so brazen. As usual, the songs that normally tumbled through his head at any time of the day or night eluded him when he stepped on to the stage. So he sang *I See the Moon*, as well as he could with his voice now much gruffer, and remembering that it was a favourite of Pauline's and looking briefly and shyly over to her. But the song also made him think of Margie and he felt miserable when he sat down, though he managed a laugh with the rest of the crowd because Bill had deliberately carried on clapping after everyone else had finished.

"You're famous," Debbie told him.

"Not yet," he smiled, "I feel too stupid when I'm up there to be famous."

"One day," Caterina said, and again melted his heart.

But he said, "Thank you," stiffly and formally.

George was reading in bed when Peter arrived home, which was lucky, because his brother got quite upset when he was woken up to be asked anything.

"Put the wood in the hole," George told him.

Peter closed the door softly so not to disturb his parents. "You know this beautiful girl I was telling you about today, Caterina?"

"No," said George, lifting his wide eyes from the book.

"Well, I did, and she's going to become a nun."

"You did what?"

"I did tell you."

"And she's agonna whatta?"

"She's becoming a nun."

"I don't blame her if she's been going out with you," George said. "You would have that effect on young women."

"I'm trying to ask something serious."

"I am being serious," George told him. "When I am comfortably tucked up in my bed and reading a book, I take being disturbed very seriously. Now tell me what you want before I get out of bed and thump you."

"Are you still doing your new coming thing?"

"Of course, what do you think this is?" George turned the book so Peter could read the title: it said *Pathways to Perfect Peace.*

"I've forgotten what I was going to ask you," Peter said.

"This is part of the grand plan," George spoke very softly, which sometimes was a danger signal. "I'm being tested, aren't I?"

"It won't take me a second to remember . . . it was something to do with becoming a nun."

"You can't," George said, his eyes growing larger.

"I know — Chico told me that . . . I knew anyway. I would have to become a priest."

"I don't think Church of England people can become priests," George said, frowning as though in deep thought, "you would have to become a vicar or something . . . Oh no, I'm wrong, of course they can become priests".

"I don't want to become a priest or a vicar," Peter told him.

George sighed, "What the fuck do you want?"

Peter remembered: "Can nuns dance and flirt with men before they . . . I mean, while they are still in training?"

"You've come to the right person with that question," George said, for the first time showing some enthusiasm, "I happen to be an expert on the non-breeding habits of the nunnery."

"Don't talk like that," Peter gasped, "for goodness sake!"

"Did she tell you she was training to become a nun when you tried to root her?"

"No! I wouldn't try anything with her. Don't talk like that."

George grinned, "I'm only being honest. If you studied this book you would find that honesty is one of the inner pathways — a shortcut to truth and happiness."

"I don't want to study that book," Peter told him, "I'm reading a Carter Brown mystery thriller at the moment."

"What I can't understand," George said, "is why a person so well read as you would bother coming to me for advice. You must lack confidence, I suppose."

"I can't know everything," Peter pointed out.

George furrowed his brow, "What was it you wanted again?"

"See," Peter said, triumphantly, "you forget things as well."

"I can't really help you about the nuns," George explained, "I was pulling your leg. I would like to help, but my knowledge of church matters is, strangely enough, fairly limited."

"That's all right," Peter said, "just thought you might know — goodnight." He left the room, closing the door silently behind him and leaving George staring a long while into space.

Chapter 19

Fever

"Please tell me about them. Tell Caterina about your thoughts."

A middle-aged woman stopped and looked at them disapprovingly. Peter pulled his tongue out at her and she went away.

"I know a secret," he said.

"That was my mother," she said. "I was waiting for her."

"I don't think it was," Peter replied, in soft, soothing tone.

"I think it was."

"I'll explain to her next time I see her, then," Peter said.

"What's your secret?"

For the life of him, Peter couldn't remember what it was.

"I don't know."

"What's your secret?" She persisted.

"My nose has grown."

"That's because you tell lies," she taunted him.

"I don't ever tell lies," he said. "I'm not allowed to tell lies."

"Shall we go?" She got up and smoothed her short skirt out, gazing down at him lying on the concrete.

"I know a place," Peter said. "There's a tree there as well."

"Did you like kissing me?" She asked.

"Yes, I like that – do you?"

"Always and forever."

They followed the path, his arm round her shoulder, stopping now and then to kiss.

"I'll cut your hair one day," he said. She seemed pleased about that. He struck a match when they got there. "Here's some grass," he said.

"That's marvellous," she cried in delight.

They lay down and he lit a cigarette. "Do you want a puff?"

She took the cigarette from him and drew a couple of deep drags of it.

Peter took it from her and buried it into the grass. Then he gently rested his hand on the back of her head and kissed her, tenderly at first, but with mounting passion until they were kissing hard and hungrily at each other's lips. Slowly, fearfully, he moved a hand to her breast and was rewarded by little moans of pleasure as she quickly undid her bra. He tore his own clothes off and suddenly she was naked too. He took her breasts in his hands and caressed them gently until her moans became gasps of total desire. They lay down and she cried "Now, now." He tried to enter her but something wouldn't let him. He tried again and she cried "Now, now". He pushed hard into her and broke through and she gave a small cry and he knew absolute ecstasy as he climaxed in long, fiery spurts inside her. Then they kissed and he fondled her breasts, her body, and moved his hand gently to caress between her legs until she demanded to be entered again. They made love again and again until, finally sated, they lay together and slept.

The police found him lying on the bench by the shops at 3 o'clock in the morning, moaning and shivering in his sleep. They picked up his singlet and underpants from the pavement and told him to put them on and then they took him home.

"The police said you should wear pyjamas in bed if you're going to sleepwalk," his mother told him the next morning.

"I will," Peter promised fearfully. "Don't worry, I definitely will."

"I think he's totally mad," George said through his cornflakes. "One minute he's in my bedroom talking to me about nuns and the next thing you know he's running round the neighbourhood starkers."

"Sleepwalking has nothing to do with madness," his mother said. "It's caused by an overactive mind."

"He's not normal," George said. "Or, if he is, no one else in the world is."

"Eat your cornflakes, George," his mother said, firmly.

After breakfast Peter shut himself in his room and prayed that none of the gang would find out about his escapade.

He had one of his strangely detached feelings for the rest of the day. By evening, Peter had half-convinced himself that he had made love to Caterina by the shops and it hadn't all been a dream. It was quite possible, he told himself, that she had slipped away after their lovemaking, leaving him to fall asleep on the bench. Perhaps he hadn't sleepwalked. Perhaps he had seen her from the window of his house and gone to her, kind of half asleep, so that he had not remembered doing it. He would know when he saw her whether it had been a dream. Then he realised that it all seemed so real because he wanted it to be, and that of course it hadn't been real at all.

He put his pyjamas on before getting into bed that night but forgot to say his prayers.

They lay together in the grass, looking up at the stars.

He was the first to speak. "Are you all right?"

"Yes," she said, her words soft, like a warm breeze.

"You should have told me."

"Didn't you like it?"

"It was wonderful, but I would have been more careful had I known."

"You won't have to worry any more, will you?"

"True," he said, feeling a wave of sadness. "I was quite gentle anyway."

"Yes, you were." Moonlight caught the curve of her breasts as she turned towards him, "I want you again."

They made love again and again — each exploring the other in mounting crescendos of passion, Peter marvelling at his own physical strength and ability to quench her many burning fires. Finally, she fell asleep and Peter covered her with his jacket. Then the police came and took him home, but this time even they were in his dream, and he woke up sitting naked on the side of his bed.

So that was true love. The next time he saw her he would propose marriage. They would have lots of children and he would bring one of them up to be Lord Mayor of Adelaide and the others would be wealthy business people or scientists.

Everywhere they went, people would say, "There goes a man who has found true success" and "isn't his wife beautiful". Then he remembered that she was training to become a nun and he wondered what he was doing sitting stark naked on the side of his bed in the middle of the night. He got back between the sheets, glowing with a strange quietude. He didn't want to think of Margie or Pauline or the others. He thought only of the lovely Caterina, the virgin goddess who had so pleasurably burst into his life. He fell into a deep, exhausted sleep.

"You look like you've lost a shilling and found a pound," his mother said at breakfast. "You have a peculiar smile on your face."

"He's got malaria," George said. "Or he's in love."

Peter suddenly had a vision of an occurrence some years before when his mother had poured a cup of tea over George's head for making a smart comment.

"You're too young to be worrying about girls," his mother said, fixing him with her gimlet eyes. "There's plenty of time for courting when you're older and when the right girl comes along."

Just like his mother, Peter thought. How could she know that the right girl hadn't already come along?

"It's that blond girl at the hostel," George said. "Or is it the brunette? Or is it the thin, smiling one?"

"She's not thin," Peter said.

Mr Mitchell, who rarely spoke at the table, said, "Stop pulling his leg and stop talking at the table."

They ate in silence for a little while, then George said, "I can't understand why his face is so red."

Peter fled to his bedroom.

"Make your bed while you're in there," his mother called.

A new week went by. Peter visited the hostel a couple of nights to see Pauline, and went out with Bill and Chico, Debbie and Gayle one night. There was no sign of Caterina and when he once ventured to ask Chico of her whereabouts, the other youth shrugged and said, "How should I know?"

By the Saturday morning, he could contain himself no longer. He would have to call at the Baglianos and find out where he stood with Caterina. But he knew he wouldn't summon the nerve to boldly knock on the door and ask for her, so he would ask for Chico and hope to see Caterina there. He felt that if there was the tiniest prospect of Caterina's changing her mind about being a nun, then his presence should bring her closer to him.

First, though, he walked over to the shops and sat on the bench. There was always a chance she would turn up, especially if he sent thought waves out. But she didn't turn up, so after nearly an hour he half-walked, half-ran to the Baglianos. His steps slowed nearing the house, as his nerve began failing him and he contemplated the likely scenarios that might follow his knock on the door. If Mr or Mrs Bagliano opened the door, he would ask for Chico. If Chico answered the door, he would pretend he had called for him.

Despite having mustered all the will in the world when he had set off for the Baglianos, he realised that his only hope of getting anywhere with this errand of love was going to be if Caterina herself came to the door. He slowed a bit more, yet still the yards seemed to be gobbling themselves up and all too soon he was at the Baglianos. He bent down at the gate to make sure his shoelaces were tied. They were, so he undid the laces and retied them into a bow and then double-tied the bow. His socks were a bit droopy so he thought he should straighten them out, too. It was incredible how long you could fiddle with a gate latch if you wanted to, and how long you could take to close a gate behind you.

Chico opened the door before Peter was halfway down the path. "Come in and have a beer."

Peter followed him to the fridge, where the youth took out a beer and reached to the cupboard for glasses.

"Are your parents not home?" Peter asked as casually as he could. "They help round at the church on a Saturday," Chico said, pouring them both a beer. "I can get out of church these days."

"So can I," Peter said. "Mind you — I still get nagged now and then to go. They shouldn't be too long, should they?"

"Hours yet, they go visiting afterwards, bringing cheer to a few old people in Salisbury. You've really hit it off with my parents, haven't you?"

Peter breathed beer up his nose causing him to sneeze and splutter. "Sorry about that," he said. "Where's errm . . ."

"Caterina?"

"Yeah, yes, Caterina."

"She's at the Sisters of Mercy," Chico said, "should be back about five." Peter was halfway through his glass of beer, which wasn't sitting too well in his stomach, when Bill knocked and entered in a rush of cool air. "It's too early for that," he indicated the beer, "we've got places to go, people to see."

"Where are we going?" asked Chico.

Bill put his hands up in mock Italiano, "Any-a-where-a, every-a-where-a and some-a-where-a."

They both grinned at Bill's ebullience.

"Where's your darling sister?" Bill asked. "Still in bed? Shall I go in and wake her up?"

"She's out training to be a nun," Chico said.

Bill swung the fridge door open, "Bullshit."

"She's at work — should be back around four." Chico frowned, "Have you guys come to call on me or my sister?"

"Your sister," they both said together, laughing.

"I thought so," Chico replied, with mock glumness.

"What's the Sisters of Mercy?" Peter asked.

"A hospital," Chico said. "My sister is a nurse or trying to be one." He turned to Bill, "She looks like a nun with her uniform on, doesn't she?"

"She sure does," Bill said, "enough to terrify you in her uniform."

Peter sighed, "I thought you were serious when you said she was training to be a nun."

"I know," Chico said, "you were supposed to."

"The protective brother," said Bill.

"Don't tell Caterina for goodness sake," Chico implored Peter. "She'll never speak to me again."

Bill poured himself a beer from the bottle on the table, having found there was nothing more tempting in the fridge.

"It's too early for this," he said, taking a big gulp. "I've managed to borrow the car again, despite forgetting to put petrol in last night. We should get going — we have to pick up Debbie and Gayle."

"Can you drop me off at Smithfield?" Peter asked, not wanting to be a gooseberry.

"Come with us," Bill offered, "the more the merrier."

"What about you and the girls — you don't want me around."

"We're only taking them out to Gawler," Chico said, "we don't actually go out with them. We aren't canoodling with them or anything."

"Oh, for the chance," said Bill. "One day Debbie will come across, I reckon, as Chico will no doubt testify."

"Shut up about that — you'll get me shot," said Chico.

"What happened?" Peter couldn't resist asking.

"It's something that nearly happened when we were both too young, put it that way," Chico said, awkwardly.

Peter let the matter rest, not wishing to embarrass Chico further. He didn't really want to go to Gawler. There was too much on his mind for him to socialise. But he went with them anyway and Debbie took his arm and he pretended to enjoy himself.

After tea, George asked him the name of his latest girlfriend.

"How do you know I've got a new girlfriend?"

"You told me about her — that's how I know and I can see her in your eyes and in the food you leave on your plate."

"You mean Caterina Bagliano," Peter said.

"Don't be ridiculous," George replied.

"Her parents are Italian."

"Caterina sounds Spanish to me," George said. "Perhaps they're from Gibraltar or Malta."

"The mother's half-Spanish," Peter said. "But they are very Italian. They look it and act it."

"I don't suppose it matters where they're from," George said in a philosophical tone. "When you think about it — if you're not British, then it doesn't matter where you're from."

"You shouldn't make fun of your own country," Peter said. "I know the British aren't perfect . . ."

"Of course we are — it's written in history. It's written in blood, but it's definitely written."

"Anyway," Peter said, "I'm not sure if she is my girlfriend now. Bill fancies her and I've hardly seen her."

"What about the blonde you were seeing at the hostel?"

"I still see her — she's a friend."

"Which one are you rooting?"

"None — for goodness sake!"

"What happened to the nun?"

"That's Caterina, only she isn't a nun and isn't going to be one."

"Did she get thrown out of the order?"

"No, she just changed her mind."

"It's a big responsibility being a nun," George said, without elaborating.

"She's really beautiful," Peter said, "I can't believe how . . ."

"Why don't you ask her out then?"

"I don't know. I was going to today, but she wasn't in."

"You'll have to hurry if you want to beat the other guys to her."

"I think Bill already has her. Mind you, he might not know it."

"You would be much better off with the blonde one. She looks like a homely sort."

"She's quite pretty," Peter said.

"They're all quite pretty," George said. "I'm not getting involved with women until I'm about thirty."

"What happened to your inner pathways?"

"I'm still doing that," George rolled his eyes. "Have more respect in your voice when you say, 'inner pathways'."

"I'll remember that," Peter assured him.

"Actually, I've been studying you, again," George said. "You're not from this planet are you?"

"No, I'm from Mars."

"There's no life on Mars."

"They don't know for sure. What about the canals? Anyway, my men are stationed there at the moment."

"Conditions are too bad for life up there."

"Then I'm from another planet, aren't I?"

"Which one?"

"I'm not allowed to tell."

They sat in silence then, a silence broken only by the muffled sound of the radio in the lounge where his parents were enjoying a quiet evening. George had almost gone into a trance when Peter asked: "Should I be thinking of sex all the time?"

"Not all the time, no," George replied, still looking as though he had tunnel vision. "It means you've got an unhealthy mind."

"All the time, just about," Peter told his brother. "I just wondered whether everybody wandered around thinking of sex all the time."

"People do think about sex," George said, patiently, "and quite often they do more than think about it — that's how the world goes round — but they don't think about it all the time. There are other things to do and to think about."

"All the time, I think about it, when I'm not commanding my men," Peter spoke almost to himself. "Perhaps I should take up a sport or something."

"Have more cold showers," George said. "Now sod off so I can gaze into space privately."

"I do that," Peter said in surprise, "I stare into space sometimes."

"Yes, I know," George said, "but I'm doing it for a reason."

They walked hand in hand through the streets of Elizabeth, stopping now and then to gaze into each other's eyes or to murmur sweet words. She wore an expensive bone-coloured suit: the jacket, fastened by two large leather buttons, had slipaway pockets at the sides. The skirt had two small pleats from the waist and flapped gently just above the knees as she walked. Her white lace blouse was styled high at the neck with a frilly collar. And her hair, her hair poured in cascades of shining, liquid ebony over her shoulders and to her waist. She wore semi-high heeled shoes, just high enough to accentuate her calf muscles and exhibit the full beauty of her legs. He had to give credit to George, who rose from somewhere and appeared quite unmoved by the apparition before him.

"Pleased to meet you," George said, before Peter even had a chance to introduce them.

"Very pleased to meet you," Caterina replied.

Then his father was greeting her warmly while his mother looked away and said nothing.

"Please don't mention about the nuns," Peter begged of George.

"It's all right," George's tone was soothing, "she already knows."

When they reached the Gluepot Road, she turned to him and said, "Hasn't anything occurred to you?"

"Such as?"

"That I might be pregnant?"

"I didn't think of that," he said. "Don't tell my parents, whatever you do. We can send it to England anyway . . ."

Peter . . . Peter . . . Peter . . . "Bloody hell," Peter yelled sitting bolt upright in bed, "what's going on?"

"You've slept in," his mother said patiently. "You'll be late for work if you don't hurry."

"I was dreaming," he gabbled out. "I can't remember what it was about."

"I should hope you were dreaming," his mother replied sternly, "using language like that."

It rained around mid-morning and the men spent a couple of hours in the shed, playing cards and swapping yarns about the weekend. Peter wanted to tell them about Caterina and about his dream, but he was afraid they would laugh. He was pretty well trapped in the corner of the shed, anyway, and old Charlie was in a philosophical mood.

Peter suddenly remembered the purple and yellow flowers on the hills in spring.

"Soursobs," Charlie said, "soursobs, and the purple ones are Salvation Jane. Now, the Salvation Jane saved the farmers from ruin during the worst drought ever." The old man's eyes widened, "nothing would grow — no grass, no nothing, except the Salvation Jane. And that was all the cattle needed to stay alive. It was called Paterson's Curse before that. It's a noxious weed, you know. It's not supposed to be there."

"That's a great story," Peter said, hiding his disbelief.

"You're a good cobber," Charlie told him, resting a hand on Peter's knee. "You can always tell a good cobber." He left his hand there, making the boy feel uncomfortable. "The worst attitude a man can have," Charlie whirled a sandwich about in the air, "is the 'blow you Jack, I'm all right' attitude. Now if you care for your fellow man, then I reckon you'll do all right."

"Are you pissed or something?" Dave broke in. "Give the kid a break, mate."

"Hey," Clive spoke up, "don't go filling his head with all your shit."

"It's okay," Peter said, smiling, "we're just talking."

"And take your hand off his knee you dirty old bastard," said Dave. The old man gave the boy a toothless grin and removed his hand. Peter tried to look indifferent, but blushed when he caught Helmut's eyes blazing at him.

It served them right, really, Peter thought, when old Charlie began addressing everybody in the shed about anything and everything.

"I wish it would hurry up and stop raining," Clive said, looking up to the roof of the shed, "and we can get the silly old bastard back to his barrow."

"We should charge the brickies for having him," Dave said.

It stopped raining at last and the sun appeared, warm and friendly, and Peter almost lost his job. They got back to work about a minute after the owner of the company turned up for a spot check and the second-fixers were warned that they had a roof over them and couldn't stop work for the rain. Peter was among those docked two hours' pay that week, despite protests from Clive that the second-fixers had to take timber in from outside and would have got soaking wet. Apart from that halt for rain, Peter and the other second-fixers worked flat out — sawing, clamping and nailing the flooring, yet only just managing to stay ahead of the other gangs. The brickies were on piecework and the plasterers were pursuing bonuses.

He reached home tired and hungry after each working day, but recovered enough after a meal and a shower to go out in the evenings. He called for Caterina one night but asked for

Chico when the door was opened by Mr Bagliano and ended up going out with Chico, Bill, Debbie and Gayle. But at least he saw her, briefly, as she went into her room with a pile of study papers. And she managed the warmest of smiles for him before disappearing. How would he ever get to take her out if he never had the chance to ask? The thought also occurred to him that perhaps he should be studying for something. The threat of losing his job when they had taken rain time had lingered at the back of his mind and he realised his position might not be as secure as he thought. An apprenticeship would be a better option than working as an improver, at least then they couldn't fire him for five years. But did he really want to be a carpenter all his life? Could he aspire to great heights as a carpenter? And if he signed up for an apprenticeship, wouldn't he then be ensnared into the trade forever? At first, Peter tried to visit the hostel often. He had no wish to lose the friendship of Pauline and the others, valuing the bonds made since his arrival in South Australia. He wanted them all to stay friends always and when the thought crossed his mind, as it sometimes did, that one day they all might find new friends, lovers, wives and husbands, he dreamed that they might all live in a cul-de-sac of homes somewhere as neighbours, so he wouldn't lose them completely.

He didn't quite know what to do about Pauline. If she should one day walk up to him and say that she loved him and could he for goodness sake ask her to marry him, he was sure he would do just that and not worry too much about losing Caterina as a result. Pauline could take his mind off Caterina and he supposed Margie could, too. He quite fancied Debbie and hadn't failed to notice the pleasant homeliness of Gayle. But for goodness sake he already had Pauline, and Shirley as a friend if he wanted her, which he did, not to mention Donna, of course.

What Peter really needed was some good old-fashioned sex — as much of it as possible for as long as possible. However, being tied to Donna for years was too horrendous to contemplate. And of one thing he was certain, Donna would expect a lasting relationship the next time they made love together. She might give the impression of sexual openness, but she would not give her favours lightly to a guy who had been virtually scorning her advances. Most of the girls, he thought bitterly, may just as well wear chastity belts, the way they protected their virginity. It was a wonder they didn't take out insurance on it if it was that precious to them. Then, again, they managed just fine without either of those options.

Chapter 20

Caterina Confesses

The sound of chatter and laughter guided him to the boilerhouse on his arrival at the camp one night. Veronica and Lisa were trying to jive in the cramped space when he entered.

"We've been taking lessons in rock and roll," Pauline told him. "A couple of the new people are professional dancers."

"I've only missed coming here a few days," Peter said, bewildered, "how did I miss this?"

"They're giving them again next week, but we can teach you, anyway," Pauline said.

"I can already jive a bit," he reminded her.

"There's more to it than that — you've got to learn how to pick your partner up and swing her just about over your head these days."

"Probably get a hernia," Peter muttered.

"How's the new home?" Shirley interrupted. "Are we getting an invitation to the housewarming?"

I don't know yet if we'll have one," Peter said, "but if we do, then I hope to invite everybody here." To be truthful, Peter had not even thought about a housewarming. And he was sure his parents hadn't. But he made a mental note to mention it to them. Veronica was contorting her face at him in one of her more successful efforts at horror looks and he pulled his tongue out at her. "You'll stick like that," he said.

It poured with rain while he cycled home that night and he got soaked to the skin, but the rain didn't stop him from dreaming: He was a rock and roll dancer extraordinaire and had just won the world championships, partnering at times Caterina and at other times, Pauline. He was standing on the dais about to sportingly hand his large gold trophy to Pauline when a police car sidled alongside him. He brought his bike to a skidding halt. "Who are you?" one of the officers asked, shining a torch into his face.

"Peter Mitchell, sir."

"Where have you been?"

Peter explained in full, including the possibility of his taking rock and roll lessons.

"You haven't been near the building site?"

"No sir — I work there, so I know not to."

The policeman turned the torch away. "Where are you going now?"

"Home — I've got to get up for work in the morning."

"Make sure you go straight home — don't hang around the streets."

"No, sir."

The car left as silently as it arrived, leaving Peter with a dry mouth. He looked up to the inky-black sky: "Stand your men down, captain, danger averted."

"Police aren't supposed to do that," he told George. "They aren't supposed to scare you when you haven't done anything. They can't tell you to go straight home if you don't want to."

"They get bored like everybody else sometimes," George said. "All they want is for you to answer them back or be rude to them so they can get out of the car and beat the living daylights out of you."

"Then I could sue them," Peter said, indignantly.

"It's impossible to prove," George told him, "they use rubber hoses and never leave a mark on you."

"How do you know that?"

"Plenty of people I know have had it done to them. It's not like in England," George was really warming to the theme, "you daren't ask one of these coppers for the time. They wouldn't give it to you. Wouldn't give you the time of day. They'd be more likely to beat the hell out of you just for asking."

"Something should be done about it," Peter said.

"It's all part of the plan," George explained patiently. "They're all rednecks, well, most of them, deliberately chosen to keep the population downtrodden. They're all right usually, until you start spouting off about the rights of the individual.

Then they mark you down . . . and . . . one day, they get you. The Government's in on it too, of course."

"I'm learning to rock and roll," Peter said.

"I'm very pleased about that," George replied. "I'm sure Mom and Dad will be as well. In fact, they'll be delighted. They have high hopes for you. I have too, but I know you have some limitations; they don't know that. They will be very pleased you have taken this first, big step for your future."

"There's nothing wrong with rock and roll," Peter said.

"Of course there isn't," George agreed, but just think about why they changed its name. Jiving is respectable, isn't it?"

"Yes."

"Rock and roll won't be, just wait and see."

In bed that night Peter wondered whether they shouldn't import a few English Bobbies into South Australia. Import a bit of civility. Then again, an English Bobby might have kicked him up the backside just for being out in the dark. Like the one who had chased them up to the Soho Road when they were caught smoking under the Smethwick Bridge. Or the two who had tried to blame them for smashing the allotment greenhouses and would have but for one of the gardeners telling them in the nick of time that it was older lads who had done it. They still received dire warnings from the officers, despite the fact that they hadn't done anything.

Between teachers, parents, bosses, girls and police officers, Peter realised, he wasn't and had never been, as free as he had thought. Then there was the Government and the taxman and the strutting uniformed ticket collectors on the trains, and the smart-mouthed and officious bus drivers and conductors — all looking to have some say, however small, in the shaping of his destiny.

Peter didn't completely ignore the fact that a major problem looming in his life was his inability to actually do anything positive about his future. His dreams were many and varied and he found them comforting and pleasurable whenever he escaped into them. But he had no idea how to make come true those which contained some possibility of substance. If he thought about it, he might place the problem in the same category as leaving his men stranded on Mars when he fell asleep, or never actually winning the hand of any maiden he might rescue from distress. The more practical visions, such as returning to England to marry Margie, or buying a piano or writing a song, or even the vague idea that he might like to go mining in the Australian Outback and dig himself a fortune — all these things were merely bedfellows in his thoughts with the desperate battles in space and his fancy to become Lord Mayor of London or Birmingham or Adelaide or possibly of just about anywhere.

He made a mental note before going to sleep that night to sort out which one of his girlfriends he really wanted, and so remove one problem. He also addressed his men on Mars base, explaining his delay in contacting them on the fact that he had been kidnapped on Earth and taken to the other side of the planet and had only recently been able to escape. He had barely time to whisk his men from the base and into Earth orbit before he fell asleep. And again he forgot to say his prayers.

He visited the hostel every night for the next week and took part in the dancing classes there, but by the weekend had still said nothing to Pauline about his feelings for her.

Bill and Chico called for him early on the Saturday and they caught the train to Adelaide. Peter had a couple of pounds in his pocket for once, having spent little at either the Roadhouse or the camp shop. He was also stretching a packet of tobacco to last two weeks, so that was another saving. They lounged around Adelaide Railway Station for a while, but found it cold and boring so they trod Hindley Street and Rundle Street, looking in shop windows and dreaming in snatches of the day when they could afford to buy some of the tempting goods on display.

Peter was particularly taken by a galah in a cage outside a petshop and he softly whistled a tune at it until it told him to "fuck off". He glanced around nervously, hoping nobody else had heard and might think it was him who was swearing. They discovered a below-street-level coffee shop called the Black Orchid, where a tall, young Continental man served them cappuccinos and toasted sardine sandwiches in a dimly lit atmosphere of luxury. A strange excitement gripped Peter, as though he was privy to the forbidden grown-up world, as he sipped his coffee in the half-light. Then he reminded himself that he was grown-up already and should be doing such things anyway. He was probably more grown-up than most youths his age, he felt. He would bet that most of them were still virgins, whereas he had really lost that childhood condition, with Donna — well, he had in effect. Not to mention with Caterina in his dreams — dreams so vivid that they too qualified for a place in his reality. No, there wouldn't be many his age with quite his experience of women or who were quite as worldly-wise. His thoughts were racing again and he was chewing his sandwich too quickly. He slowed, chewing carefully, more deliberately and tried to allow his mind to pick up Bill and Chico's conversation.

Peter often wondered what other people thought. Did they think the same strange thoughts he did? Did their thoughts race around in a mad gallop, seeking to dash free of their heads so they could escape into the ether? What happened to all those thoughts that must at times escape? Could some of that thought energy be mistaken for ghosts? It could, couldn't it? If it all gathered in one place, surely it could appear as some ethereal presence. Peter's thoughts came to an abrupt halt as he accidentally bit his thumb instead of the sandwich — and he still hadn't a clue what Chico and Bill were talking about.

They wanted to linger there, in that little shop, so charged was it with atmosphere, but there were other things to do, other people to see. Peter wanted to ask Chico whether Caterina was home that day, but he decided not to mention her in front of Bill. Forewarned is forearmed, as his mother might say.

Caterina wasn't home when they got back to Chico's. "She's probably gone to Debbie's," Chico answered Bill. "She's not working today."

Peter wasn't sure whether his twinge of regret was for himself or for Bill or for both of them. They said all was fair in love and war, but he wasn't so sure about ignoring the rules of fair play. And he was even less sure of Caterina's affections for him — if there had ever been any.

"Shall we go round to Debbie's," he asked, casually. "There's not much to do otherwise."

"Good idea," Chico said.

"What about her old man?" Bill asked. "The prick doesn't like me."

"That's true," Chico agreed. "We'd better give that idea a miss."

Bill turned to Peter, "Do you fancy Debbie?"

"No, not particularly, I just thought it would be something to do."

Bill gave him a pensive look, "Let's go to your place then."

"Okay," Peter agreed, "Let's go to my place."

"Caterina is a bit hard to pin down," Bill said to him as they walked to Peter's home.

Peter merely nodded. He didn't want to discuss Caterina in front of Chico and for that matter he didn't want to discuss her with Bill.

Bill opened the fridge and inspected the contents. Peter glanced nervously at his mother.

"Can I have some squash?" Bill asked.

"Help yourself," Mrs Mitchell said pleasantly, "there's a glass in the top cupboard there."

Peter was about to introduce his friends when Bill did it for him, even introducing Peter to his own mother. George sat in an armchair reading the morning paper. On a Saturday, George could take hours over the paper, reading everything from the front pages to the backs of each section and commenting at length on many an item. He half-rose from his chair and shook hands with Bill and Chico.

"Are you here with anyone, or have you just popped in by yourselves?"

"That's right," said Bill, "we were just walking along the road and thought this would be a nice house to visit, so here we are."

Peter's stomach gave a nervous jump, but George was in a good mood and went back to his paper briefly with a grin on his face. Surprisingly, his mother took a liking to both Bill and Chico and made them stay for lunch. "Rough diamonds," she said of them afterwards.

Peter explained to Bill and Chico that his father had been asked to work Saturday overtime and wouldn't be home until about mid-afternoon. "I'll probably be working seven days a week when I get my taxi licence," Bill said. "Still, that's where the money is."

"Mining," George said. "Mining is the only way to make money in this country. You need some get-up-and-go, though."

"I might go mining soon," Peter said.

"You'll do nothing of the kind," his mother put in. "There are some very nasty accidents in mines."

"You pick the gold off the top of the ground," Peter explained. "You don't have to dig for it."

"If that were true," his mother said, patiently, "everybody would be out picking it up. In fact, it wouldn't be there anymore. They would have picked it all up by now."

Peter sighed in frustration and looked to his friends for support, but it wasn't forthcoming.

"Where's that pretty girlfriend of yours?" George asked his brother. "I bet she's much better looking than these two."

"Who's this?" Chico raised his eyebrows.

"I'm not sure if he means Pauline, Donna, Shirley, Debbie or Gayle," Peter said, marvelling at his own quick-wittedness in leaving out Caterina.

Bill raised his eyebrows, "How many girlfriends have you got?"

"They're just friends," Peter said.

"I've never heard of some of those," George would not be denied. "I mean the one training to be a nun."

"Chico's sister," Peter said, trying to keep his voice even. "Only she isn't training to be a nun and I've already told you that. Anyway, I hardly know her."

They changed the subject to motorbikes and were discussing whether a Velocette was superior to a Norton, when there was a knock on the back door.

"Come in and wipe your feet," George called. And in walked Caterina, Debbie and Gayle.

Relief flooded Peter that Pauline wasn't there. He would probably have gone into shock if she had been. He stood up and allowed Caterina to sit, there were enough vacant chairs for Debbie and Gayle, and he found the presence of mind to introduce the girls, who had called on the off-chance of finding some of the gang.

"Caterina, by the way, is Chico's sister."

"I thought there was a resemblance," Mrs Mitchell said.

Peter couldn't see it.

Bill drove them to the Roadhouse that night in his father's car. They bought pasties and softdrinks. Peter kept looking round nervously, expecting Pauline to walk into the garage any minute. He couldn't help a twinge of guilt now and then. Though when he looked at Caterina, he felt a glow of happiness. Nevertheless, he felt relieved when they set off for the Gawler Hall where they lounged around wondering what to do next and ended up not doing anything. Bill and Chico glared at a couple of youths who had started glaring first, but they reached home without incident at around eleven. There was something more wrong about the evening than not having anything interesting to do — something empty about it. The camaraderie Peter had so cherished since arriving in Australia was now not quite so fulfilling. He sensed that the feeling would still have been there had he gone to visit Pauline and the others.

Chico invited them in as they drew up outside the Baglianos. Caterina lingered at the gate, looking at Peter pointedly, so he waited for Bill and Chico to go into the house.

"Shall we walk?" she asked, sending a thrill of anticipation through him.

He took her hand, in wonder at the sudden turn of events. They stopped after about a hundred yards and he drew her closer to him. But she pulled away looking tearful.

"What's wrong?"

She bowed her head as though studying the footpath. It reminded him of Margie when she was about to make a big decision.

"You're not going to like this," she said, looking up at last.

There was that familiar sinking feeling. "What is it?" His thoughts flitted from pregnancy to the nunnery before realising that neither was likely.

She played with his belt buckle, but not familiarly — more in an absentminded way, just sliding her fingers over the cool metal clasp. "I want us to be friends," she said. "Is that all right?"

"We are friends," he replied kindly. "Whatever made you think we weren't?"

"I'm really sorry," she said. "I didn't mean to lead you on or anything. I really like you, Peter."

"What's the problem then?" He smiled, trying to make her relax.

"I wasn't very honest with you . . . I did it, I mean I was going to do it, to make Bill jealous." She looked at the footpath again, "I was going to go out with you just to make Bill notice me more."

"Bill couldn't notice you any more than he does now — he's crazy about you."

"But I didn't want to share him with all the boys — I got too possessive, I suppose."

"Does Bill know about all this?"

"No, I'm not telling him. I just thought I should explain how horrible I've been and why, rather than try to avoid you."

She looked so miserable Peter wanted to take her into his arms and comfort her, but she might think he was still making a play for her.

Out of the darkness rode the knight, his armour gleaming yellow fire in the moonlight, his sword raised and a cry on lips, 'Away you varlet · leave that maiden be or I'll hang your giblets out for the ravens.'

"It's all right," Peter said, taking her hand again. "It's all right. I would rather be your friend than never know you."

He wanted to tell her that he loved her and that they should try a relationship, try going steady, but he had received the message loud and clear and he wouldn't push himself on to her. He wouldn't push himself on to anyone. He could never risk rejection. At least this way, he could know that she had given him something precious to treasure for always: she had made him her friend for life. There was no rejection in that philosophy. Even so, he wanted to say, 'I'll be your friend forever, but I still want to be your lover', but he didn't. They headed back to the house.

"Tell Bill I'm walking home, I was supposed to be in early tonight.

"You're not mad at me?"

"I'm so pleased you'll be my friend, how can I be mad at you?"

He set off along the road home with a lump in his throat and tears welling under his eyelids. He wiped his eyes with his sleeves before entering the house.

"Got a cold?" George asked.

"Yes," Peter mumbled and went straight to bed. A feeling of outrage came over him as he snuggled under the blankets. He had fallen in love and been spurned. How could she not love him? How could she love Bill instead? Not that there was anything wrong with Bill, it was just that, well, if he were a girl and had to choose between Bill and Peter — Peter would be quite obviously the first choice. And yet, she had chosen him as a friend. And he supposed he should be grateful for that. It seemed that everybody wanted him as a friend. All the girls wanted him as a friend; as their guardian and comforter. Oh, yes! They could go anywhere in the dark in safety while they had a strong arm to cling to. Would any of them get into his bed as willingly? Would they heck . . . Would they bloody heck. Admittedly, Donna was more forthcoming in the other direction. In fact, Donna didn't give a hoot for his protection or company. She was more interested in his body. How he wished Caterina wanted him in the way Donna did. She was so beautiful was Caterina, so bloody beautiful. She was much too beautiful for Bill. He sat up in bed and fumbled with the radio in the dark. He lay there his mind racing, barely listening to the music, until Johnny Mathis began singing *Wonderful, Wonderful*, then he fell asleep on a pillow damp with his tears.

He awoke with a dry mouth the next morning because he had slept with it open. When his mother came in, he told her he felt sick and was going to stay in bed. She told him it was his imagination and "too many late nights". The fear of a curfew got him up. As he ate his breakfast, the words of the old school song

Barbara Ellen came to him and he was suddenly glad he hadn't stayed in bed. He didn't want to die of a broken heart.

The days turned to weeks and then to months. The hills glowed with purple and gold of Salvation Jane and soursobs and the paddocks simmered a listless brown as summer took up its lease. Chico bought his Velocette and Bill his car, a shiny black Dodge. Peter visited the hostel with increasing frequency, taking Pauline and Veronica to the city and, as summer turned on its heat, to the beaches when Bill and Caterina called with the car. With Veronica in tow, there was little opportunity for Peter to expand on his romantic feelings with Pauline. Instead, their friendship seemed to grow even stronger and they became outwardly more and more like a brother and sister. And he fell more and more in love with her.

Roger and Gayle could be seen around the town, holding hands and barely noticing the rest of the world. Debbie discovered a Dutch boy with a Triumph motorcycle and little was seen of her. And Chico provided a major surprise when he realised that Shirley was giving him and his motorbike more than ordinary attention and he promptly fell in love with her. Peter wasn't exactly ecstatic about that at first. Shirley was one of his original girlfriends. She sort of belonged to him and had been a delightful companion and he had made a place for her in his dreams in the event that Pauline might one day tell him to bugger off or something.

Peter hadn't yet recognised it, but the new, safe and happy world he had built around himself, was crumbling.

Chapter 21

Unemployed

The week before Christmas, Peter was one of thirty men laid off at the building site. The timing couldn't have been worse, with businesses about to close for the holidays. There would be no point looking for a job until about mid-January, and the way the newspapers were sounding off about credit squeezes and the economy, he feared for his future.

So many plans and so many dreams depended on his being able to work. His pride depended on his having work. How could his pride sustain the loss of work? For a couple of weeks, though, with his holiday pay, the resilience of youth and the ability to turn his mind off anything upsetting, he would enjoy the warmth of Adelaide's golden beaches and the companionship of friends.

Semaphore was not Australia's greatest beach, in fact, it was as rough as guts. So it didn't attract hordes of bronzed and muscular young men dashing through the sand and bowling over anyone slow enough to get in their way. Parents and their small children frequented Semaphore for its comparative solitude and for the shallows which stretched a long way out. It was something of a joy that the sand was strewn with seaweed and rocks because crabs and starfish lurked for young, keen eyes to discover.

There was a timelessness here in the warm, clear water, a contentment made all the more dreamy by the gentle washing of the waves and the distant cry of a gull. Veronica liked swimming and floating on her back, staring up at the endless blue sky, at times so relaxed that she would doze briefly before lifting her wide, blue eyes startled to the sky as the water threatened to lose its buoyancy. On this day Veronica had a dream — a dream which could never come true unless her sister met and fell for someone other than Peter Mitchell. Veronica thought she was in love with her sister's boyfriend. But Peter and Pauline always seemed to be together, while she tagged along like some junior chaperone or a gooseberry, more like. At 15 she was getting to an age when he could begin noticing her but for his involvement with Pauline; not that Pauline and Peter were not suited, she had to admit. Everyone said how suited they were — like peas in a pod, like the initials in their names. Yet, could it be true what Pauline had told her? Could it be true that they had never kissed? That he had never made an advance towards her and never been actually romantic with her? Could it be, hope against hope, that Pauline and Peter were just good friends and that there was room for her in Peter's life after all? Why hadn't he kissed her? Was he so terribly shy? Why hadn't Pauline kissed him? There was nothing shy about Pauline. Veronica sighed into the lapping waves and swallowed salty water . . . Now there was a dream . . . Peter, his strong lithe body, browned from exposure on the building site, cutting swiftly through the waves even as the sea tugged her to the beckoning weeds below. He reached out for her, telling her to hang on and not to panic. But who was panicking? She was too dreamy, too sleepy for panic. There was nothing to panic about, was there? But she was so tired that she must sleep now. Just a quick sleep now that she had dreamed her dream — funny that, dreaming before going to sleep. Usually . . . wasn't it the other way round? Pauline was in the shallows, trying to do a headstand on the rocky sea floor. Her legs scythed through the air in scissor motions. Peter swam over and grabbed her feet, pulling her over. She came up for air and threw water in his face. Shirley and Caterina left the water to dry themselves and Bill, still splashing around in the water, stopped to hurl a beach ball at them, only to see it carried back into the water by the wind. Chico sat on the beach, dreaming Chico dreams and idly making patterns in the sand with his fingers. As the girls approached him, he looked to where Peter and Pauline were still fooling around and he saw Bill emerging on to the beach. Everyone was accounted for, not that there was any danger at this beach, unless you were foolhardy enough to go ridiculously too far out.

"I'll tell you what," Bill said, shaking water over Chico, "there's a strong current out there in places, almost a rip. It carried me a few yards before I knew what was happening."

"Kids swim here," Shirley said. "It's pretty safe."

"Where's Veronica?" Caterina asked.

She fought against sleep, because the voice was telling her to and because it wasn't right to sleep after you had dreamed and because something was wrong. She was floating in the air. Where was she that she could float so effortlessly through the air? You couldn't float in the air, because of gravity. It was gravi ... grav—ee—tee ... grav—ee—tee ... grav—ee—tee.

She ate sand before turning herself over, fighting violently against whoever had hold of her. He was sitting astride her, his face handsome as a film star's staring intently into hers. She fought for breath and pushed his weight away, coughing up salt water.

She gasped, "What happened?"

"Thank goodness you're all right," he replied, breathing his relief.

"You were s‑o‑o‑o far out," Pauline's white face was over her.

"Lucky we found you," said Bill.

"Lucky," Chico added.

"Are you all right?" Caterina asked.

"I'm fine, I just fell asleep on the water, I think."

"Don't do that too often," Peter said, feeling some of the shock and panic ebb from him. "You gave us all a hell of a fright. I was about to give you resuscitation."

"That sounds exciting," she tried to smile.

"You've got Caterina to thank," he said, "she noticed you were missing."

Peter didn't mind too much that Veronica sat very close to him in the back seat of the car on the way home. He jammed his knee into the back of the front seat so it wouldn't jiggle.

On Christmas Eve, 1956, a Monday, they all met at Donna's place.

Each of the boys kissed her under the mistletoe hanging in the doorway before they entered. Then Bill took Caterina under the mistletoe and they kissed long and passionately, ignoring the catcalls from the others. Caterina passed a Christmas card to each of them, Peter thanked her and stuffed his card in the back pocket of his trousers without looking at it and remembered he had bought a small bottle of perfume for Pauline, which was still in the glovebox of Bill's car. Chico took Shirley under the mistletoe and then he took Pauline under there and then Veronica and Lisa. Bill did likewise, leaving Peter feeling stupid because he had so far kissed only Donna. He felt shy in front of the others, but knew he had to do something. Why didn't Pauline just drag him under the mistletoe herself, anyway? Why did he always have to make these strange, embarrassing decisions?

'Let boldness be my friend', he said to himself, and walked to the doorway, looking pointedly at Pauline. She glared, but came to him . . . It was meant to be long and tender or even passionate, but ended up as little more than a peck as the rest of the gang jeered and cheered and they both turned away in acute embarrassment. It was not only the unwelcome attention which made Peter feel stupid, he felt stupid as well because in that brief moment when their lips had met he felt a strange alienation, as though he were kissing his friend or his sister. But at least and at last, he had kissed her, if only under the mistletoe. Nevertheless, something about their kiss mildly disturbed him. And he didn't feel any better when, later in the evening, Chico and Shirley disappeared outside, soon to be followed by Caterina and Bill. He sat there feeling very lonely.

He took out Caterina's card before getting into bed that night. On the front was the Virgin Mary holding the baby Jesus and inside the simple inscription, "Christ the King was born today" and underneath, "Love and friendship, Caterina". He placed it under his pillow and remembered again that he had left the gift for Pauline in Bill's car.

Christmas brought socks and underwear for Peter, but no gift of money. The New Year dance at the hostel was held the following Monday and Peter gave Pauline the bottle of perfume before they entered the hall, apologising for forgetting it the previous week. She gave him an uncharacteristically shy look and tucked it into her handbag. She hadn't bought any presents, she explained, because she was trying to save for clothes.

"I can't bludge off my parents forever."

"I know what you mean," Peter said, "I'm the same. Mind you, they won't let me bludge off them at all."

The distant roar of Chico's Velocette drew them outside. He cut the engine at the gate and glided to the hall. It wasn't only Shirley who liked the roar of motorbikes — Pauline and Donna also showed what Peter thought was rather excessive interest. And he felt peeved when Chico promised to take Pauline for a ride later.

Peter sat and poured him and the other boys a beer while Veronica winked and pulled faces at him. He winked back, stuck out his tongue, and looked away.

She was trying to make him laugh but he had an unfortunate habit of often going into giggling fits and now that he had grown up, he didn't think it was seemly to giggle. Men should laugh outright, not giggle. Unfortunately, he felt a giggling fit coming on and made the mistake of looking back at Veronica, who was still staring and winking at him. He burst into laughter and hid his face in his arms to hide his embarrassment. Pauline asked him what was so funny, which made him laugh even more. Once he had recovered, he refused to look at Veronica for fully an hour.

They drank to absent friends in England and then Peter asked them to drink to Jim and Wendy. He was just realising that Jim should actually have been there, when the words "what a pack of drunken fuckin' wombats" sailed through the noise.

"That's amazing," Peter said, "we were just drinking to you."

"Don't drink to me — go and get me a drink," said Jim, who wore a black patch over one eye.

"Get your own," Pauline told him.

Jim went round the table and asked Pauline to get up, pulling her up by her arm as he did so. He promptly sat in her chair, grabbed her round the waist and sat her on his lap.

"It's been a long time on the trail, darling."

"Don't you dare darling me."

"Not tamed yet, then, I see," Jim grinned at her. "Peter not tamed you yet, then?"

"Don't be silly," she said.

"Yeah, don't be stupid," Peter said.

"Listen, dickhead," Jim said, "this lovely lady won't let me get up, so how about you getting me a beer."

Peter went off meekly to get his friend a drink. When he got back to the table, Jim was engrossed in the rock and rollers on the dance floor. "I've just seen someone's knickers," he said conspiratorially to Peter. Pauline dug him in the ribs.

"Have you heard from Wendy?" Peter asked him.

"There was a card from her when I got back home. She's got a job in a boutique, whatever that is."

"It's a clothes shop," Pauline said."

"Then why didn't she say that?"

"There are clothes shops and there are clothes shops," Pauline replied.

"Thank you, darling, that explains everything." Jim took a long drink.

Shirley leaned over and slipped a folded envelope into his jacket top pocket. "It's from Wendy," she said. "She sent it to me in case you weren't getting her mail."

"Haven't you written to her yet?" Pauline admonished.

"No — I haven't had time. All I've been doing is working and sleeping — mostly working. Sometimes I get a chance to eat."

"What about opal mining?" Peter asked.

"I don't know. This is good money, bloody hard yacker, though." Peter nodded and croaked because his voice was playing up again, "A bird in the hand is worth two in the bush."

"Dead right," Jim actually agreed with him.

Pauline interrupted, "You should write! Just think of Wendy looking for the mail every day in the hope of receiving a letter from you." Peter made a mental note to write to Margie.

"I don't think she's all that fond of me," Jim said. "If she was, she wouldn't have gone back to England."

"She had no choice," Peter reminded him. "She's not very old, don't forget."

"She could have run away with me. I asked her to," Jim said gloomily. "I would have looked after her and they would never have found us."

Veronica leaned over to Jim, "Don't you realise what a terrible choice she must have faced?"

Jim grunted and poured another beer.

As though by some prearranged signal, Chico and Pauline rose and went outside. Peter crossed his fingers for Pauline as the deep roar of the Velocette cut through the hall. They were gone for more than an hour, and he didn't uncross his fingers until they arrived back. Pauline looked windblown and happy. Peter felt a stab of jealousy.

"Wow?" she exclaimed as she sat. "Wow?" And she punched Peter on the arm. He looked at Jim for some explanation of her behaviour, but the other youth merely rolled his eyes and looked away.

"It's only a motorbike," Peter said to her.

"Oh, you!" She gave him a frustrated look, "Don't you ever have any fun?"

"I always have fun," Peter was genuinely surprised. "I have fun all the time."

"Then where's your motorbike?" Chico asked, grinning and putting his arm round Shirley.

"Hey," Jim said, "who are these people anyway? And why has he got his arm round one of my sheilas?"

"I'm not one of your sheilas," Shirley was indignant. "Do you mind?"

"Not if you don't, darling," Jim said, wriggling his shoulders at her. Peter belatedly introduced him to Chico, Bill and Caterina and everyone laughed when Jim reached across the table and kissed Caterina lightly on the back of her hand and Bill replied by grabbing Jim's hand and kissing it noisily.

"Gerroff?" Jim growled. "I don't fancy you."

Peter followed an ill-looking Jim outside later in the evening and watched uneasily as his friend was noisily sick in the paddock at the back of the hall.

"Fuckin' rum," Jim said, "I knew I shouldn't have drunk it." Another violent spasm gripped him and he threw the rest of his stomach contents on top of the first lot.

"Shit a brick, that's better."

"You should have had Coke or something with it," Peter said.

On the way back into the hall, Jim beckoned Peter to his car and switched on the headlights.

"I've got a letter from Wendy here," he said, pulling out the envelope. "Shirley darling gave it to me. I can't read properly at the moment because I've got a fuckin' welding flash in my eye, can you read it to me? Peter read with difficulty in the headlights:

Dearest Jim,

Surprise, surprise, I'm writing yet again. I hope one day you will come out of the bush and read my letters. Shirley said she gave you my first letter, so why haven't you answered?

Well, I have settled back with all my friends, but I don't really want to be here. Roger is having second thoughts as well. I've told my friends about you and the gang and then I started missing you all so much. Shirley says people are moving into their own homes now. I really, really miss you, Jim. Give my love to everyone and I send it especially to you. Please write. I lie in bed at night thinking about you. Do you still love me?

I wish I could come over to you right now. I think Mom and Dad are regretting coming back, but I'm not sure. The weather is terrible and there is so much unemployment. Remember Aunty Aida I told you about? Well, she has offered to pay my fare back to Australia but Dad won't let me go. It might be easier if you saved and came over here. Anyway, Mom's just yelled out, we're going shopping so I'm scribbling this in a hurry. Say hello to Pete and Pauline for me. Tell her and Donna I'll write soon.

Love and heartaches, Wendy.

PS. Miss you.

"That's all I fuckin' need," Jim growled. "Love and fuckin' heartaches."

"Women get emotional about romance," Peter said. "You have to understand that. By the way . . . I thought you were doing plastering."

"Am I fuck — I'm welding now."

"You should write," Peter said. "Write and tell her you love her and you want her to come back."

"That's a good idea," said Jim sarcastically, "then I can break her heart again, can't I?"

"Just trying to be helpful," Peter muttered.

The letter did the rounds between the teenagers. Veronica said it was "sweet". Jim said it was a load of "bullshit", but everybody knew he didn't mean it.

Peter never let anyone read his letters from Margie.

He stood between Pauline and a man he didn't know for Auld Lang Syne and felt stupid holding the man's hand. He wished he could be the other side of Pauline, holding Veronica's hand. He wanted to give Pauline a New Year kiss before going home and hung around her in the hope that the chance would present itself. He caught Veronica staring at him and thought that he should probably give her a kiss, too, but he didn't. Lots of people came up to him and kissed him and lots of people kissed Pauline, but Peter didn't. All he did was gently touch her elbow and say, "Goodnight, happy New Year". He really must become more positive, he told himself.

Chapter 22

A Brief Job

Peter slept like a log and woke refreshed. The local shop was opening for only two hours so he skipped breakfast and went over to buy a milkshake. A notice in the shop window told him it was the best milkshake he was ever going to buy. A canning factory in the wine and fruit famed Barossa Valley wanted men and women to help in the peach season. Good money, it said, and a bus would pick up workers in Elizabeth at 11 am and drive them back to the town by midnight. Peter rang the factory from the public phone box and was rewarded by a maintenance man who told him to merely get on the bus the second Monday in February.

January quickly began fulfilling the promise of a South Australian summer. Sweltering days and hot, sticky nights enticed the young and not so young to the beaches. There were barbecues where guitars could be played and songs sung around an illicit fire. Pretty girls in thin dresses or shorts, their long legs, white or tanned, attracted the eyes of the boys, and couples could be dimly seen embracing under the piers at night.

The month began kindly for Peter. George bought a car from another migrant who was packing up and taking his family back to England, and Peter was able to beg a lift on occasion to a friend's place or to the hostel. George offered to teach him to drive at the weekends, along the dirt tracks between Elizabeth and Salisbury. Peter learned quickly with the knowledge that he was out of a job and his money was dwindling rapidly. At least he might bluff his way into a driving job if they didn't want him at the canning factory when he got there. Such work was not part of his grand plan, but a man had to crawl before he could walk and walk before he could run. If only he could get to the starting blocks.

He answered the questions correctly and got his licence. He didn't even have to show the police he could drive.

As his friends drifted back to work, Peter began the task of hunting for a permanent job. He studied the paper each morning and gleaned from the few jobs advertised one or sometimes two for which vaguely he might be considered. He crossed his fingers as hard as he could in the waiting rooms, and exerted silent, mental pressure into the minds of the employment officers of various companies as he sat across from them. He answered their questions politely and tried his hardest to look intelligent, which sometimes gave him a headache. But all to no avail. After a fortnight his mother stopped lending him money, though she paid for a weekly train ticket. George stopped lending him the car, because Peter couldn't afford to help with petrol and George hadn't much money himself.

Peter rang the Labour Exchange from a public phone box and inquired about registering for the dole. He was told it would take six weeks for the money to come through. It also meant constant visits to the Labour Exchange to see if a job had become available. He arrived on his first visit to the Adelaide Labour Exchange at 8.30 one Monday morning and joined a queue of mostly New Australians which stretched about four deep along the street. He waited more than two hours before getting to the counter, along which were small glass screens to allow some privacy. He had noticed while waiting that those who reached the counter before him were each given forms to fill in and then directed to more queues further along. It could take all day, Peter realised. But he soon found that his accent opened more doors in that place than the accents of those born outside the English-speaking world. Apparently, only the New Australians were being shunted to another queue. Peter was told to go to a cubicle around the side of the counter and to take a seat. The interviewing officer was a man in late middle-age, balding and with horn-rimmed glasses. His face was friendly but tired and thin.

"And how can we help you?" he asked Peter, which Peter thought was a silly question.

"I'm out of work and need a job," Peter said, hoping the man didn't know about the vacancies at the canning factory. "And I want to know if I can sign on for the dole, because I haven't any money." He didn't like asking for money and looked quickly away, over to the counter and the gaunt mass of foreigners, their faces deadpanned with vacant hopelessness. He thought suddenly of Dopples and the Cypriot's dreams for the future in a strange land. He hoped Dopples would make it all right. He hoped they all would. He hoped all their dreams would come true.

Peter realised with a start that the man was smiling and had obviously spoken to him.

"I'm sorry," he apologised quickly, adding, "it's hot in here, isn't it?"

"How did you do at school?" the man asked.

"Three years' secondary education and I was very good at English and science."

"Do you have school reports?"

"No, they got lost coming over on the boat. I think an Egyptian has got them."

"An Egyptian has your school reports?"

"I don't think he meant to steal them," Peter said, trying to loosen his tie, "I dropped them at Port Said. And I didn't realise until it was too late and I saw this Egyptian person pick them up and I couldn't get to him in the crowd."

"You were lucky to have visited Port Said, with all the trouble there."

"I know, but I was with my parents and George."

"And your school reports."

"I had them in my wallet which my girlfriend gave me before I left England."

"I see — I was wondering why you would take your school reports around Port Said with you."

"Would you be able to find me a job?"

"I have a couple of forms for you to fill in, and then we will have a look at what is available. What sort of work have you done since leaving school?"

"I was a trainee carpenter at Elizabeth and I worked in a grocery shop in England. Oh, and in an office at Canning's — that's a big Birmingham company."

"Sport?" the man eyed him quizzically.

"Pardon?"

"Sport — were you good at sport?"

"Very good," Peter lied easily, and at last managed to get the top button of his shirt undone. "I was good at cricket, soccer and swimming."

"Excellent," the man said, getting up from his chair, "excuse me for a moment."

He disappeared somewhere into the nest of offices at the back, leaving Peter nervously wondering at the relevance of his sporting attributes. Australians were good at sport, especially swimming and cricket. Perhaps there was a coaching job for him. He could probably coach school kids all right . . . Perhaps one day he could coach the Aussies to beat England at cricket — not that they needed much coaching for that . . . or he could train youngsters for Olympic swimming . . . If he dreamt his very hardest, he could definitely see himself coaching kids to reach the pinnacles of success in sport. Why hadn't he thought of this before? It would have to be more interesting than being a stuffy Lord Mayor of somewhere.

The man interrupted Peter's reverie.

"Now," he said, giving the youth an important look and handing him a form. "Fill this in and we'll arrange some money for you. It takes six weeks to come through. I have three possible jobs here. If you don't have any luck, come back and see us."

Peter filled in the form, thanked the man and hurried out, squeezing quickly and carefully between the rows of New Australians still waiting to be attended to. He tried to look disappointed, so they wouldn't guess that he had been given jobs to go after. He felt ashamed as he stepped out into the city heat, but there was nothing he could do about it. Anyway, as his mother would say, you could never look a gift horse in the mouth.

The first job listed was at Parafield, which wasn't far from Elizabeth. Another job was at Gawler and the other at Port

Adelaide. Peter decided to try for the Parafield job first. The vacancy was for a young man who was good with his hands and had an interest in aircraft. Peter had no interest in aircraft, but felt he was good with his hands in some areas.

He was interviewed by a young, pleasant German, whose father owned the business. The job, from what Peter could gather when he managed to concentrate long enough on what he was being told, was helping to make large, model aeroplanes. He was taken into the workshop to meet the workers, none of whom seemed to speak any English at all. They nodded and smiled at Peter and shook his hand. He was shown the beautiful, scale-model planes and told he could start work the next day. He was elated, barely slept a wink all night and got to work, armed with his tools, a good fifteen minutes early. He realised when he looked at the task properly that his carpentry tools would be useless. The pleasant man gave Peter the job of glueing stanchions to the wings of a biplane. The job was awkward and Peter managed to get glue everywhere, but he expected to improve as he got used to it. He had been working for about an hour, when another young man entered the workshop, carrying sheets of balsa wood. The man looked at Peter in surprise and went over to the pleasant man and talked with him in German, at first in a low voice and then in a loud, angry tone. Finally, he glared at Peter and walked into the small office. The pleasant man continued with his work, seemingly unruffled. At about 10 o'clock, the other workmen sat down and unwrapped their sandwiches. Taking this as a cue that it was morning tea time, Peter did likewise. However, before he had taken a bite, the angry young man stalked out of the office and confronted him.

"What do you think you are doing?"

"I thought it was morning tea time," Peter gasped, fear rising inside him. "Sorry."

"You are here to work, you lazy bastard," the man screamed at him. "No breaks. We can't afford breaks. You have only just got here."

Peter quickly rewrapped his sandwiches and went red-faced back to work, hoping the man wouldn't notice the mess he was making of the stanchions. No one else spoke to him, and a peek around the workshop showed that no one was looking at him, either. At about midday the other workers drifted back to the bench and their bags, ready for lunch. Peter didn't know what to do. Surely he could sit and have lunch, couldn't he? That was the law. As he pondered what to do about his rumbling stomach, the outside door swung open with a blast of hot air and in stepped an elderly, white-haired man with square, Germanic features and gold, wire-framed spectacles. He wore light brown overalls and a short-sleeved pink shirt from which rippled powerful arm muscles only lightly tanned from the summer sun. Peter judged him to be well into his sixties, yet still enormously strong and fit despite his bulk. He gave Peter only a cursory glance and went to the office to speak to the angry young man. Peter decided to carry on working and not risk taking a lunch break. After a little while he heard the elderly man speaking in German to the pleasant man who had hired Peter. He fancied the man who had hired him was explaining that he had hired the youth because he was out of work and needed a break. But when the elderly man suddenly stalked from the workshop, Peter knew his job was at an end. The young man who hired him was apologetic, "I'm very sorry, but my father and brother don't think we can afford to hire anyone new for the present."

"Thank you anyway," Peter said. He picked up his tool box, turned to say cheerio, saw that no one was looking at him, and left the premises. With anger and wounded pride, he waited in the stinking heat at Parafield station for a train to take him home. He had a long wait — two trains went by without stopping and he was almost passing out with the heat by the time the dull brown diesel squealed to a halt. He stepped groggily into a carriage, lugging his toolbox in front of him. An Italian porter, resplendent in black uniform and peak hat, strutted up to him and asked loudly for his ticket. Peter wondered about uniforms.

He had a splitting migraine by the time he reached home and felt slightly delerious. His explanation for losing his job sounded far-fetched even to him.

"You couldn't have been doing your job right," his mother sniffed.

"It had nothing to do with that," Peter explained patiently. "The old man was German and hated English people ... probably shot down during the war or something."

"The war's been over a long time," his mother said. "Someone should tell the old bugger that. He's probably planning a new one."

"Will you lend me some money to go to the hostel tonight?"

"I haven't got any money — and you don't need it to go to the hostel."

"It's just in case I want to get a drink with the others. I can't be the only one without money."

"You should have thought of that before you lost your job."

Peter sighed wearily, "Even when I was little you gave me money for sweets or an ice cream."

"You were lucky to get any sweets at all then," his mother said, distantly, "with the rationing and food shortages. You don't know how lucky you were."

"I don't need much money — just enough to buy something from the shop."

"You're grown up now. You have to stand on your own two feet. Don't ask me for money — if you're that desperate, take some bottles back to the shop."

"We haven't got any bottles."

"There must be a dozen or more under the laundry tub — go and look. Funny, Peter thought as he made his second trip over to the shop with the holdall crammed full of bottles, it's funny how embarrassed you get when you're older. As a child he would have thought nothing of taking bottles back to the corner shop in Thornhill Road, but now he found the task completely beneath his dignity. Nevertheless, dignity aside, there were so many bottles in the cupboards under the laundry tubs that he scooped the princely sum of eight shillings and six pence from the shopkeeper, who paid up cheerfully enough.

"I'll probably be spending it back here anyway," Peter told him generously.

He informed his mother he had made nearly six shillings from the bottles and she told him to make it last the rest of the week. He put four shillings in his tin box, emptied a couple of weeks before by summer activities, and jingled the rest in his pocket as he waited outside the house for Bill to pick him up. After about an hour, Bill hadn't arrived and Peter was getting eaten by mosquitoes, so he walked to the hostel. He went into a big explanation with Pauline about losing his job and how hard it must be for some people to forget the war.

"It was because I'm English," he said, winning some sympathy.

"Some people can't forget the war," Pauline said.

"It probably didn't help that my father built Spitfires and is doing secret work at Weapons," Peter added. "George says there are spies everywhere and they know all about certain people."

"Your father's a sheetmetal worker," Veronica said.

"Spoilsport," said Peter, "but he did work on Spitfires."

They walked up to the Roadhouse and Peter bought a Cottee's lime and offered to buy the girls a drink but they paid for their own.

"What will you do now?" Pauline asked him as they stood outside the garage and watched the occasional car zoom by.

"I might go and work with Jim, at least it's good money."

"You shouldn't do that," Pauline said, "I don't think Jim would appreciate anybody dogging his footsteps."

Peter was puzzled, "Who's dogging his footsteps?"

"I mean . . . if you go to Whyalla, he might think you're trying to horn in on his job."

"Not his job," Peter explained, "there must be other jobs there. You couldn't possibly think I would try to pinch his job off him."

"You shouldn't follow Jim around," she said with finality.

It was quite obvious to Peter that what Pauline really meant was that she didn't want him to go away. Mind you, he hadn't thought for one minute that she would be happy about his going to Whyalla. She needed to have him close-by, just as he needed her to be around for him. Perhaps he had better not upset her with thoughts that he might go away. She shouldn't be made to feel insecure about something that would probably never happen.

"Are you staring into space or something?" Veronica asked him.

"I was miles away," Peter grinned.

"I saw you go," Pauline said.

"I probably won't go to Whyalla, anyway," he said.

"You had better not if you're going to keep going into a trance," Pauline said. "You'll end up getting lost."

The comment worried Peter.

He arrived home at about eleven when the rest of the family had gone to bed and knocked on George's bedroom door.

"Whaaateryawan' . . .," came the muffled voice.

Steeling himself, he stepped into his brother's room. George was lying half-awake with a book opened face down across his chest. He studied Peter with one eye open as though he were investigating a specimen in a laboratory.

"What?"

"Do you think I'm normal?"

"I thought we had already established to the contrary." George kept one eye wide open and the other tightly shut.

"What does that mean?"

"It means that you're anything but normal."

"I'm serious," Peter whispered so not to wake his parents.

"They aren't asleep," George said, "so you needn't whisper."

"Why are you looking at me with one eye?"

"I find you can see things in a different perspective with one eye shut. It helps you to get away from three-dimensional viewpoints. And it also enables you to rest one of your eyes."

"But you're putting extra strain on the other one."

"Not if you do it right," George said. "It takes practice, but you can learn to do it properly in a comparatively short time."

"What's your book?"

"Oliver Twist — it's very good."

"We had that at school."

"So did we," George explained, "but I hated it. I hated it because I was forced to read it. Now, I am reading it because I want to and I love it. The characterisation is so strong, you can feel and see all the people as though they were in the room with you."

"Wow," Peter said, "I wish I could write like that. I wish I could write like Carter Brown, even, and make a lot of money."

"You're serious, aren't you?"

"Why?"

"You're a mercenary sod. All you think about is money."

"Girls," Peter said, "all I think about is girls."

"Money and girls," George said.

"Are you reading that book with one eye closed?"

"Yes — I'm reading the left-hand pages with my right eye and the right-hand pages with my left eye. It's an exercise to help strengthen my resolve and fortitude."

"Jim hurt his eye," Peter suddenly remembered. "What about the inner path thing?"

"I've put that on hold — I'm not ready for it yet. The world isn't ready for it yet, either."

"Did you hear about me losing my job?"

"What happened?"

"They were all German and when they found out I was English, they fired me."

"The Germans don't hate the English," George said. "They never really did hate the English. The English are a bastard race, you know. Most of us already have German blood, not to mention French and Italian and goodness knows what else."

"They must be the same, then," Peter said. "They must all have English blood as well."

"No, no," George said patiently, "we didn't go out and root Europe, Europe came and rooted us."

Peter fell asleep that night while attempting to manoeuvre his Spitfire to get a good shot at the Messerschmitt, the pilot of which bore an uncanny resemblance to the white-haired man who had sacked him.

Chapter 23

A Crumbling World

The summer furnace drove them to the beaches in search of relief, but one day there were shark warnings all over the radio. Peter remembered the waterhole Redbanks and talked everyone into going there for a swim instead.

A few children splashed around at the far end of the waterhole, further confirming for Peter the safety of the place. He had put his togs on under his clothes before leaving home and undressed quickly, beating the others into the water with the biggest splash he could make. They dived, swam and splashed for more than an hour before Peter became aware of painful tingling sensations on various parts of his body. He thought small fish might be trying to nibble at him and threw his arms about in the water to ward them off. But the tingling continued. One of the children, who had been watching him, swam over and yelled, "Leeches!"

Horrified, Peter shot from the water and tried to wipe the black, slimy sucking things off with his hands but most of them refused to budge. "You've got to burn them off," the child said, "that's why we carry matches."

Peter dug a box of matches from his trousers pocket and Pauline worked quickly, burning off up to a dozen of the creatures, while Peter tried to appear unaffected by the appalling episode. Nobody else had been attacked by them, which didn't surprise Peter.

"I've found a new creature that likes me," he told George bitterly that afternoon. "Leeches — look at the red marks on me. Leeches like me as well as mosquitoes."

Doctors used to put leeches on people to suck out poison," George said, helpfully.

"They didn't go for anyone else," Peter said, "just me. I bet if we had gone to the beach, the sharks would have made a beeline for me."

"It's the price you pay for popularity," George pointed out. "Girls, mosquitoes and leeches — what more could a man ask for?"

Following his mother's bidding he dabbed a weak solution of Dettol on the blotches, following it up with copious quantities of the good old standby, calamine lotion. Calamine and Dettol were about the only medicinal substances carried in the Mitchell household, though there was always bicarbonate of soda and vinegar for use on various stings. Peter couldn't remember seeing anything in his St John handbook covering leeches.

February began as January had left off, so scorching that Peter wondered how anyone could work anyway. He left home early in the mornings and arrived back at teatime, tired and hot and still jobless. His money had finally disappeared and there were no more bottles to take back. The job at Port Adelaide had already gone by the time he arrived at the factory and he was interviewed for the Gawler position, in a small shop learning to make jewellery, but never heard back. They told him at the Labour Exchange that his first dole payment, when he received it, would be six weeks' worth — about £8.

He sat on the small shelf at the rear of the boilerhouse, next to Pauline who remained standing. She was close beside him, her arm touching the top of his shoulder. But she was like that — she always stayed close to him. He never really thought of their physical closeness as having any particular romantic significance. It was just her way: perhaps a need for security, despite her apparent independence, or the big brother she never had. He knew that she liked him and that he loved her, but he didn't know whether she actually loved him, though he allowed his mind to believe that she did.

"Any luck with a job?"

He sounded dismal, "I've been looking, but there just aren't any around. I might have something for a few weeks at a canning factory, though."

"Cheer up," Shirley said, "you'll get one."

"The chances aren't good," he said, catching Shirley's eyes in the gloom. She looked particularly attractive and happy and he looked away quickly when she smiled. He felt like a leper, being the only one of the crowd unemployed.

"Have you seen Chico?" he asked her.

"He should be here soon . . . Did you know I was moving?"

"No, I didn't."

"Dad's got a house at Henley Beach, through his work."

"It's nice there," Peter said. "We'll miss you."

"I'll be visiting," she smiled and melted his heart.

So he was losing her altogether, he thought. He had already lost her to Chico, but now she would drift out of his life for good, along with Chico. He thought suddenly of Debbie and Gayle; he had sort of lost them before even having the chance to know them properly. He would lose Bill and Caterina, too, and he wondered about the mostly absent Jim and he wondered about Pauline and if he would lose her and a familiar loneliness swept over him.

"I don't like being out of work," he said. "We were told there was plenty of work in Australia — that's why we came."

"That's why we came, too," Pauline said. "You'll get a job, so why worry?"

"Have you seen Bill?" he asked.

"He's coming as well," Shirley said.

"Are you all going to the dance or not?" He had found them in the boilerhouse, which was unusual on a Saturday night, obviously heavily involved in girl talk, judging by the way they fell silent at his appearance.

"We were just discussing our romances," Veronica said.

"And a certain other person's," Pauline added, without elaborating. They left the boilerhouse and entered the rec well before 8 o'clock yet there was already a good-sized crowd inside. Many of the people were strangers to Peter and he guessed there had been a new intake of immigrants: more British cattle for the Great Australian Stud Farm. There was no sign of Jim, but Peter, who had risked life and limb to wheedle ten shillings from George, was determined to enjoy himself. Pauline seemed to be in a romantic mood and danced close to him. Chico and

Shirley sat awkwardly together, looking as though they didn't know what to do with each other. Veronica was happily sharing a joke with Caterina and Peter caught her looking at him and Pauline on the dance floor, and he wondered whether she was talking about him. He hoped Caterina wasn't saying too much to Veronica.

Donna arrived with a bit of a swirl at the doorway, holding the arm of a bearded young man. She introduced him to them both in the middle of the dance floor and then took him to the table. His name was Ian and he was from New Zealand. Peter had never met a New Zealander before, but he looked like an Australian or Englishman anyway. And he thought it better not to pay much attention to him. He didn't want to precipitate any comment even slightly embarrassing from Donna. So she had found a man at last. Peter felt strangely relieved. He wished he knew what to do with Pauline. They were going steady, but it was really an arm's length thing. A bolder man would long ago have swept her off her feet. He wished he could hold her very tightly to him right now and kiss her long and passionately — like he used to do with Margie.

"How's your song going?" she interrupted his thoughts.

"My song?"

"The song you were writing."

"Oh, I'm still working on it. I think it's really good so far."

"Sing it tonight."

"I haven't finished it yet. And I can't even remember what I've written. I haven't done any music for it yet, either."

Over at the table Bill was sitting with his arm round Caterina and Chico and Shirley were just getting up to dance. Veronica was staring wistfully around the hall.

"It's hot in here," Peter said. "Let's go outside for a bit." She punched his shoulder and they carried on dancing. He suddenly wondered whether she was really dancing with him or with the man of her dreams. Like sometimes when he was dancing with someone he didn't really know he would imagine her to be Pauline or Margie or Wendy or Caterina or Shirley. He asked Veronica up to dance next — her wistful look having not been lost on him. They danced quite wide apart, of course, which was right and proper considering her age. But Veronica loved to dance and, he felt, she seemed to particularly love to dance with him. She probably felt safe with him, he guessed.

The ride home was uncomfortable and scary. Bill, who had insisted on giving him a lift, drove with one arm round Caterina while Peter sat in the back on his own. Chico roared past them and then zigzagged in front of the car as they approached Elizabeth, having obviously said his goodnight to Shirley. It was another balmy night for some.

"I had all these girlfriends," Peter told George, "and now they seem to be disappearing."

"You're better off without them," George said. "They only cramp your style. A guy of your age should be out with the boys not worrying about girls."

"I'm out with both," Peter retorted.

"It's your sex drive that's the problem," his brother said. "Control that and you'll be much happier. Take up sport if cold showers aren't working." Peter had heard it all before. He sprayed his room with the unwieldy pump sprayer before retiring for the night. "One flit and they're gone," said the radio advert. He sprayed several times to make sure there would be no mosquito dive-bombing when he went to bed.

He began his prayers immediately his head touched the pillow: Dear God, I'm sorry I haven't spoken to you for a while. I'm out of a job at the moment. Please don't let me lose all my friends again. I want them to be happy, but let there be room in their lives for me. Please bless everybody and Margie and Pauline. And if Shirley isn't happy with Chico, please send her back to me to look after and the same with Caterina. But please bless Bill and Chico and Donna. Help me to find a job soon, because I don't like being out of work and having no money. He fell asleep before his prayers could get any more complicated.

He surprised himself the next day by working on his song, thanks to the inspiring *Unchained Melody*, which played on the radio while he was eating breakfast. He found the sheet of paper on which he had made a start to the lyrics:

I'm lonely without you, so lonely
I write and you don't reply
That's why I'm lonely without you
That's why.
I catch a glimpse of your face
In every secret place
But shadows fall and hide you
That's why I'm lonely without you
That's why.

A strange excitement ran through him as he wrote:

Lonely Without You
By Peter Mitchell

I'm lonely without you, so lonely
I write and you don't reply
I'm lonely without you so lonely
Please tell me the reason why
Nothing can be the same
Oh, no, nothing ever the same
I'm lonely without you, lonely
Among the Salvation Jane
Picking Salvation Jane.
That's why I'm lonely without you
That's why.
I catch a glimpse of your face
And bluebells clutched to your breast
In every secret place I look
Only a glimpse of your face.
But shadows fall and nothing
And nothing is ever the same
Shadows fall and hide you
Among the Salvation Jane.
Shadows fall and hide you
Among the Salvation Jane.
One day I will try to find you
To hear your laughter again

And when I find you, when I do
The bluebells will bloom again.
Where now there is only Salvation Jane,
Bluebells will bloom again.

"What are you crying for?" George interrupted him. "Are you writing a silly love letter or something?"

"Of course not," Peter choked, grabbing his manuscript and fleeing to the bedroom.

The air was giddy with the sweet, cloying smell of peaches. A long line of mostly hostel and Elizabeth women sorted, stoned and steamed and skinned the fruit on a conveyer belt. Peter's job was to help the other men supply the women with full boxes of fruit and to keep the floor reasonably free of peach juice and skins. His pay was £8 ten shillings a week — a small fortune. The buses took nearly an hour and a half to get to the factory, stopping as they did to pick up people on the way. The Elizabeth people were dropped back at the town just before midnight.

It was stinking hot in the factory and the floor ran rivers of peach juice and skins as the evening progressed, defying his efforts to keep it clean. Sometimes he would be too slow with the crates of fruit and the supervisor, a large Germanic man, would smile kindly at him and say, "Get a move on, though". It was hard work but Peter didn't complain. He was too pleased to be working to complain. And the tasks weren't mentally demanding, so he was able to do what he liked doing best – dream. But it was hot, so stinking hot, and he felt drunk on the peach smell. And he wondered whether he would see out the entire season there.

He dreamed of England and of playing in the snow with Margie and the others. Dreaming of the snow made the heat almost bearable.

With his first week's pay he gave George some of the money he owed him and paid his mother £3 for board, keeping more than two pounds for himself. On Saturday night he went to the Salisbury Cafe with Bill, Chico, Shirley and Caterina and they drank cappuccinos and listened to the jukebox until closing time. He revelled in the sheer, simple enjoyment of being out with his friends, but wondered whether he really fitted in any more as they drove him to the corner of his street afterwards and tooted goodbye. While he walked the couple of hundred yards to his house, he realised that he must be getting in the way now the others were so romantically involved. They had called for him, and they seemed always pleased to see him, but how long would that last? He was definitely becoming a gooseberry.

It was difficult to believe that the weather could get any warmer, but it did. Stepping from his house reminded Peter of opening the oven door as a child to inspect the cake his mother was baking and singeing his eyelashes. It was that hot now — Peter would swear.

The canning factory was the very bowels of hell. He survived there first with his dreams of England and then by getting his men out of Earth orbit and discovering a new planet, Hosirus, circling Sirius, the Dog Star. A kindly king and queen ruled much of Hosirus, whose people spoke English, with a mediaeval accent. Peter's adventures on Hosirus revolved mainly round the royal couple's 16-year-old daughter — the beautiful Princess Nariana. Not only was his time taken up with wooing the Princess Nariana, but she managed to get herself into the most incredibly dangerous situations from which she needed constant rescuing. He wondered how she had survived before he and his men rocketed down from the heavens.

Many of the workers at the factory wore thick Wellington boots, which they called gumboots. Peter could not afford such a luxury and wore ordinary shoes. His one pair of trousers were constantly under siege from spillings and splashings of juice. During his second week of working in the factory, Peter put his trousers through the washing machine upon reaching home and the noise woke the rest of the house. Tired and irritable himself, he explained bitterly that there was no other time for him to wash them. They couldn't expect him to do it early in the morning. George said he should wash his trousers at the weekends, a suggestion that won approval from his parents. Peter hung the wet trousers out on the line overnight and pressed them the next morning. They came up looking wearable, though they acquired a velvety sheen, despite the use of a damp cloth under the iron. And they shrank about half an inch.

His trousers suffered more and more peach stains, but for peace in the household, he decided to wait until the weekend to wash them. For some reason, though, he never quite got round to it at the weekend. If his trousers acquired a sweet, sickly smell, nobody mentioned it.

The garment continued to soak up peach juice until one overbearingly hot night, they finally solidified. He took them off by lying on his back on the bed and lifting his legs into the air. Then he actually stood them up on their own on the bedroom floor. He was so excited about the phenomenon that he got George out of bed to have a look. "You can't wear those," George said, "you'll bring disgrace to the family."

Peter had nightmares that night about his trousers stalking the streets of Elizabeth on their own.

Feeling anything but refreshed the next morning, he nevertheless had to attempt to bring his trousers back to some semblance of wearability. He sprinkled in far too much Rinso, flicked the 'On' switch, and grumpily ate toast and marmalade while the machine hummed and crashed about its latest challenge. It took no time at all to dry them in the blast-furnace heat of another day. The trousers shrank a further two inches and while he waited for the canning factory bus, they solidified. He had to strap-hang all the way to the factory because his trousers were too stiff and tight for him to sit down and he was frightened of tearing them. That they didn't reach his ankles was the least of his worries — his crotch was suffering strangulation.

On the Wednesday of his fourth week at the factory, he skidded in the peach juice and fell heavily, smashing his elbow into the concrete floor. He lay there in silent agony until the supervisor and some of the women helped him to his feet. Pale and shaken, he clutched his elbow which had swollen up like a balloon, and everything swirled dizzily around him and he almost fainted. They told him to have a few days off and to see a doctor in case anything was broken.

The doctor didn't think anything was broken when Peter presented his blue and green elbow to him the next day. He gave him some clear, liquid-glass like ointment to rub on it regularly. "It will turn even more vivid colours than that before it starts getting better," he told Peter. "When it starts turning yellow, it will be on the road to recovery."

As well as using the ointment, Peter packed the elbow with ice and some of the swelling went down. That night he tried to fix up his bike which had a buckled wheel among other maladies but finally he kicked one of the spokes in and walked to the hostel, pulling his trousers ridiculously down past his hips so they wouldn't look quite so short, and bringing immense relief to his groin. He sat with great care in the armchair at Pauline's. They were surprised but pleased to see him and they didn't blame him for taking the night off when he showed them his elbow. They told him there was a rock and roll dance on at the Presbyterian Church Hall the next night, a Friday, and they wanted him to take them if he wasn't working.

He had no trousers to wear to the dance and his parents had no money to spare that particular week. However, his mother promised he could buy new clothes the next week. He couldn't get anything on time payment until then because nobody had the time to go into a shop and sign as guarantor for him. So he borrowed a pair of George's old trousers and stitched the turn-ups a couple of inches higher, which left them only a bit long. They were too loose around the waist, but he tightened his belt and decided they would have to do. George said he couldn't borrow his newer ones in case he decided to go to the dance himself.

Luckily for Peter, George did go. The hall was packed with teenagers. Bill and Chico were there with Caterina and Shirley. Donna was there with Ian who was the oldest person on the dance floor. Peter rolled up his shirt sleeve and showed off his elbow, and Shirley said she felt faint.

A "toughie" called Stone, who had moved into the town about the same time as Peter, was also present that night. Peter normally made himself invisible when anywhere near people like Stone. But the youth sat only two chairs away and was paying undue attention to Pauline. Peter got Pauline up to dance and hoped Stone would disappear or find someone else to annoy by the time they got back. As they danced past the foyer exit, a youth from Salisbury wearing cowboy clothes, whom Peter had seen around the shops a couple of times, swaggered over to them and asked in an almost American Wild West accent: "Hey, pardner, who's Stone?"

"The chap in the red shirt," Peter said, pointing across the hall.

"I hear he's reckoned to be the toughest guy in these parts," the youth drawled.

"I think he's fairly tough," Peter warned him.

"Go and tell him I want to see him outside," the youth ordered.

"Go and tell him yourself," Pauline snapped. "If you're so tough, you tell him."

The youth hesitated only momentarily before tucking his thumbs into his belt and swaggering across the dance floor. Peter and Pauline danced quickly over to where Stone was telling the youth in a strong Scottish accent that he had promised not to cause any trouble because the girls didn't like violence. Peter thought Stone sounded as genuine as Scotch mist.

The youth persisted: "If you're as tough as you think you are, why not come outside to prove it?"

"Why should I? What's your argument with me feller?" Stone didn't sound a bit scared.

"There's only room for one tough guy around here — and I reckon that's me."

With a sigh of exaggerated weariness, Stone rose and accompanied the youth outside, followed by everybody else in the hall, except George, who carried on dancing with a girl Peter didn't know. Stone took about four minutes to dispose of Billy the Kid who, vanquished, bruised and bleeding, disappeared into the night. Stone, playing up to his audience, loudly proclaimed that if there was anyone else who wanted to take him on they could step forward. Nobody did. They all filed back into the hall as the bemused reverend who had organised the dance, held the door open for them. They couldn't get quite the same seats, but Peter sat down next to Pauline and Veronica sat the other side of her sister. Peter's elbow was hurting and he wasn't quite thinking straight, which was probably why he had sat in Stone's seat.

"Shift yourself," Stone said, looming over him suddenly.

Normally, Peter would have apologised and moved just for the sake of peace, but he didn't want Stone sitting next to Pauline. So instead he simply said "no", as his face drained of colour.

"Fuck off," Stone said.

"I'm staying here," Peter said.

"Fuck off or come outside."

"I can't fight you — I've hurt my elbow."

"Then shove off."

Peter glanced around the hall, hoping to catch George's eye or even the attention of Chico or Bill. He didn't know what to do. He doubted that his elbow would stand up to a fight. And he would certainly need both arms working to protect himself against Stone. Reluctantly, he stood up. "There you are then, I don't want any trouble." He turned to Pauline and Veronica, "Let's go and squeeze in with Bill and Chico."

"Don't take the girls away," Stone said, sitting down, "because then I'll get really upset."

"We want to join our friends over there," Peter said meekly, wishing he could be more assertive. Live or die, he could imagine what Jim would have said to Stone.

"Then you go, and leave them here," Stone's voice was getting quieter and meaner. "I could fuckin' do you for dinner."

"We're going anyway," Pauline said, "we can sit where we like."

"I'm taking them with me," Peter said.

"You're coming outside," said Stone.

"All right," Peter gasped, "let's go."

The hall emptied again and everyone stood in a large, silent circle around Peter and Stone. Peter realised that if he beat Stone in a fight, he would win fame in Elizabeth. He had always wanted to be famous, but his elbow was hurting like hell now.

Bill came up to Stone and said, "He's a mate of mine, Stone, let's go back inside."

"Fuck off!" Stone said, and then to Peter, "I'll give you one chance — you apologise in front of all these people and I'll forget it."

"I don't owe you an apology," Peter said as casually as he could, "you started this, you owe the girls an apology. You know I've got a sore arm. How brave are you fighting someone who's been injured?"

"He needs to be taught a lesson," Stone said to the assembled onlookers. "And I saw him up dancing and waving his arm around, now he says he cannot fight because his arm is hurt."

"He has hurt his arm actually," George said, stepping forward. "He fell and damaged it at work."

"Who the fuck are you?" Stone said.

George spoke low, so low that those nearby had to strain their ears to catch what he said, "I, my friend, will be your nemesis if you don't leave my brother alone."

"Oh, yes?" said Stone, puzzled.

George again spoke, even more softly, "I don't want to embarrass you in front of everybody, so shall we all go in?" Peter shivered at the deadliness in George's voice and he fancied that the same shiver ran through the crowd.

Stone obviously possessed a strong survival instinct. He suddenly turned to Peter and extended his hand. Peter shook it thankfully, if painfully.

"I don't want to fight this guy while he's injured — let's get on with the dance before the police come and close the place." There were murmurs of assent from the throng and everyone again filed into the hall. Peter was relieved that George had rescued him and relieved that he hadn't mentioned his trousers.

Peter woke the next morning to find George fixing his punchbag on to the ceiling of his bedroom.

"Why are you doing that?" Peter asked.

"Because I keep banging into it in my room."

"Won't I keep banging into it?"

"Not if you're careful," George said.

At the end of March the nightmare of the canning factory came to an end for Peter and most of the other casual workers. A few people were kept back to help with maintenance but they were all local country folk. So he was once more unemployed, and he hadn't saved a penny.

Autumn threw its gorgeous gold and russet-brown cloak over the City of Adelaide, revealing to the north a sight of breathtaking beauty as the many deciduous trees played out their final glorious act before shedding their leaves. Peter's eyes bathed in the city's beauty, allowing it to fire the romantic kindling within.

There were still few jobs around, but Peter was lucky. One of Bill's friends was the foreman of a roof tile factory near Dry Creek and he got Peter employment there. It was a marvellous job. He had to oil the metal plate moulds before they went on to a circular table to be filled with cement, squeezed and heated into tiles. It paid an incredible £11 ten shillings a week and wonderful pop music blared out at the workers all day. The men worked at breathtaking pace; but Peter, driven by the music and calling on his physical fitness, soon found a rhythm that enabled him to keep up with them on the circular table. They told him he was the fastest oiler they had ever had. There were always piles of freshly made tiles for the big trucks to reload with each morning.

The teenage population of Elizabeth swelled. Britain, which had lost the cream of its youth and been brought to its knees financially by two world wars, was inexplicably unloading a new generation of young people into its former colony.

More and more teenagers joined the Elizabeth gang. There were more girls to smile shyly at and more boys to converse with. One night, Mrs Mitchell expressed concern when six carloads of teenagers drew up outside the house; though they had pulled up in comparative silence because of the seemingly ever-present police car tailing them.

There were so many friends to go out with now and so many things to do, Peter found himself visiting the hostel less frequently. The Elizabeth gang began organising Sunday trips away to Morialta Falls, in the Adelaide Hills, and once to the holiday resort of Victor Harbour. The trip to Victor Harbour ended before any swimming or adventures could begin, because when they got there, more than thirty of them, they were told to turn around and go home by an overzealous police officer. They had not caused trouble, nor were they looking to, but the police state had its way. The young people read the newspapers, and caught trains and buses and knew the state was being run by pompous asses in uniform — and out of uniform if you counted some of the magistrates and politicians.

Morialta became a favourite visiting place, despite its popularity at weekends with family groups. The teenagers spent whole days there — tramping, picnicking and climbing craggy cliffs before heading home tired yet sated.

An unspoken code forbade romance within the gang. But the code could not last forever and it did not stop Peter from falling secretly in love with a couple of the girls. It was a long time before he realised that the other boys must have had secret loves and desires too.

Peter had money and wore good clothes again because his mother had been true to her word and opened a time-payment account for him. He was deliriously happy with his lot. So happy that he suffered with good grace being woken each morning to the sound of George thumping hell out of the punchbag that swung crazily over the foot of Peter's bed. He even forgot about England for much of the time and kept forgetting to write to Margie. He found only a couple of spare nights through that winter to visit Pauline, who had at last moved with her family to a house in Elizabeth North, and he put down to his imagination the feeling that she no longer seemed to be quite so pleased to see him. She never joined the gang, so he didn't think it was his fault that he saw her only rarely. But she was just about always on his mind when he was away from the gang and he was sure he still loved her.

Chapter 24

A Car at Last

He put money regularly into his tin box, but little of it stayed there for more than a week. Some of the crowd were heavily into Mantovani and pop songs, while others were just as heavily into jazz, so Peter tried to buy a mixture of records. He still relied on Bill or some of the others for transport. How would he ever afford a car of his own?

One Friday night, Peter took time off from his friends to go with George and a couple of neighbours to the Gawler harness racing track. He had never been to a race meeting before, nor was he particularly interested in horse racing of any kind. However, being invited out by George was an honour he had to accept. He had been paid that afternoon so had plenty of money. George told him not to go mad with his wages, reminding him that the next pay day was a full week away.

Peter was immediately caught up in the race-night atmosphere. He thrilled at the sight of bookmakers displaying tempting odds under their colourful umbrellas and at the peculiar antics of the tic-tac men.

He was too young to bet and looked it, so he gave George ten shillings to wager on a horse whose name he liked in the first race. It started at odds of twelve to one and stayed in sixth place all the way. George told him with smug satisfaction that he should have bet on the favourite. Peter chose the rank outsider in the second race — a ten-year-old grey mare — because he felt sorry for it. In a show of bravado he gave George £3 and asked him to wager it for a win only — "on the nose". George told him he was wasting his money but put the bet on for him, securing odds of thirty-three to one. The ticket would be worth over £100, including his original stake back, if the horse won.

Peter had never forgotten the time his father won the football pools in England, nor the excitement in the household at the prospect of untold riches. The plans made for the future, including a "we'll see" half-promise to buy him an astronomical telescope, which he felt would go very nicely with the newly dreamed of mansion and its ever-so-high attic roof in Gloucestershire. But dreams crashed with the news that just about everybody else had won the pools that week and the dividend was a mere £8 and not the hoped for riches. Peter remembered that disappointment vividly when he saw the sum scribbled on his betting ticket and he remembered his mother saying, "Dreams are for dreamers". So as the race started he gave George his ticket to hold for him and went off to buy a hotdog with lashings of tomato sauce and deliberately blotted out the words of the race commentary by humming to himself and thinking of other things. He got back to the others to find George tearing a ticket into tiny shreds and singing *The Old Grey Mare She Aint What She Used To Be*". Peter philosophically reached for more money to bet with.

"Yours won," George said, "led all the way. The others must have been drugged. I'm sure mine was drugged or the driver is a crook or both." Peter was rich. He gambled a little on the other races and won a further £20 as well as ending the night with his wages intact.

Bill and Chico took him round the saleyards to choose a car. Peter had gone through a bit of soul-searching with them beforehand. He had enough money to return to England with some to spare. He could stay there and work until Margie was old enough to travel back to Australia with him. She would join the gang and they would get married and she would be his forever. But the pragmatic Bill pointed out the obvious to him.

"First of all your parents might not let you go. Second, it will take you years to save enough money to bring yourself back here, never mind the two of you. But that's all right because it will take you years to win the hearts of parents who find some spotty-faced twit suddenly turning up on their doorstep with the intention of whisking their daughter, who I believe is still at school, to the other side of the world."

"I haven't got spots," Peter said.

"No, but you are a twit," Bill and Chico said in unison.

"And," Bill continued, "how do you know the Australian Government will even let you back into the country. You got here on your father's skills. You are unskilled. And you would be an adult by then, and, by the way, there might not be any gang by then, either. Think of the fun you will have missed."

"Another thing," Chico put in with a measure of his own blunt wisdom, "a car is far more important than a trip to England."

Peter scraped up £140 for the car plus two £5 notes he secreted at the back of his wallet so he wouldn't be broke when he bought it. A total of £150 had him feeling quite light-headed.

They spent most of the Saturday inspecting English and American models. Peter was pleased his friends were with him, because he might have been talked into buying the first car he saw had he been alone. The salesmanship was high pressure and it fell to Bill to fend it off.

"They could sell me a fridge in the Arctic," Peter admitted.

"They do their training selling fridges to Eskimos," Bill said. By mid-afternoon, though, all three agreed on a 1950 Chevrolet, in excellent condition except for a large dent in the rear. But the price was too high for Peter at £200, including a tankful of petrol.

The salesman winked at Peter and said, "It's even got layback seats." And added that he was virtually giving it away because he had been young himself once and knew what it was like trying to find a decent car. Bill said he didn't think they had invented cars in those days, which made the man laugh.

"I'm not that old you cheeky prick," he told Bill, but with humour. Peter was pleased the man had a sense of humour because he was about twice the size of Bill.

"Could you knock the price down?" Bill asked unabashed.

Peter shuffled his feet nervously and gazed with feigned interest at a car about twenty yards away.

"Knock the price down? This is a steal at two hundred," the man wore a look of practised astonishment. "Where would you get a car like this for two hundred?"

Bill shrugged, "It's just a bit expensive for what he wants — he isn't loaded with riches."

The man turned to Peter, "You can't afford this car?"

"Not quite."

"No," Bill interrupted firmly, "he's only just got himself a job and his parents haven't much money. They're just poor immigrants."

The man grabbed his chest in mock anguish, "shall I play the violin for you now, sport?"

"Play the bloody violin if you want," Bill told him, "we'll go and look somewhere else."

The man scratched his head. "How much can you afford, Pete?"

Peter wasn't sure what Bill might want him to say. "I suppose . . . A hundred and forty," Bill interrupted. "It's all the money he's got and he can't get into debt."

The man turned on Bill, "Is your name Pete as well?"

"No, my name's Bill."

"I can't bring the price down that much, but," he slapped his hands together and the noise cracked through the car yard, "all right, you can have the car for a hundred and eighty."

"He hasn't got that much," Bill persisted.

Peter wished Bill would shut up. His friend had succeeded in bringing the price down and he felt he could talk his parents into signing up for a loan to pay the rest. He was worried that the man might get annoyed and walk away from the deal. He knew he shouldn't show it, but Peter now wanted that car more than anything else in the world.

The man stepped back and looked long and hard at Bill, "Why don't you lend him the money — you're his friend aren't you?"

"I've only got a few quid on me," said Bill. "I'm a poor immigrant as well."

"Zing-zing-zing-zing," said the man, playing an invisible violin. He turned to Chico, "What about you — can you lend your cobber some money?"

"I'm even worse off," Chico said, "I'm an Australian."

"I know what you mean," the man grinned. And then, "Okay, you can have the car for a hundred and sixty cash with no tankful of gas and only because you're holding me up from other customers."

"A hundred and fifty," said Bill, and Peter's heart sank.

"You're a bloody burglar," the man snorted. "Just to finish this daylight robbery — a hundred and fifty-five."

"Done," said Bill.

Peter felt giddy.

His friends scraped up £10 of the extra £15 needed, telling Peter when he magically produced the two £5 notes from the back of his wallet to keep £5 for petrol and oil and "whatever".

While Peter went to the office to complete the sale, the man took Bill to one side for a private word.

Bill and Chico followed Peter back to Elizabeth in case there were any problems, but the car ran sweetly all the way.

"What a marvellous shagging wagon," Bill said when they had stopped at the Elizabeth shops. He was running his hands lovingly over the soft leather seats in the back. Peter was still in a state of euphoria and only dimly heard him.

"He got offered a job," Chico said, pointing his thumb at Bill. "Good money, too, by the sound of things."

"Good money if I sell cars," Bill put in. "I'm not sure I should take it. At least what I'm doing now is fairly safe."

Peter thought wistfully of his own former "safe" job on the building site. "I thought my job was safe. I thought I was going to be a carpenter."

"You still can be," Bill said. "You can be anything you want to be if you want it badly enough."

"It's not that easy," Peter and Chico said.

Bill shrugged, "I never said it was easy. Who wants easy? Where's the challenge in easy?"

"Easy come, easy go, as my mother would say," Peter gave him a grin.

"Your mother's right," Bill said.

"I want to be a writer," Peter sounded dreamy. "I want to write songs and books. Songs that everyone can sing to and the kind of books that make people feel sad to have turned the last page. Or even a journalist — a war correspondent maybe, getting out the news to millions of people."

"You don't want much," Chico told him. "I was hoping to be a motor mechanic."

"You have to experience life before you can become a good writer," Bill said. "You have to write about life as you have tasted it. All the good books I've read . . . you can tell the authors have been there."

"You have to have been there and done that," Chico put in.

"What about Carter Brown, Mickey Spillane and Agatha Christie?" Peter smiled.

"But they have experienced life, too," Bill said. "You can tell that. Where do you think they draw their characters from?"

"From life — you're right," Peter agreed. And how could he, living in his dream world most of the time, ever hope to draw on his experiences of life? Didn't he deliberately protect himself from them? "You're right," he repeated.

That weekend he leafed through a song book for an address and posted his song off to a music publisher in the United States. He was to wait expectantly for several weeks and then hopefully for several months, but he never heard back.

His mother once told him that money could never buy happiness, though she had added wryly that she wouldn't mind the chance to find out for certain. Money had bought Peter his car. And his car was pure happiness. No more did he have to run for the train in the mornings, nor suffer the embarrassment of having a kindly train driver wait for his just appearing figure while hundreds of faces pressed curiously and impatiently against the windows wondering why he didn't run faster.

His standing in the gang rose considerably. He was immediately more important and useful. He could now help to chauffeur some of the carless members and they included lots of girls whose pay did not stretch to such grandiose dreams as having an automobile of their own. They liked the style and the comfort and security of a car, did the girls. His responsibilities increased, too. If you were a car owner you could be sent to buy hamburgers or drinks or be the one to deliver petrol to a friend's empty tank. Not that you could phone any of the gang if your car broke down or it ran out of gas. Telephones were a luxury most of the people of Elizabeth had yet to indulge in. Messages of such nature were usually carried on two feet. He had been so busy since buying his car that it was fully a fortnight before he got round to visiting Pauline.

"Hiya, stranger," she yelled from a window as he turned into her driveway. "Nice car."

"Thought you might like to go for a drive," he muttered, feeling his face warming up. He got out and opened the front passenger door as she emerged.

"Where did this come from?"

"Just a bit of a windfall," Peter brushed it off. He didn't want to tell her he had won money at the races. A fool and his money . . . "Do you like it?"

"Of course — it's very nice."

He was about to tell her it had layback seats but thought better of it.

He drove her several miles west to the town of Two Wells and they sat on the top of an old farm gate chatting about work and the latest happenings. And when Pauline spoke of work, he found himself waiting half expectantly. He had the vague impression that she wanted to tell him something. But his expectancy disappeared when she wriggled precariously closer to him and said, "Guess who's going to Melbourne." She didn't wait for an answer, "Caterina and Bill."

"No they're not," he said, in disbelief. "Wherever did you hear that?"

"Shirley told me. Caterina's parents are moving to Melbourne and Bill has got a transfer through the company he works for."

Peter was stunned, "I wonder why he didn't say anything. The last I heard he had been offered a job in a car yard."

"Perhaps he is working out how to. Shirley said Caterina cried her eyes out when she was telling her."

"Why is she going if she doesn't want to?"

Pauline turned her face to him and the gate creaked ominously. "I suppose she would rather stay here with her but doesn't want to leave her parents yet. Or, more precisely, her parents don't want to leave her behind. Your parents wouldn't leave you behind, would they?"

"Not wouldn't — didn't," Peter said. "I wish they had, though. Well, I used to wish that, now . . . I'm not sure."

"Sometimes you sound like a boy and at other times you sound like an old man," she said.

"'Tis folly to be wise," Peter said.

"And you're very strange."

"I know, I'm a lunatic."

"Caterina should get a job in a Melbourne hospital," Pauline said distantly. "I bet she would stay if Bill refused to go."

"This is really bad news," Peter said. "Bill is one of my best friends, so is Caterina. What's Chico doing?"

"From what I can gather, Chico plans to board at Shirley's in Henley Beach. They have a spare room."

Peter frowned, "You knew that I didn't know anything about this — how?"

"Because," Pauline said.

"Because what?"

"Because you're not supposed to know."

"Who said?"

"Shirley said that Caterina said that Bill said he wanted to tell you himself."

They now sat close to each other on the gate. She pressed hard against him. Pauline's news had swept him with a new loneliness and he had the sudden urge to draw her to him. As his arm went to her shoulders she jerked her face round to look at him. He thought about kissing her a second before the gate collapsed and they both sprawled laughing in the paddock.

Peter was starving by the time he reached home, but would have swallowed his food in double-quick time anyway. He had to get to Bill's place and confirm that the news was true. And would Chico be stuck at Shirley's in Henley, where Peter would rarely see him? Perhaps he should visit Chico first.

Shirley was at the Baglianos. Both she and Chico were in high spirits. "What's all this bad news I've been hearing?" he asked them. "We'll have no friends left the way things are going."

"They're off to Melbourne in about four weeks," Shirley replied. "But Chico is staying here."

"I am," Chico agreed. "Bill says he will come back and see us as often as he can."

"It's a long way to travel," Peter said. He put his hands in his pockets and surveyed them with an air of importance. "What brought it all on?"

"It's a big job for Dad," Chico grimaced, "general manager. But Bill and Caterina should stay — I reckon they have their own lives to lead."

Peter nodded his agreement. "And what about you — moving to Henley?" Chico grinned shyly and hugged Shirley, "If you had arrived an hour earlier you would have heard me propose to my darling here."

A strange thrill of terror ran through Peter. He forced a smile, "That's wonderful — that's marvellous news."

Shirley looked grim, "How do you know I accepted?"

Then she smiled gorgeously and extended her left hand, "Do you like my ring?"

He gazed hypnotically at the large, shining stone mocking him from the cluster of smaller diamonds. They were a girl's best friend. His mother had never said that. Diamonds were forever . . . forever and ever, amen.

"It's beautiful," he breathed. "Congratulations both of you." Then he blushed.

"We haven't decided on a date for the party yet," Chico said. "But I thought we might combine it with Caterina and Bill's farewell."

Shirley screwed her face up. "That sounds too sad. We want to have a happy party."

Peter agreed, "You don't want tears at your engagement."

Chico persisted, "I think a combined party is a good idea and it would save money — after all, I haven't got any, especially after buying the ring."

Shirley took his hand, "Let's discuss it later."

Peter felt quite depressed by the time they reached Bill's house. Why was everything changing so quickly? Why couldn't these precious times be kept cocooned, safe from time and change? If only things could stay like they were forever. There was that loneliness again, dogging his footsteps, never far away, always waiting to pounce.

Caterina looked out of place in the kitchen helping to dry the dishes. He would definitely dry the dishes for her, or rather, one of the servants would, if she married him. She would never have to do housework if she didn't want to, because the servants would do it. But Caterina had no idea how famous and wealthy he was going to be. And that was her fault — she had never asked him.

"You've just missed tea," Bill told them.

"Had some, thanks," Chico replied, turning to Peter. "Have you eaten?"

Peter patted his stomach, "Like a train."

"You mean like a horse," Bill said.

Peter frowned, "I think it's 'you could eat a horse', not 'eat like a horse'."

"Then you ate like a pig," Bill said.

"I'm too well-mannered for that," Peter said.

"Do we gather that you're not hungry?" Caterina put in.

"Yes," said Peter.

"Yes, you're hungry?" asked Bill.

"No," Peter grinned, "I'm not hungry." His spirits rose.

They sat in the lounge and listened to records. Johnny Ray sang *Please Mr Sun* and Peter thought of Margie. Then Max Bygraves sang *Heart of My Heart* and he remembered that Bill and Caterina would be leaving them and he hadn't even mentioned it yet.

"There seems to be a song for every occasion," he said above the music. "So you and Caterina are leaving us?"

Bill rose from the settee and went over to Peter. They shook hands silently and awkwardly.

Peter tried to clear his throat, "I'll . . . we'll really miss you both. The gang won't be the same without you two."

Then the Jimmy Young song *Too Young* ran through his head. "Too young, he blurted, "Too young to really be in love."

"Not us," Bill chirped. "We're not too young — are we Cat?"

She turned her smouldering eyes on Peter, "Love has nothing to do with age."

Peter cringed, "I didn't mean you two," he explained hastily, "I was just musing."

Chico laughed, "You do a lot of that."

"What a stupid word," Shirley said, "What does it mean?"

"It's like thinking, I think," Chico replied with a frown.

"It's like half-thinking," Peter said.

Caterina smiled, "Peter Mitchell definitely does a lot of half-thinking, don't you Peter?"

"No muse is good muse," Bill intervened, earning a slap from Caterina. Her hand caught the comb in his jacket top pocket and she began restyling his hair with it.

"It doesn't matter how old you are," Peter was unable to quite let the matter rest, "it's whether you're in love that counts."

Caterina turned her eyes on him again, "That's what I said."

"I'm going out with Cat for her money," Bill said, trying to duck a sudden twist of the comb. "Hey, leave my hair alone, will you," he yelled, covering his head with both hands.

"You've got knots in your hair," Caterina scolded, but she left Bill and crossed the room to work on Peter's hair instead. He let her tease and comb it. Bill got up and put on *Unchained Melody*, which started Shirley and Chico off snogging.

An evening such as this was sublime happiness, but Peter knew it must all end one day. Everybody would drift off into marriage and lives of their own. And with all the romance going around these days, it might not be long in happening.

Not only did Chico get the engagement-farewell he wanted, it turned out to be a double engagement-farewell. Bill popped the question too.

Both girls looked stunning. Caterina wore a russet English tweed suit with a high-necked white blouse and red cravat, which emphasised her dark eyes and black hair now cut to just reach her gold gipsy earrings. The ever-smiling Shirley appeared in a lemon dress which finished a little above the knee in ruffles of white petticoat. A white mohair stole clung to her shoulders under cascades of shimmering honey-blond hair. Most of the other girls wore colourful dresses or skirts finishing demurely above the knee in ruffles upon ruffles of white, pink and yellow petticoats which swirled and crackled as they danced.

Peter arrived with Pauline, Veronica and Lisa. A mature-looking Donna and Ian were among the sixty guests.

Veronica sat in the corner with Lisa for much of the evening. Both wore a touch of make-up, but were dressed soberly compared with the older girls. The favourite record of the evening was *Party Doll*, with *Peggy Sue*, *Rainbow* and *Too Young to Go Steady* also played more than once. Caught up in the enchantment of the evening, Peter found himself wondering whether he could summon enough courage to ask Pauline to marry him. He drank a lot of beer early and then switched to lemonade and ate plenty of food. He wanted to be reasonably sober when the time came to take the three girls home and he wanted to be able to walk the white line if picked up by the police. The beer helped his nerve but it didn't stop him worrying about how he would handle the embarrassment should Pauline decline his proposal.

In fact, the worry of being embarrassed kept him from proposing, though the idea of it stayed heavily somewhere in his chest as though he had swallowed a large chunk of newly baked bread. He didn't kiss her goodnight when he came to a halt outside her home in the early hours of the next day. Yet as he held the car door open and Pauline got out, she squeezed his arm and whispered, "Goodnight dreamy".

So Bill and Caterina went to Melbourne. Peter was to see them only once more — when they returned for a weekend some months later for Chico and Shirley's wedding at the Salisbury Catholic Church. Chico looked uncomfortable in his charcoal grey suit, white stiff-collared shirt and pale blue tie. Shirley was radiant in her white wedding dress and whisp of a veil. The bridesmaids, Veronica and Lisa, charmed the gathering in red and tangerine taffeta and silk. Bill was best man and Peter, groomsman. Peter had scoured the shops for a gift within his budget. He ended up buying them an ornate spice rack but wished it could have been more. At the reception, Chico spoke of his plans to seek out a good job in Perth, where workers were urgently needed, and perhaps one day buy a house there.

As the bride and groom were about to depart for their honeymoon at Victor Harbour, Peter shook hands with a very nervous Chico and gruffly wished him all the best for the future and then he accidentally kissed Shirley on the nose and told her everyone would miss her.

He never saw them again, but heard a year or so after the wedding that they had moved to Melbourne and were flatting near Bill and Caterina, who had themselves recently tied the knot in a quiet ceremony at a Melbourne Catholic church. Peter meant to send all four of them a letter or a card, but he never got round to finding out their addresses.

Chapter 25

The Snowman

He sat in his car at the shopping centre one Monday night, just waiting in the hope that even one of the gang might come by. It was a night-school night for some and a night for staying home for those wishing to avoid a curfew later in the week. Monday could be a boring night for Peter. He was toying with the idea of calling on Pauline, who would probably be ironing or washing or thinking of an early night, when a police car sidled alongside and a torch was shone into his face.

"Good evening officer," he called, screwing his face up.

"Mitchell," the policeman said without inflection.

"Yes, officer?"

The policeman got out, banging his door against Peter's car. "Why are you hanging around here?"

"Waiting for some friends, sir."

"Just waiting for some friends?"

"Yes, sir."

The tall, thickset man shone his torch into Peter's car and studied the dashboard before shining it into the back. Then he switched off the torch. "There's been a lot of hooliganism around here lately, Mitchell. You wouldn't know anything about it would you?"

"No sir, we don't cause trouble."

The officer stood back against the patrol car and studied him. Peter waited with bated breath.

"Why are you waiting for your friends?"

"I'm sorry," Peter was genuinely puzzled, "I don't know what you mean."

"Isn't that a simple question?" The officer bent to gaze into Peter's face, his peaked hat scraping ominously against the metal of the boy's car. "It's a very simple question: why are you waiting for your friends?"

"Because I want to," Peter gasped at last

"Now you're being cheeky," the officer snarled. "Don't be smart. I'll give you one more chance: why are you waiting for your friends?"

In the long silence that followed, Peter felt the first tear trickle down his cheek and nestle between his lips. He licked away the salty taste and had a sudden urge to swear at the officer and get it over with. Instead, in quivering voice, he said, "I'm sorry . . . I just don't know how to answer."

The officer's voice was softer, "Why don't you go and call for your friends instead of hanging around here where you are going to get into trouble?"

"All right," Peter said, daring to feel relieved.

The officer straightened himself. "You're too good to be true, Mitchell. We'll be keeping an eye on you. In the meantime, don't be here when we come back or you might get a ride in the patrol car."

"Yes, sir," Peter gulped.

He watched the car move away with the two men inside laughing over some shared joke. He had heard about the police car "rides". Peter wasn't sure what happened on them, but he was sure that he never wanted to find out. He started his car engine and switched on the lights, knowing that the policemen would keep checking their rear-vision mirrors until they had turned out of sight. Nevertheless, he was going to wait as long as he dared before leaving — just to get back at them. He lit a cigarette and wondered how the officer had known his name.

A girl walked out of the delicatessen. Despite the coolness of the evening she wore short-shorts and a thin white blouse knotted at her bare waist. Her auburn hair fell in waves to her shoulders and he didn't need broad daylight to know her pleasant, open face was covered in freckles. He sucked in a deep breath, having hardly breathed since the arrival of the police. She stopped beside his car and delicately tore the wrapping from an iceblock. Nothing ventured, nothing gained, hadn't his mother said?

"You must be freezing," he called.

"Hello." She allowed a touch of surprise in her voice.

"Aren't you cold?"

She took a couple of licks of the iceblock, "It's not exactly tropical." Her cultured private-school-for-girls accent with just the merest touch of Old London Town, made him want to say something intelligent and wise. "Are you new here?" he asked.

"About a fortnight," she replied. "Tell me, are you the only boy in this place?"

"Yes," Peter heard himself say. "It gets quite lonely sometimes." The song *If You Were the Only Girl in the World* popped into his head.

"What about you," she asked, "have you been here long?"

"About a century," Peter said.

"Thought so."

"Errrmm," said Peter.

"Spit it out," she said.

"Pardon?"

"Spit it out. Daddy says that if you have something to say, you should say it." With an exasperated air she threw the partly licked iceblock into the litterbin. "Didn't much care for that," she said.

"Do you want to come for a ride?" Peter blurted out. "We could go to the Salisbury Cafe."

"Sounds exciting," she said, "the Salisbury Cafe."

"Well, we could go anywhere you want," he gasped.

"The Salisbury Cafe sounds fine. I was dying to go somewhere — and if you are the only boy in town, then whither thou goest . . ."

Peter got out and opened the passenger door for her.

"I'm Dianne Hodges."

"Pleased to meet you — I'm Peter Mitchell, and I'm not really the only guy in town."

"I didn't really think you were." She smiled, "Pleased to meet you, too."

He liked her, but found her terrifying for no good reason. Pauline was sometimes scary, Shirley used to make him nervous, he was sometimes awkward with the girls in the gang and Donna was a pain. Dianne terrified him. He got back into the driver's seat and started the car up with a roar but drove off slowly in case the police were in the vicinity.

She read his thoughts, "I saw the police talking to you."

"Oh, that . . . it's a bit of a nuisance, but my father is a nuclear scientist at Weapons Research. The police check on us now and then, you know . . . Russian spies and all that."

He jumped a foot off his seat as she screamed, "Daddy is a nuclear scientist there as well." Then disappointment edged her voice, "No one has been to check on us, though."

"They will," he assured her, "just wait and see."

Mercifully, she changed the subject, "Where are you from?"

"Birmingham," he tried to say it without an accent. "You?"

"Oxford."

"And Cambridge," he said automatically.

"No," she laughed, "just Oxford."

Suddenly she jerked upright in her seat, again startling Peter, "I know who you are," there was wonderment in her voice, "you're the Snowman."

"Not me," Peter said, turning the car sharply into Salisbury.

"Peter Mitchell." She said it softly, as though talking to herself. "That's right — you're the one they call the Snowman."

He laughed, "Who told you that?"

"A girl I work with — Pauline. She lives in Elizabeth North."

"Pauline's my . . . I know Pauline," Peter said, "but she's never called me that — what does it mean?"

"Who knows, who cares about a nickname."

"I don't," Peter replied.

He was a sobbing eight-year-old being comforted by his mother because a gang of kids had been taunting him and calling him Goldilocks. 'Sticks and stones will break my bones but names will never hurt me', his mother told him.

"Sticks and stones," he muttered as he brought his car to a halt outside the cafe.

"I hope I haven't upset you," Dianne sounded concerned.

"I'm not sure if my father is actually working on nuclear things," Peter told her as they sipped their coffee. "Something to do with rockets — like the Blue Streak and Bloodhound."

"Do you think they will ever get one to go to a planet?" Her voice was serious. She sat opposite him at the small, round table so must have noticed that his cheeks had turned a bright crimson. He was trying to concentrate on the fact that she wasn't holding her cup with little finger slightly extended as his mother had said he should do.

"One day they will," he said. "George says they have to get one to stay up in the air first, though."

"Who's George?"

"My brother: he's a bit strange sometimes, but he knows just about everything there is to know about anything and was a champion boxer until Mom made him give it up."

"Just as well," Dianne said. "I don't think intellectuals should be boxing."

He felt relieved when she changed the subject. "How does one get to know the other teenagers in Elizabeth?"

"I know them all — I can introduce you to my gang," he added generously. "A really good bunch."

"That would be wonderful, thank you!"

"You're welcome," he murmured self-consciously. Dianne would certainly fit in well with the gang, he thought, feeling a sudden possessive urge. "I don't suppose you want to go to the drive-in movies on Friday or Saturday?"

"I would love to — I've never been to a drive-in. What about Friday?" She sounded almost eager.

"I'll pick you up just before seven," he said. "If I run you home tonight, I'll know your house."

Peter arrived home to find George cleaning his shoes over a newspaper spread on the kitchen floor.

"It's about time you cleaned yours," he told his younger brother. "They haven't been cleaned since you bought them."

"Yes they have," Peter protested, "a few times."

"No they haven't. You can clean them when I've finished mine, and I'll make a pot of tea."

Peter did as he was told and was surprised at the amount of dry mud which lay scattered over the newspaper. None of it had come from George's shoes.

He was standing in a line of boys in the school corridor. The headmaster was berating them: "You are all a disgrace to the school, your shoes are filthy, your hair is untidy and some of you haven't washed for a week. Look at your shirt collar, Johnson — don't you ever change your clothes?"

"Yes, sir," said a hapless Johnson.

"And you, Mitchell — I want to see a shine on those shoes tomorrow."

"Yes, sir," said a hapless Mitchell.

"You will all write a hundred lines after school: 'I must keep myself clean and tidy'."

"Yes, sir," chorused the line of hapless boys.

Peter looked up from polishing his shoes, "What's a snowman?"

"You should know," his brother said, pouring boiling water into the teapot. "You used to build so many you terrified the neighbours."

"That was only that woman who had bad dreams and told Mom my snowmen were marching up Thornhill Road after midnight. I don't mean that kind of snowman, anyway. I mean, if someone called you the Snowman, what would they mean?"

"Who's calling me the Snowman?"

"Not you!" Peter was exasperated, "I mean anyone — if anyone was called the Snowman?"

George wore his wisest look: "Now let me see . . . they could mean you are cold and aloof or they could mean you melt easily, which is the opposite . . . or they might mean that you wander around with a big red and black check scarf round your neck, have pebbles for eyes and have a clay pipe stuck in your mouth."

"Thanks," Peter couldn't keep the sarcasm from his voice, "I only asked you because you're supposed to be an intellectual."

"We don't call ourselves intellectuals," George said modestly, turning his gaze to the ceiling, "the word is a label used by the masses to explain people who actually think things out."

"Dianne says you're an intellectual."

"She would know," George spoke mildly. "Who the hell's Dianne?"

"My latest girlfriend," Peter said.

There was never going to be any major romance between Peter and Dianne. The main problem as always was Peter's shyness and his feeling of inadequacy when he was with her. Not that he found her the slightest bit snobbish, once he became used to her referring to her father as "Daddy". She didn't have to say "touch me if you dare", either. The wrapping and ribbon of her friendship had opened for him, but the contents were for someone she had yet to meet.

They arrived at the drive-in about an hour too early and sat in the kiosk with a hotdog and milkshake each. Peter pretended not to notice the sly looks Dianne was getting from other boys. He was never one to exhibit his jealousy.

She surprised him when at last they were in the car and the movie was beginning by resting her head against him. He slipped his arm behind her neck and allowed his fingers to dangle just above her shoulder. He kept his other hand on his knee, not really knowing what else to do with it. It might have been a natural thing with another girl to lean over and place his spare arm round her waist, before perhaps trying, ever so slowly, to reach and caress her breasts, but not with Dianne. As well, he wanted to show a touch of class. He wanted to show that a working-class school dropout from Handsworth could behave in an exemplary manner with a privately educated girl from Oxford. Not that he ever told her his father was not really a scientist, but he suspected she would one day find out. When he reached home he wondered if he was the first boy to take a girl to a drive-in theatre and know what the movie was about.

He lost her in any romantic way after introducing her to the gang. She proved popular with the other girls and became unreachable to him. Yet something lingered between them for a long time. It hung will-o'-the-wisp over them. Once, as they all struggled up a steep hill at Morialta, he took her hand and helped her the few remaining yards. She turned to him at the top, red-faced and breathless but looking deep into his blue eyes, and said, "Thank you, Snowman", and let her hand linger for just the barest moment in his. But he didn't know what to do about it.

So he lost her to the gang and became known as the Snowman. And no one ever seemed to know why he was called that, least of all Peter.

"Commander Mitchell calling Earth Orbit One, come in please.

"Commander Mitchell here . . . do you read me Earth Orbit One?"

The transceiver crackled into life, "Mitch, where have you been? We were getting worried you might have run off with one of those damsels down there."

"Too busy protecting them to have any evil designs, Jake. Listen, we have a new ship — the Salvation Jane — a star voyager, and she's ready for our galactic rescue mission. Tell the men that transfer time will be 0400."

"Aye, aye, Mitch.

"She's a big ship, Jake, so allow for space loss when she comes alongside."

"The Salvation Jane, Mitch?"

"It's a good name. That's our mission — the salvation of the planets of Aldeberan."

Wendy came back in the winter of 1959. Peter had been squeezing in some time to visit Pauline, knowing that he might be coming close to losing her. He managed to see her most Monday nights, and occasionally found a couple of hours for her at the weekends. His was a happy time — his wages had risen to £16 a week and he had actually been putting away a couple of pounds a week for the past few months. There was more than £30 in his tin and the thought of returning to England and bringing Margie to South Australia was once more at the forefront of his mind. He lost some of the desire to stay in England. His voice had broken more fully and, he thought, spoiled his singing voice a little, but his accent had smoothed out and there was a hint of Australian on his tongue.

Jim had been back in Elizabeth a few weeks and was staying with his parents. He drove a brand new shiny red Holden ute and got a job straight away as a plasterer with the Housing Trust of South Australia. He had matured since being away and cut down on his swearing, but used the word "frigging" a lot.

Wendy turned up at the Nicholls' house without warning one Tuesday night. She had stepped off the ship only the day before with her parents and brother.

Peter thought something dreadful had happened when he found Pauline tearful.

"I'm not upset, I'm happy," she told him, smiling. "Guess who's in the lounge?"

"Elvis Presley?"

"Don't be silly." She yanked him into the room, Wendy rose quickly and went straight to his arms. Barely given time to realise whom she was, he hugged her self-consciously in front of Pauline's parents.

"Welcome back," he choked out. "Welcome back . . . have you seen . . . ?" She stepped back and shook her head.

"Let's go to the shops," Pauline interrupted, giving her bemused parents a meaningful look, "we can talk there."

They walked the hundred or so yards to the shops. The girls wore overcoats and scarves against a chill wind whipping through the streets.

Peter turned up his coat collar and nestled his ears into it. "Colder than this in England," he reminded Wendy.

"It's warm there now," she replied, "but the winters are terrible."

"But when we were kids, we didn't mind the winter and we loved the snow," he said. "We dressed up warm when it was freezing cold."

"For goodness sake!" Pauline exclaimed, "Here we go again."

Peter changed the subject, "Some of our friends are starting to disappear. Mind you — you should see the number of teenagers around the place now."

"People are getting engaged and married far too young." Pauline said.

Wendy nudged her, "Whatever happened about the boy at work?"

Peter gave them a startled look, "What boy at work?"

"None of your business," Pauline smiled mysteriously and gave Wendy a glance which told her to drop the subject.

Girls could be infuriating at times.

"What about Jim?" Peter fired at Wendy.

"I was hoping you would know where I could find him," she replied.

"He's in Western Australia somewhere," Peter said in devilment.

"I thought so," Wendy said dismally. "I thought he would be far, far away by now."

"Everybody's lost track of him," Peter rubbed in.

Wendy sighed, "He wrote to me from some strange place a few months ago and said his work was running out and he would have to move on. Anyway, I didn't expect to find him easily."

Peter sounded sympathetic, "It's a big place, Australia, but you'll find him eventually."

Pauline gave him a quizzical look, but she didn't say anything. He waited until they finished their softdrinks.

"I know how you might find Jim," he said, "I know where his parents live. They could have his address."

"I was going to look them up," Wendy said, "Can we go there now?" Peter wasn't very good at practical jokes. Often they backfired on him and even when they didn't, he got embarrassed so easily that he couldn't pull them off with any panache. So he began to get a bad feeling as the car neared Jim's place. What if Jim had another girl there? Unlikely as it was, but what if? And if Jim wasn't home, how could he stand there and let Wendy ask Mr and Mrs Brown for his address? After all, he called on Jim most days. They would think he was loopy.

"Listen," he said, slowing the car the last few yards, "I'm having a joke with you — Jim's been back a few weeks. He's living at home."

"Swine!" Pauline thumped him on the arm.

"I can't stand it," Wendy gasped, "you've scared the hell out of me telling me that."

Peter shot her a nervous grin, "Don't worry — you're about to scare the hell out of him."

They parked on the street because Jim's car was in the driveway. The sight of the gleaming new ute made Wendy even more nervous. Peter and Pauline spent the next quarter of an hour trying to coax Wendy out of the car. Only when she had smoked one of Peter's cigarettes and become light-headed and giggly because she didn't smoke, did they finally troop up to the house and go round, expectantly, to the back door. Wendy tried to hide behind Pauline who was trying to hide behind Peter who was trying to become invisible. Peter knocked gently and no one answered the door. He knocked louder, but still there was no answer.

"Funny," he whispered, "there's a light on inside and Jim's car is here."

"Shall we try the front?" Pauline whispered.

"I don't like this sort of thing," Wendy breathed.

"Nor do I," Peter said. "Let's try the front door."

A sudden flood of light from next door and the sound of Jim's voice yelling "goodnight" froze them in their tracks.

"Hi there!" Peter called as Wendy made a bolt up the back steps to hide behind the flyscreen door.

"I thought I heard something, Jim called back, "just been chatting to the neighbours. See you round the front."

"Wait there," Peter hissed at Wendy who had no intention of moving, "we'll surprise him."

"What if he doesn't like me any more?" she groaned.

"Wait there," Peter urged.

Peter and Pauline met Jim as he entered the gate.

"The old people are next door," he said irreverently, "would you like a beer or something?"

"A beer," Peter squeaked because he was holding his breath.

"A glass of water for me," whispered Pauline.

Pauline sipped at her water while the two boys drank half a bottle of beer each. There had been no knock at the back door, Pauline began glancing at Peter.

"I'm starting to feel a bit silly," Peter said.

"Beer's like that," Jim observed, "it makes you feel how you really are."

"Thanks very much," Peter sniffed.

Jim took a long swig from the bottle, "Don't tell me you two are getting engaged or something?"

"Don't be daft," Pauline said, looking rather overly taken aback, Peter thought.

"I had some bloody awful sherry next door," Jim said. "I had to leave in case I was sick on their dog."

"What's their dog ever done to you?" Pauline asked.

"Nothing, but it sits between your knees all night and tries to trip you over when you get up."

"Can I use your toilet?" Peter asked.

He stood on the toilet seat and pressed his face close against the mesh window. "Psst," he called, "pssst". Then, ever so softly, "Wendy, Wendy . . ."

"Can you hear something?" Jim asked Pauline.

"It's only Peter going psst, pssst," she said.

"He's bloody bonkers," Jim said. "I always thought he was."

The loud knock startled even Jim. He opened the back door and slammed it shut again, the colour drained from his face as he turned to Pauline and the re-emerging Peter, "Am I dreaming or what?"

"It's no dream," Pauline told him, "you have just shut the door on Wendy."

She opened the door and walked in, her bottom lip trembling, "Fancy slamming the door on me."

"Where the hell did you come from?" Jim's face turned from white to crimson.

"Where do you think? From England, of course."

He took her gently in his arms as she burst into tears. "Hey," he said, "hey, I can't believe this. This isn't happening."

"You didn't write much," she sobbed.

"It's not easy when you've only got a gum tree branch for a pen," he told her. "But I'll make it up to you — you can bet on that."

He held her tighter and looked in bewilderment at Peter and Pauline, who were standing awkwardly in the middle of the kitchen floor, "Frig a kangaroo," Jim said simply.

"We should leave you two alone," Pauline said. "You've got a lot to talk about."

In bed that night Peter found himself thinking about the boy at Pauline's work and wondering how much she fancied him.

And in a far distant part of the galaxy, a small spacecraft hurtled towards warp-seven speed for a jump through the time-space continuum which would take it into another zone of the Milky Way, near the planet Earth.

Jim and Wendy knocked around with the gang for only a little while. Peter soon found he was seeing less and less of them. Many times he would call on Jim only to find he was not at home. Eventually, he stopped calling. They got engaged, Jim and Wendy, on Christmas Day, 1959. In the 18 months that followed before their marriage, they saved enough money for a deposit on a lovely Tudor-style home in Elizabeth.

September 1959 brought a warm, if showery spring. Two or three other couples in the gang were showing signs of pairing off and the unwritten rule no longer existed. As well, some of the girls had caught the fancy of boys from outside the gang.

Peter looked upon it all with a happy-sad philosophy, but mostly he felt a bit sad. He called on Pauline a couple of times and took her to the theatre in Adelaide and once to the drive-in movies. He felt the urge for a new aim in life and wrote off for information about various correspondence courses. Television had arrived in South Australia and one warm evening he brought Pauline and Veronica home and they used an extension cord to watch the small screen in the back garden where it was cooler. Peter got eaten alive by mosquitoes and spent much of the evening scratching himself and standing on a chair to marvel at the zigzag glow of televisions in all the other back gardens on his side of the street.

He decided that night to really start things moving with Pauline. He would ask her to go steady with him, and if this time she said: "I thought we were already going steady," he would be firm and tell her exactly what he meant.

He drove them home at 10 o'clock, sending thought messages to Veronica, telling her to get out of the car first and go inside so he could speak to Pauline alone. But it was Pauline who hopped out of the car first when he pulled up, not even waiting for him to open the car door for her. With a quick "Thanks, goodnight" and a smile, she disappeared into the house. He climbed out, opened the back door of the car and gently helped Veronica out.

"See you later," he mumbled.

"Alligator," she replied cheerily.

He drove home feeling a mixture of anger and frustration. He walked past his father in the kitchen and his father sang, "Have you ever seen a dream walking?"

He sang *The Loveliest Night of the Year* under the hot shower, but stopped when George banged on the door and asked him if he was in love. Then he sang *Mocking Bird Hill* and *Return to Me*, wondering if his voice would ever come right again, and he burst into tears and cried into the jets of water and just as suddenly started laughing and laughed and laughed until George banged on the door again and told him there were a couple of men in white coats waiting outside.

The following Monday a letter and photograph arrived from Margie and his whole world crumbled. She was wildly beautiful and grown-up looking and standing beside her handsome beau. His name was Richard and they had just become engaged. His little Margie . . . how could he have not realised she would have grown up by now? How had he allowed her to sneak into womanhood without him? How had this happened? He had waited for her through most of his childhood and she for him. Now fate had betrayed him. Someone else had wooed and won her heart. Tears streaming down his face, Peter walked blindly outside and kicked the side of his car and nearly broke a toe.

Their childhood song haunted him in bed:
At the end of the day
Just kneel and say
Thank you Lord for my work and play
I tried to be good
For I know that I should
That's my prayer at the end of the day.

In troubled sleep he saw visions of the bluebell woods and in flashes he and Margie were climbing a tree, then crossing a brook, holding hands over slippery wet watch-your-step stones and running pell-mell through the trees, laughing and shouting "catch us if you can" as the others in the gang chased vainly and breathlessly behind.

"I'm losing everyone," he told George the next night; "everybody's courting or getting married."

"Have you decided which girl you want to marry?" George asked, looking up from his racing form with slitted eyelids.

"I can't make up my mind," Peter said casually, "it's such a big decision."

"Tush," his mother interrupted.

"You've got so many to choose from," George agreed. "It must be very difficult for you. I'm glad I don't have that problem."

"I just don't know which girl I want to go steady with," Peter was completely caught up in the charade. "I suppose I have to decide one day."

"Don't be a chump," George said, tiring of the conversation, "you're far too young, anyway. You want to see the world first."

"Of course you're too young," his mother put in, "Too serious too young."

"You were only eighteen when you got married," Peter reminded her.

"That's beside the point," she replied primly. "And don't be cheeky."

"If you wait too long," Peter said, "you'll end up losing them."

"You must realise," George said, "there are millions of females in the world. You don't have to run off with the first one you meet."

"That's quite enough, thank you," his mother looked reprovingly at George. "You shouldn't be filling his head with such things."

"Definitely not," Mr Mitchell joined in with a wink at Peter. "Hang on to your freedom while you can."

He wrote a last letter to Margie, wishing her luck and happiness and finishing the single page with "all my love, Sir Lancelot". But he didn't put down any kisses and he resisted the temptation to scrawl SWALK on the back of the envelope. He sent it air mail and with heavy heart yet firm resolve quickly and deliberately turned his back on the postbox after plopping the letter through the slot. The sweetest of all his dreams so far had ended.

A few nights later, when they were alone in the kitchen, he again tackled George.

"I haven't really got a lot of girlfriends to choose from," he told his older brother.

"I know," George said.

"I mean . . . once I did, sort of. Once I had a lot of girlfriends and maybe I could have made a choice. But they all sort of disappeared."

"I know," George said.

"Except that I probably couldn't have made a choice because I don't think they were ever interested in me romantically. It was just my ego."

"It doesn't matter," George said. "None of it is real anyway — it's all make-believe."

"What do you mean?"

"Everything you do is make-believe." He stepped across the kitchen and lifted a large, brown package from the top of the fridge. "This is reality. This is your correspondence course. Inside lies the key to the real world," Peter sniffed, "Don't worry, I was going to study."

"No you weren't," George told him. "You might have got round to thinking about it, though." He handed the package to Peter, "You probably are not fully aware of this, but next year you will be twenty-one. Next year you will become officially an adult. If you studied now, you could start making something of yourself by then."

SALVATION JANE

The hills were bathed in purple and yellow and a warm breeze stirred from slumber as he helped her out of the car. They spread a blanket in the middle of a paddock run riot with Salvation Jane and soursob. Peter had brought salmon and lettuce sandwiches and a flask of cordial and Pauline cheese and biscuits and some fairy cakes she had made. Around them, grasshoppers, locusts and a couple of magpies sang, hummed and squawked about spring and the approaching summer. They sat each end of the blanket, looking down on Elizabeth and marvelling at how much it had grown.

The picnic was Peter's idea. It was silly and romantic and impulsive but he had fallen in love with the scheme the instant he thought of it. They ate the food and drank the cordial without saying much, content with their own thoughts and to gaze at the view of the town and beyond, where the already stark brown paddocks shimmered in the sun's warmth.

She wiped the crumbs from her mouth and lay down on the blanket. He spoke first, "Remember making daisy chains?"

"Everybody has made daisy chains," she replied dreamily.

"Are you falling asleep?"

"No . . . I could, though, it's so nice here."

"You're sitting on top of someone's house," he said.

"You're sitting in someone's fireplace," she rejoined.

"One day," he said, "all these hills will be covered with houses."

"I suppose so."

"That worries me," he said.

She stifled a yawn, "It doesn't worry me, because I might be living in one of them."

He was sure she was falling asleep. He rose from the blanket and began gathering the wildflowers. "I'll make you a daisy chain," he said. "You don't need daisies for that."

He unclasped his penknife and began slitting into the stems. The soursobs were soft and slimy and the Salvation Jane, hard and brittle.

"It's not easy," he told her.

"That's why they use daisies," she pointed out. "That's why they are called daisy chains."

He thought there might have been an edge of sarcasm to her voice.

"But there are no daisies in South Australia," he reminded her.

It took a long time to make the chain. A stronger, cooler breeze crept up the hill, rustling the wildflowers and playing in her hair.

"We should leave soon," she said, "that breeze is getting up."

"Won't be long, nearly finished."

He wondered what he was doing playing with flowers at his age. "This is really stupid, me making daisy chains." Then he held the garland up to her with a cry of "finito!"

"It looks lovely," she said, and burst into laughter.

He smiled, "What's the joke?"

"You're so funny sometimes. So sweet and funny."

"Put this round your neck," he said, lifting the flowers towards her, "and I'll be yours, sweet and funny, forever."

Her face dropped, "Are you proposing to me?"

A thrill of terror ran through him and he suddenly knew.

"I mean as a friend forever," he explained quickly.

"I don't have to wear this to be your friend forever," she said.

He spoke in his most important tone, but awkwardly, "Men and men can be friends, once each has married, and women can be friends with other women, but a man and a woman can't be friends the same once they have married someone else." He ran a finger slowly and delicately over the petals of the Salvation Jane. His lips trembled, "It's the guy at work, isn't it? She shrugged, "We've been out a few times. It's sort of getting serious."

"I guessed, I guessed that."

"You know something," she said gently, "once upon a time . . ."

"I know," he replied, "I know . . . once upon a time . . . me too." He glanced deliberately up the hill so she wouldn't see the mistiness in his eyes. "Soon there won't be any room in your life for me," he said, turning back to her. "So put it round your neck just once to remember me by." He trembled as he watched her bring the garland down over her head and on to her shoulders.

"It's beautiful," she said. "You will stay my friend forever, won't you Peter?"

"Always," he whispered. Then, "You can take it off now if you want to." But she kept it on.

"Star warp control . . . star warp control . . . Salvation Jane calling star warp control."

"Come in Salvation Jane — reading you loud and clear."

"Commander Mitchell in trouble, sir. Request rescue red one."

"You're a bit big for Earth rescue, Salvation Jane, but if you think you can mount an accurate mission, without taking up half the town, go ahead and good luck, Jake."

"By the way," Peter said as he turned the car into Elizabeth North, "where did the nickname Snowman come from?"

"I can't remember," she replied. "It just appeared, I think."

"No one knows," he said, "quite ridiculous really."

He brought the car to a halt outside her house, climbed out and opened the door for her.

"Au revoir," he said.

"Au revoir." She looked sad.

He took her hand and ever so lightly kissed the back of it, the way Sir Lancelot might have done.

"Hey kid," he mimicked her accent, "look after yourself."

"I always do," she replied. "You . . . you look out for any loose gravel." And she was gone. She was gone before he could say all the things he wanted to say, like thanks for being there when he had needed someone to talk to and thanks for making him feel important when the rest of the world conspired at his insignificance. And he hadn't quite said, 'Thank you for being my friend'.

He drove to the Elizabeth shopping centre not even realising he was whistling the song *You Don't Know Me*.

"Salvation Jane entering Earth atmosphere . . . rescue red one has begun."

"Calling Salvation Jane . . . Calling Salvation Jane."

"Reading you control, hurry, Salvation Jane reading."

"Abort rescue red one, Jake. Royal Hosirus starship entering green sector. Repeat, abort rescue red one.

Peter spied Donna and Ian at the end of the shops, so he dodged into the deli and ordered a milkshake. He stood listening to The Platters singing *The Great Pretender* on the shop radio before stepping outside with his drink. A large cloud scurried across the sun, bringing an eerie gloom. A sudden strong wind whipped at his legs and he fancied that, for the briefest instant, it had lifted him off his feet.

Bits of ice in the drink kept clogging his straw so he made loud sucking noises as he drank. Then the wind died as suddenly as it had sprung to life and the sun shone again.

She came up behind him and placed her hands over his eyes, "Guess who?" He turned quickly. Gosh, he thought, gosh you've grown up.

"You look different," he said.

"I've just had my hair done."

"It really suits you, it's nice."

"Thank you," she sounded demure. "What are you doing with yourself these days?"

"Having one hell of a time," he said. "I've actually been on a picnic with your sister, as well." He wanted to ask her out, but George's face kept appearing vividly in his mind. So he said, "I'm starting my studies tonight. I'm doing a correspondence course in journalism."

"That sounds worthwhile," she said. Then she crossed her fingers and held them up in front of him, "I'm hoping to go to university next year, but I have to study really hard between now and then."

That was what many young people were doing, Peter realised, studying so they could find a rewarding future for themselves. He was glad he had told her about his correspondence course.

"I hope you make it," he told her. "Good luck." He turned towards his car.

"Good luck to you, too," she called after him.

"Can I give you a lift?"

"No, thanks — I'm waiting for Lisa."

Those few yards to the car were the hardest he had ever walked. He should ask her for a date. He really should. Surely she would accept. She had pulled enough faces at him, hadn't she? Then again, she was deep in study; wanted to go to university. What if she refused to go out with him because of her need to study? That was fair enough . . . and there was George's face again . . . "You'll be an adult next year." Officially an adult, at least.

As he started the car engine, strangely eager to get home, Donna and Ian walked by. She stopped and bent her head at the open window.

"Hello," Peter said, smiling his friendliest smile.

"I've got a real man now," she grinned and walked on.

He cut the engine and called softly, "Donna, sweetheart."

She turned and came back to the car, still grinning, "What?"

"Donna sweetheart," he said, "get fff . . . have a good life."

The end